Max Cossack

Zarah's Fire

The song *"It Ain't Gamblin' When You Know You're Gonna Lose"*
Words and Music by Joseph Vass; Copyright © 2018 Joseph Vass All Rights Reserved

Other Novels by Max Cossack:

Khaybar, Minnesota
Simple Grifts   A Comedy of Social Justice
Low Teck Killers

Other books published by VWAM include:

By Susan Vass:

Ammo Grrrll Hits The Target (Volume 1)
Ammo Grrrll Aims True (Volume 2)
Ammo Grrrll Returns Fire (Volume 3)
Ammo Grrrll Home On The Range (Volume 4)
Ammo Grrrl Is A Straight Shooter (Volume 5)

Acknowledgment: Many thanks to Constable Glenn Morrison for his tour of the area southwest of Phoenix, Arizona, and his explanation of illegal immigration and drug smuggling there. Any inaccuracies are mine and not his.

WHAT READERS SAY

about Max Cossack's consensus
5-Star Debut Novel
"Khaybar, Minnesota"

"Frighteningly possible story, well told."

"A fast-paced pleasurable read."

"A great read, a great story and (unfortunately) extremely topical."

"You won't be able to put it down."

"Tremendous first novel."

"An entertaining tale which I enjoyed enough to read twice."

"Great read! Hard to believe this is the first book by this author. He hit all the high notes with a timely, believable plot, interesting characters and authentic dialog...Get this book, you won't be disappointed."

DEDICATION:

For My Mother

Minna Blankfeld Vass

מינה בת יעקב וחשה גיטל

זכרונה לברכה

Author's Note

Early readers of *Zarah's Fire* have asked me how much of it is fiction. The answer is: not much. I may have imagined Zarah and her friends, but I did not imagine the real world they confront. The compound where terrorists have imprisoned Zarah is based on real terrorist camps, right down to the stacked black tires on its perimeter. A three-year-old boy really did die in an Islamist compound during a failed exorcism. Scouts for drug cartels really do hole up in the desert hills of the Southwest to guide drug smugglers and human traffickers into the U.S.

And during the Syrian Civil War, the Israeli military really did helicopter more than 3,000 Syrian civilian casualties into Israeli hospitals to treat them of their often-calamitous wounds, and really did smuggle them back home into Syria by night.

Sometimes I wonder if today's headline writers plagiarize them from my fiction. I don't claim *Zarah's Fire* is a completely true story, but if it isn't yet, it may become one very soon.

-Max Cossack, April, 2019

1 Zarah

After little Omar died Zarah decided to die too. She stopped eating or drinking. She lay down on her mattress on the hard ground in the girls' tent and pulled her thin ratty blanket over herself and closed her eyes tight and concentrated on not breathing.

Zarah had tried with all her prayers and all her strength to protect Omar. She watched over him just the way her own long-lost mother had watched over her. The other children teased her. The few with Arabic called her "Walida Omar"—Omar's mother. Other children teased her in the local language Spanish as "Madrecita"— little mother.

Zarah didn't mind. She liked being called someone's mother. She wanted to be a real mother someday anyway. So in the moments she could sneak away from her obligations of work and prayer she shepherded Omar all around the Compound. When Aida doled out the meager rations of rice and beans, Zarah got a slightly bigger ration than the other children, and Zarah shared her extra food with Omar. If it happened that Omar napped in the heat of the day, which he did more and more as he got sicker, Zarah made sure he slept in the shade of the tire stacks or tent walls and let him lay his dark curly head on her thin chest. But in the end she was too young and weak to protect him from grownups like Ali and Aida.

Ali and Aida tried to make her get up from her mattress. They threatened to beat her. Zarah believed them. They'd already beaten her many times before. But their threats no longer scared her. And then Aida did beat her but Zarah didn't care since she planned to die anyway. She just lay there and took it without a single whimper or tear.

Zarah had started out thinking it should be easy to die. After all, little Omar had done it, just like so many other smaller children she had seen do it before in so many other terrible places she'd been.

But dying turned out to be hard. No matter how much she tried not to, in the end she always breathed again. Maybe it was easy for

Omar to die because he'd been only about three or four years old. Zarah just lay there broiling in her own sweat and thirst and helpless anger at the mean stupid grownups who had killed him and the mean stupid way they did it.

The day Omar died, Ali had gathered all the children in the compound to what he called his "school." But it was nothing like the school where Zarah's parents had sent her back home before someone burned it down. That school was indoors with desks and a kind lady teacher who taught the children to read letters and count numbers and never talked about killing people.

Besides Ali and Aida, there were twelve in the compound, all of them children, from Omar's age up to Zarah's, which she guessed at about nine or ten. She'd lost track of her own exact age since they took her from her mother.

Aida made all the children squat on the filthy ground while Ali explained in English, which was the only language he spoke, and which Zarah had learned from two of the other children: "There are demonic spirits called "jinn" inside Omar. We will banish them. We call the treatment "ruqya." Omar is too young to perform his own ruqya. I am a raaqi and I know how to perform ruqya."

Then Ali began to mispronounce Surahs from the Koran in an Arabic so barbaric Zarah couldn't understand him. She knew Koran Arabic was different from the Arabic regular people spoke, but Ali's didn't resemble any she'd heard anywhere.

Ali put a *taweez* around Omar's wrist. It was an amulet something like the one Grandmother had given Zarah years ago, which Mother had called "superstition" and thrown out the first time she saw it—although Zarah had retrieved it and hidden it and wore it on a string around her neck ever since—even now, sitting cross-legged on the dirt with the other children watching Ali make a fool of himself one more time.

Then Ali filled a glass with water. He spit into the glass and made Omar drink from it. He poured the remaining water from the glass over Omar's head and did a bunch of other water things with

3

more glassfuls. Ali kept looking in a book for what came next and Zarah knew he was just bluffing his way through. He stumbled over any long word and stopped and started the ruqya over and over again, until Zarah noticed even Ali's pet John stirring in obvious impatience in his place on the ground near her.

Throughout the ruqya Omar kept fainting. Ali and Aida kept standing him up for more but he kept keeling over in the heat. Each time he fainted Aida said that was good because it meant another demon had left Omar and soon Omar would be free of all of them. Then Aida woke Omar and stood him up again and then he fainted again. This happened many times.

Zarah didn't believe any of it. Omar fainted because he was tired and weak and sick. Zarah had seen many children die and it was always those reasons. Nothing so powerful as a demon was needed to kill a sick little child in the blistering heat of the desert. The beings Ali called "ayn" and "sirh" and "jinn" had nothing to do with it.

Finally Omar fainted one last time and didn't move at all. Ali and Aida tried to stand him and then when he keeled over again they pretended he was sleeping and Ali carried him away.

"See?" Aida stood facing the children. "Omar is fine now. Our ruqya worked."

But Zarah had seen many dead people and she knew Omar was dead. Although she hid her feelings from Ali and Aida, she burned with sadness and anger, sadness for Omar whose helplessness had made her try to protect him and anger at Ali and Aida who were grownups whose job it was to take care of children and not kill them.

After Zarah had lain on the ground in the girls' tent for two days and nights and discovered that dying was painful and hard, she recalled it was forbidden to kill yourself. It would be better to escape. If she could get away and find some good men she could tell them about Omar and this place and the good people would come rescue the children and if they were really good punish Ali and

Aida.

Zarah knew there were good men and women. She remembered her own parents very well and they had been good. They never beat her and their speech was kind and beautiful and not crazy and stupid like Ali's and Aida's.

Of course, escaping was going to be hard. She had no idea where she could escape to. She didn't know what country she was in or if its people spoke languages she knew.

Once she'd been in Ali's big tent and she'd peeked over Ali's shoulder and glimpsed a computer screen with a picture taken from above of the compound and the area all around. Hills lay to the east and on the other side of the hills were many buildings. Buildings meant people. Maybe good people.

Zarah was strong. Hadn't she proved it over and over just by staying alive through kidnapping and slavery? She could surely take a simple walk through a desert. After all, she came from a desert people. Grandmother had taught her things about the desert. And Grandmother was a Bedouin and Bedouins knew deserts better than any other people in the world.

When Zarah caught daytime glimpses past the tires guarding the Compound perimeter, she saw a desert dotted with green in every direction and not just endless barren sand dunes like in the desert back home. Where there was green there also must be water and food.

She thought, I'll plan and wait for my chance. I'll escape and find adults kind and good like my parents and bring them here and they will free all the children.

The sweet ache of remembering her parents made her clutch the amulet under her abaya. She should never say or even think their names or even the words mother or father. She needed all her strength to run away.

Zarah lay on her mattress and cradled her amulet in her hands and planned her escape.

2 *Lily Meets The Press*

In the living room of her house in St. Paul, Minnesota, Lily Lapidos curled up in the junction at the two sections of her big brown L-shaped sofa, sipping Pinot Grigio from her crystal goblet wine snifter and thinking about picking up her book to read some more.

The television droned a Twins game. Lily only occasionally cared about baseball and the Twins sucked yet again this year, but she did appreciate the relaxed summer ballgame rhythm, especially in June, by which month Twins games nearly never mattered. And Lily enjoyed the blather of the Twins play-by-play man Dick and his color man Bert, in particular their natural unforced jocularity.

Lily felt she needed any help she could get in the jocularity department.

Lily took another sip of her wine. The book was something about something. By someone. Lily had reached only page fifteen and it hadn't sunk in the first two times. Maybe she should start over. Maybe she should slow down on the wine.

The white iPhone on the marble lift top coffee table rang.

Should she answer? Might be a client.

But answering might lead to work and working again might require her to leave her house, something she'd hardly done in months.

If you don't leave your house, how are you planning to feed your beautiful daughter and pay for her school? Nat's broke, you know that, and it's not fair to Sam to make him foot all the bills for Sarai forever. Maybe Sam would like to retire from the law sometime.

That idea made her smile to herself. Sam would never retire. An old soldier, he'd just fade away.

The ringing stopped.

On the TV Bert quipped a quip Lily didn't catch and Dick couldn't stop chortling. Missing out on the fun again.

She picked up her goblet and took a slug of wine. Decent.

6

The iPhone rang a second time.

Lily set the goblet down on the absorbent stone coaster and picked up her book. Ah, yes. "The Armies of the Night", by Norman Mailer. It was about this big anti-Vietnam War demonstration in 1967 where beatniks and hippies and communists banded together to levitate the Pentagon with some sort of hocus-pocus wizardry. She'd read it a few years ago and it had engaged her then. Mailer had a lively prose style.

Sam had known Mailer. Sam said Mailer had been a jackass. "He never stopped talking about himself," said this other man who never stopped talking about himself.

Unfair. Her father could be rigid minded and rude but he was no jackass, and he adored his granddaughter Sarai and showed her only a tender loving side. If he talks about himself every so often, it's only because there's a lot to say.

The ringing stopped again.

Dick shouted something and she glanced at the screen. The Twins shortstop had connected on a long high drive. Naturally it fell short; the left-fielder pulled it in just in front of the wall—a "can of corn," Dick called it. Why corn? Lily wondered. Why not peas? The green mushy overcooked kind you get out of cans? Was she getting drunk? The TV went to commercial. Did that signify the game was over, or was it just the end of the inning?

Wait two minutes and see. Lily lay her book face down next to her on the sofa and picked up her goblet.

The iPhone rang again.

She set her wine down on the coaster again and picked up the iPhone and thumbed the virtual white button on the screen and entered her six-digit code and touched her index finger to the screen.

"Hello," a woman's voice. "This is Lauren Goodwell. May I speak to Lily Lapidos?"

Lily said, "Sorry. Things have been crazy lately and I keep meaning to get back to you but something always interferes. I'll make it up with a discount in my next bill."

"Oh, no, we haven't spoken before."

Not a client. Relax.

Lauren said, "I'm from ZNN. You know."

"No, sorry, don't."

"The cable news network."

Antennae up. "I see."

"I was wondering if I could have a few moments of your time."

Lily picked up her goblet and took a smaller sip than before. She curled her knees up in front of her and pulled them to her chest and leaned back onto the thick comfy sofa cushion. "Why?"

"I'm doing some roundup coverage on the incident this past January in St. Paul."

"What incident was that?"

"I'm sure you recall. Your client Tariq Daghestani was killed outside the Jewish Center and you were right there. In fact, the police reports say you ran him over yourself."

"They do? Interesting."

"You're not claiming you don't know that? Oh, I suppose you're joking."

"Haven't read the police reports myself. But I'll take your word for it."

A pause. "Have I called at a bad moment?"

"Actually yes. I've talked about it fifty times, to the police, the FBI, the District Attorney's office, the U.S. Attorney's office, to everyone. It's all public record."

"Of course, but I'm coming at it from a different angle. And there are some loose ends."

"Loose how? Daghestani drove a van loaded with explosives right up to the Jewish Community Center. My ex-husband Nat Wilder was trying to stop him."

"You see, there's one loose end right there. Your ex-husband is Hack Wilder, right, but you call him Nat?"

Lily noticed the woman's persistent, silky and ingratiating voice. Sort of like Dad's when he was nailing a witness on cross-examination. Careful. She took a sip so small it barely moistened her lips. "There's only one guy. Hack's his nickname. I call him by his birth name—Nat."

"Does anyone else call him that?"

"I think maybe his mother did."

"And you divorced him, right?"

"Which is why I also call him my ex-husband."

"And you divorced him because of his history?"

Maybe Lily should learn what this woman was about and maybe warn Nat. "What history is that?"

"Well, his employer Gogol-Chekhov fired him because he was creating a hostile work environment, right? For minorities and women?"

"Nat Wilder can barely summon up any hostility to anyone. Not even me—even when I deserve it."

"For divorcing him?"

"You must want to weave a lovely new sweater out of that particular loose end. But I think by now it's all knotted up."

Another pause. "Maybe I'm getting off topic."

"Which is?"

"What?"

"Your topic?"

"You know, when any controversial event, happens conspiracy theories and theorists pop up. So there are conspiracy buffs who say Dr. Daghestani was framed—a patsy—you know, someone set him up to look guilty. Like Lee Harvey Oswald. That you ran your car over him and killed him to silence him."

"And you take this seriously?"

"Regardless what I think personally, it's my professional obligation to give you a chance to tell your side."

"I did what I needed to do when it needed to be done. I ran over Tariq Daghestani because he was standing in the street pointing a gun at Nat, who I had just personally witnessed stop Daghestani's pal Khaled from using his assault rifle to shoot up a school bus full of kids."

A pause. Then Lauren said, "But Dr. Daghestani was your client, right?"

Lily took a big slug of wine and thought a moment. "Yes, he was. And the bastard never paid his bill."

"That's an odd joke to make, if that's what it is."

Which gave Lily a scary thought. "Are you recording this? You have to get my permission for that, you know."

"Really?" The voice was innocent.

Shit.

Lauren continued, "So that's another theory I want to give you a chance to knock down. It's rumored you killed him for personal reasons and that Tariq Daghestani was your lover."

"Is that how you got your job?"

"My personal life doesn't enter into this."

"But mine does, right? He and I were not lovers. And it's an obviously sexist theory you as a purported feminist representing a self-designated progressive news network ought to reject out of hand. Ours was a business relationship. He approached me to work for him as an image consultant. He said his image needed burnishing. I consulted and burnished."

"Let's say I accept that. There are people who say you've let your business slide since then. Like it was never real in the first place."

"Your questions are all ridiculous. I stopped what turned out to be a bomb attack on the Jewish Community Center when it was full of kids. I was as surprised as anybody."

"But what would make a respectable academic and professional like Dr. Daghestani even think of bombing a JCC? The JCC's not a military target."

Lily took another sip. "I've thought about that a lot. It might have been a copycat attack."

"Copycat?"

"You know, the 1994 bombing Iran committed at the Buenos

Aires A.M.I.A."

"Really?"

"You don't know about that?"

"There was nothing in the materials my researcher gave me."

"How can you consider yourself qualified to cover this story or any story involving Islamist terrorism against Jews if you don't even know about the 1994 bombing in Buenos Aires?"

"Well—"

"Give me a second." Lily pressed a few keys on her phone. "Here it is. Ten seconds Internet research: On July 18, 1994, Iranian government agents bombed the Buenos Aires A.M.I.A. building."

"A.M.I.A.?"

"The Asociación Mutual Israelita Argentina. A Jewish Community Center like the JCC in St. Paul, where Jews and other people go for basketball and kids' parties and art festivals and concerts. The bomb killed eighty-five people and injured hundreds."

"But why?"

"They hate Jews. Get it?"

"But—"

"Wait. There's more. A judge in Argentina has indicted their prime minister Cristina Kirchner for helping Iran cover up the massacre. This came after Argentine government agents murdered the prosecutor Alberto Nisman who planned to indict both Kirchner and the Iranians together—see, there's your conspiracy—the real thing."

A pause. "I wonder—"

Lily cut her off. "If you'd done the same ten seconds' research I just did you might have started your so-called roundup coverage with some notion what happened in St. Paul."

Lily jabbed the fake red "End Call" button as hard as she could, but sadly it was just an image on the iPhone screen, and poking a picture of a button—no matter how hard—felt wimpy and inadequate to her developing rage.

She considered taking a hammer to the phone, but that would

require getting up and going to the basement to look for a hammer, so she settled for trying to squeeze the electrons out of it with her left hand. Her tiny hand felt impossibly weak against the rigid metal and plastic. Just one more futile effort—the high-tech geniuses really ought to invent a way to hang up a cell phone with some balls.

The phone rang again.

Lauren Goodwell again. Lily wasn't quite finished with the woman. She answered.

Before Lily could speak, Lauren said, "I'm sorry." Her voice was just as soft and calm and even as before, as if nothing had happened. "I think the call dropped or we were disconnected or something."

"It was something."

"Pardon?"

"The call didn't drop and we weren't disconnected. It was door number three—I hung up."

Lauren's voice finally lost its silkiness. "Your choice. But you should consider, millions of people watch my network and I'm going to run a story with or without your cooperation and it might profit you to use your chance to tell your side of the story."

"I hung up, get it? I don't want to talk to you. I don't care about your network or your conspiracy theories. I hung up!"

"Your choice. But there can be consequences. Especially in your line of business."

Lily made a conscious decision not to scream. She said in the quietest and most even voice she could muster, "And now I'm going to hang up again."

"Perhaps I've caught you at a bad time."

Now Lily did scream. "There's no good time! None. Never call me again. I'm going to hang up one last time and you will never call me again. Never!"

Lily pressed the crappy little red fake button again and sat rigid, clenching the iPhone. She wondered for a moment if her head might explode. Her precious living room—her favorite place in the world—her sanctuary—blurred. Her favorite possessions—the marble coffee table with its classy accoutrements, the matching hand-woven Afghan rug on which the table sat, the Jacquard silk window panels—all danced before her in that blur.

Inner discipline. Calm. Equanimity. She breathed deep, first in, then out. Then in and out again. Then one more time. She leaned her head back against the plush cushion and stared at the ceiling. She mustered her self-control and cradled the phone in both hands and leaned forward and settled it on the coffee table like a Fabergé egg she feared she might shatter. She wondered if she was going crazy. Probably.

3 *Stymied For The Interim*

By the time Hack slipped through the back door of the nearly empty courtroom and tiptoed to an empty chair on the back right, his ex-father-in-law Sam Lapidos had already begun his direct examination of Sam's client Amos Owens.

Hack was grateful he and Mattie had accepted Sam's offer to fly them down from Minnesota to Phoenix instead of making the two-thousand-mile drive in his 1973 Audi Fox. That relic's exhausted air conditioner barely ruffled its passenger compartment's air. Its fans puffed out only the final feeble exhalations of a dying emphysemic. In a Minnesota June, a defunct air conditioner was an inconvenience; in Phoenix it was a potential death sentence.

At almost one P.M. Hack and Mattie had ducked out of the cab they'd taken from the airport and dashed through the blazing heat into the coolness of the Vauxhall Arms Hotel. They stopped and gawked at a lobby as alien to their home town's green woods and fields as the brown Sonoran Desert they'd seen from the air flying in.

Mattie said, "You could put my house in here five times." She pointed up to where the atrium ceiling loomed far above them like a distant blue western sky.

Hack pointed to a shelter on the horizon. "That must be the front desk."

Elegant gentlemen and businesswomen strolled about in slick business and sport wear cut in exquisite fabrics. Hack and Mattie ran the gauntlet of chic to the front desk in their souvenir Minnesota tee shirts and Walmart jeans, which was all they'd packed, since it was also pretty much all they had.

If the sight of the two hayseeds trespassing on his opulence bothered the front desk clerk, he never let on. His face beamed welcome. When Hack handed the platinum credit card Sam had overnighted him, the man's face phosphoresced to near stellar radiance. He stuck the magic card into the front slot of his machine and handed it back to Hack. "Welcome to the Vauxhall Arms," he said. "We hope you'll enjoy your stay."

Hack himself was hoping to sidestep the obligation for a tip. He'd planned that Mattie and he would port their two vinyl suitcases up to their room on their own. But the clerk was too quick on the bell, and a bellman appeared and snatched up their luggage and smiled a smile almost as brilliant as the clerk's.

Hack opened his wallet. He handed Mattie Sam's credit card. "Eat something," he said. He pulled out his last ten-dollar bill. "Here. For the bellman. I'll see you later. I've got to check in with Sam."

Mattie whispered, "Where do I go?"

"Wherever this guy takes you," Hack said, and kissed her cheek.

Hack dashed out of the hotel and squinted against the white Arizona sun frying his eyeballs and followed the map he'd printed to the Federal Courthouse. It was almost four by the time he made it through the security checkpoint and up the elevator and down the hall to the courtroom to watch Sam in action.

Sam was standing on the left of the courtroom in front of his table. Sam was wiry and half bald, with a weathered olive-skinned raptor face. He wore a gray sharkskin suit that fit him like the snug abrasive skin on an actual shark. He shot Hack a flicker of eye contact and turned to face his witness.

Behind the high bench, a gray-haired woman judge in customary black robes was eying Sam with an expression Hack read as a kind of alert but slightly jaded amusement. Her name plate read "J. Muriel Zernial." At Sam's table a tall slender black man sat facing forward. Hack couldn't see the man's face.

Sam had told Hack something about the case. Amos Owens was a Freshman at Southwest Arizona State University on a basketball scholarship. The University had dumped him from the team and then expelled him.

Owens was a thin young black man who sat on the witness stand upright, stiff and somber. He'd buttoned up all three buttons on his

15

dark gray suit. He wore a wide black tie with red and green stripes. He had clamped his hands together on his lap. Every so often he unclenched them and then right away clenched them again.

Sam: What happened then?

Owens: I went to that Thursday's practice and Coach Wilson met me outside the locker room and said he was sorry but I couldn't come in. He said I had to report to Dean Stamp in his office. Which I did.

Sam: And then?

Owens: Well, first I had to wait for an hour in a chair outside Coach's office not knowing what was going on. And that put me into even more of a fret.

Sam: And then?

Owens: Dean Stamp finally came out and took me in and he sat down behind his desk and I sat in front of him and then he told me that I couldn't go to practice any more.

Sam: Did he say why?

Owens: He said there was a complaint.

Sam: What did you say?

Owens: Well, naturally, I asked what was the complaint?

Sam: Did he tell you?

Owens; He wouldn't say. I asked him over and over and I said how can I answer this complaint if I don't know what it is? He just said it was policy. They had to protect the person making the complaint.

Sam: What did you say?

Owens: I say I don't see how it makes a problem for the complainer if I just know what the complaint was. I don't need to know who made the complaint, just what the complaint is.

Sam: Did he tell you?

Owens: No. He just let drop at some point—I don't know when exactly—that it came from something he called the "Bias Response Committee."

Sam: Did you know what this Bias Response Committee was?

Owens: Never heard of it. So then I'm thinking out loud, and I go "Is it about this or that thing?" and he goes he can't say but he took notes on what I guess.

Sam: For example?

Owens: I don't remember them all now. Like I guessed whether this girl I asked out was offended or something because I came on too smooth or something. But I know that girl and since then she say "no problem" and she still my friend.

Sam: So what did you do next?

Owens: Well, I left and went back to my room and to be honest I was almost crying. I stewed for a while and tried to think back to anything I'd said or done to anyone that would count against me as bias and I couldn't think of anything. And I asked around from my teammates and my friends if they could think of something and no one could.

Sam: So you were stymied.

Owens: Stymied is the right word. It's a good new word for what I was going through. I came to college partly to learn new words and I guess it turned out SWASU is a perfect place to learn what stymied means.

Sam: Let the record reflect that "SWASU" is a commonly accepted nickname for defendant SouthWest Arizona State University. Then what happened?

Owens: Nothing for the next week. I just went to classes and fretted about practice. Then Dean Stamp called me in again and said I could continue to attend classes but I had to sleep off-campus.

Sam: For how long?

Owens: For the interim, he said. Another good new word. But I tell him I can't afford to do that. My mother doesn't make much money and my father has passed. The scholarship is all I have and it's supposed to include on-campus housing.

Sam: What did he say to that?

Owens: He said that was too bad. And of course I say why can't

I stay on-campus and he say because other students might not feel safe.

Sam: Did he say who these other students were who might not feel safe?

Owens: No. He's saying if he told me he would be violating their confidentiality.

Sam: Have you ever been convicted of a violent crime?

Owens: No.

Sam: Ever been arrested?

Owens: Nothing serious. You know, teenage stuff. Like a few fights after school. I got to defend myself, right?

Sam: And you were arrested?

Owens: No, sorry, I mistook the question. I wasn't arrested. Just suspended for a day along with four others.

Sam: Thank you. At the time Dean Stamp said this to you, could you think of any reason why any other human being ever might feel unsafe around you?

Owens: No sir. And I can't now.

Sam: What did you do next?

Owens: I found a friend off campus and stayed with him and slept on his floor. I came on-campus just for classes and left right away afterwards like Dean Stamp says.

Sam: Even though you couldn't play in any games or even practice your basketball, during that interim you kept on studying?

Owens: Right. Studying. And feeling stymied. Stymied for the interim.

Sam: Did there come a time when you met with Dean Stamp again?

Owens: Yes, two more weeks later. Professor Morgan met me outside my first-year composition class and told me I had to go see Dean Stamp again.

Sam: And?

Owens: So I did and Dean Stamp told me I'd committed a very serious act of Islamophobic bias and I was expelled.

Sam: And did he finally tell you what specifically you'd done?

Owens: Yes.

Sam: Which was?

Owens: Something I said in a team meeting.

Sam: Which was?

Owens: There was some talk about a possible team tour over in Asia. Malaysia and other places. And I say I'm not sure I want to go.

Sam: Why not?

Owens: I say I'm gay—which I'm not, but one of my teammates is secretly gay and I don't want to say who, so I pretend it's me because everyone knows I got an active social life with women—so I say I'm gay and I'd be afraid how they might do me in Malaysia because I heard how they treat gay people in some of those Muslim countries. They hang them or throw them off buildings and stuff. That's what I heard, anyway.

Sam: Did you know whether that ever actually happens in Malaysia?

Owens: No sir. That's why I was asking the question.

Sam: Did you ever get an answer?

Owens: Coach said he'd look into it. That's all.

Sam: Did Dean Stamp give you any other reason for expelling you besides the concern you expressed in the team meeting about being a gay man—even though you're not actually gay yourself— going to Malaysia?

Owens: Not at that time when he told me I was expelled: I guess they've ponied up some other reason or two since then.

An heavy-set balding lawyer at the table on Sam's right jumped up and said, "Objection!"

The Judge said, "Sustained." The SWASU lawyer nodded and sat down.

Sam: At the time Dean Stamp explained your expulsion to you, the one and only reason he mentioned was that single question you asked about treatment of gay people in Malaysia?

The SWASU lawyer jumped up again and said, "Objection!"

19

The Judge said, "Overruled." The SWASU lawyer sat down.

Owens: Yes. Just that. It was only later I saw they'd thrown in all those things I told on myself when I was guessing out loud what I might have done wrong in front of Dean Stamp and he wrote them all down. And then they put them in the writing they gave us after I hired you as my lawyer and started the lawsuit.

Sam: Including your asking that friend of yours on a date in an allegedly offensive way?

Owens: They say that now.

Sam: And she'll be testifying on your behalf later in this trial.

SWASU Attorney: Objection!

Judge: Sustained.

Sam: What has happened in your life since your expulsion?

Owens: You mean besides having lost the scholarship and any chance of getting an education or advancing in basketball and feeling depressed and miserable all the time and not sleeping?

Sam: Let's slow down, please. I think we'll need to break those down piece by piece and go over them in detail.

Judge Zernial said, "It's pretty close to five. Mr. Lapidos, is this a good point in your examination for a break? That is, before you and your witness delve in meticulous detail into each and every damage Mr. Owens will say he has suffered—a process I'm confident will consume many hours."

Sam said, "It's a perfect time for a break, Your Honor."

Judge Zernial said, "We'll recess until ten tomorrow morning, when we'll resume direct examination of Mr. Owens." She tapped her gavel once on its hardwood sound block and stood and disappeared through her door at the back of the courtroom.

The few scattered spectators near Hack stood and drifted out the front exit. Amos Owens got up from the witness chair and walked to the plaintiff's table. He and Sam and the third man conferred with quiet voices Hack couldn't hear. SWASU's lawyer and a man in a dark suit Hack assumed was there to represent SWASU opened the little gate that divided spectators from gladiators and frowned their way down the front aisle and out the door.

Hack met Sam and the other two men at the little gate. Sam introduced Hack to Amos Owens as his "crack investigator." Hack shrugged in sincere modesty about the characterization and shook hands with Owens.

Sam said, "Hack, you remember Jacob Laghdaf," and Hack now recognized the third man as Laghdaf, the tall slender African who'd guided Hack to Sam's house for a secret meeting when Hack had been on the run in January.

"Of course," Hack said. The two shook hands.

Laghdaf smiled a big smile. "Amos, you are a very fortunate client. This is a very resourceful man. You have no idea what he accomplished."

Sam said, "You mean got away with?"

Laghdaf's smile somehow widened. "The same thing."

Sam said, "Now that we've got the entire resourceful team together, let's go to dinner."

"You guys go without me," Hack said, "I better see how Mattie's doing at the Vauxhall Arms. Opulence is a new experience for her."

Sam said, "As you wish. But seven tomorrow morning come to my office. I've got something needs doing right away."

Hack said, "Already?

Sam nodded. "Already. May call for your special skills."

Hack hurried back to the Vauxhall Arms and Mattie, wondering what those special skills might be.

4 The Mujahid

What the Mujahid wanted most was peace in his soul. He could attain peace in his soul only by submission to the will of Allah. It was the will of Allah that Muslims war against Khaffir leaders who opposed Allah and against their stubborn rebellious followers.

With all his soul, the Mujahid wanted to do the will of Allah and to be a good Muslim. The Mujahid therefore made the war that Allah willed. The goal of his war—his jihad—was to bring all human beings everywhere into sublime, peaceful and happy submission to the will of Allah, as expressed in the holy books and explained by scholars and the Mujahid's teachers.

It is the nature of war that there will be frustrations and failures, so despite his temporary frustration at the failure of his recent *"Khaybar, Minnesota"* operation and at the heroic death of his lieutenant and friend, the martyr Tariq Daghestani, the Mujahid felt optimistic about the progress of his jihad. He had developed several dozen compounds spread from northern Mexico into the rural United States. His network was accumulating an ever greater treasury and developing ever more profitable business contacts with the narcotics cartels, as well as with the networks of human traffickers and weapon smugglers intertwined with those cartels.

His political operation thrived. The American media treated the "Anti Islamophobia League" he had helped found as their go-to source for understanding Islam. Politicians were beginning to bend from their previous unwavering allegiance to the Jews. On university campuses it seemed a Muslim could do no wrong.

The lawsuit at the university by that homosexual student was probably only a nuisance, but he should keep an eye on it anyway. His key ally there was a woman and an intellectual and therefore doubly unreliable. The Mujahid preferred converts who had committed their lives and deaths to the Prophet, especially convicts, who in general were already experienced in violence, as opposed to western leftist blowhards like this Intersectionalist professor.

One very exciting development was a recent upturn in the Mujahid's human trafficking enterprise. He'd lined up a filthy rich Hollywood customer for his next special delivery. The Mujahid was proud of his English and he had developed an appreciation for American slang. The Mujahid could "kill two birds with one stone." In one transaction he could take further sweet revenge on the family of the betrayer who'd been his nemesis back in Iraq and simultaneously rake in a huge profit. Once the Hollywood customer saw the girl's photo, he had immediately doubled his bid for Amir's daughter.

5 *Sarai*

While her mother sipped wine downstairs, Sarai sat at her little desk in her upstairs bedroom and drew pictures in her sketch book. Sometimes drawing helped Sarai focus on a problem. The problem right now was fixing her mom, so Sarai had set aside her favorite book—her big book of spectacular James Audubon bird paintings— and instead of copying the paintings drew pictures of her mom.

Mom had suggested once that Sarai could call her "Lily" if she wanted, but Sarai never called or even thought of her as anything but "Mom."

That's who Lily was, right? Her Mom. Not a friend, certainly not a pal or a buddy or a bestie. Sarai had plenty of friends including three best friends at school, and could get more any time she wanted, but she had only one mother. Sarai adored Lily as a mother, but she didn't think much of her skills as a friend—although of course Sarai never said that out loud.

Mother or friend, Sarai worried about her. Tonight Sarai was sticking to paper and flare pens, mostly the plum colored one. Of all the colors Sarai could choose from, the plum ink gave her the hue closest to the red wines Mom been favoring the past few months.

Sarai ignored the computer sitting on the desk in front of her. With a computer, you could copy and save and erase and paint with any of a zillion colors and that was great, but Sarai enjoyed the smell of the ink on the paper and the crunchy noise you got when you crumpled up the paper and tossed it if you didn't like the picture. Sarai had already thrown a bunch of wadded-up Mom drawings towards her waste basket in the corner.

Sarai also enjoyed the satisfied feeling she got when she made a swish in the basket. Just this moment, a few wads she'd missed with lay on the carpet near the basket. No hurry. Mom had totally slacked off on her inspections of Sarai's room. When Sarai got around to it Sarai could collect the crumples and dunk them all at one time into the basket.

Her drawings were mostly just cartoons. Sarai sketched Mom lolling about the house in plum sweatpants and a plum tee shirt instead of the fancy outfits she used to wear when she went out almost every night, or Mom eating a pop tart—she never used to eat things like that—as well as Mom crying for no immediate reason, big round plum colored tears streaming down her face. The sketch Sarai was working on just now showed Mom sitting in a purple chair staring at a ringing purple phone in her hand but not answering it.

Enough sketches of Mom looking sad. Sarai could see the real thing any evening just by opening her bedroom door and strolling downstairs. Sarai crumpled the half-finished picture and threw it towards her waste basket and banked it off the wall for two points.

Sarai stuck her plum pen back in the pack and took out an olive one to start her new subject. It was Uncle Amir's face, kind and warm and with a silly little mustache, pretending to glare at Sarai over a chess board.

Sarai recalled every detail of Amir's face because she'd loved it. His had been everything a grownup's face should be, patient and kind. He was usually sad, but once in a while he flashed a quick smile when she caught him off guard and said or did something he thought smart or funny.

His smile always seemed to flare for an instant and then disappear. It was like he never actually decided to smile. The smile just came out of him on its own and disappeared an instant later without his having anything to say about it one way or the other.

That's how she knew Uncle Amir's smile was real; it was nothing like that fake painted-on expression that always overstayed its welcome, the phony thing adults wasted on her when they tried too hard.

The best part was that even though Sarai was only nine, Uncle Amir had treated her like just another regular person. He argued with her and made fun of her and in their chess games he never let up or took it easy on her. When she finally did beat him once after months of trying, she knew she'd earned it. And although he pretended to be upset, she knew he was even happier about it than she was.

The chess pieces were harder to draw. They were just lifeless wooden things cut in weird jagged shapes. They kind of took over the picture too. She didn't want that.

She wanted them small. Uncle Amir's face had to be the most important part of the picture. But she'd drawn the pieces too big. Maybe it had something to with perspective. Sarai's art teacher Ms. Collins had mentioned perspective but hadn't explained much about it.

Sarai needed to learn more about perspective. Then she'd be able to paint her complete memory of Uncle Amir and the chess games at Dad's house and the fun they'd all had together before Mom's client Tariq Daghestani helped murder Uncle Amir and framed Dad for it.

Dad wanted her to call him "Dad." He did not pretend he wanted to be her friend. Dad wanted to be her dad and did okay at it even though Sarai lived with Mom in St. Paul and Dad lived ninety minutes away in Ojibwa City.

Drawing Uncle Amir gave Sarai an idea. She put the sketch into a drawer to look at later and fix up once she figured out how to draw the chess pieces better. Maybe she'd even paint it in.

Her new idea was to draw Amir's daughter Zarah. Then she'd have pictures of both.

The problem was Sarai had never seen Zarah or even a photo of her. Sarai thought of Zarah as her cousin—but only sort of, because Amir had been a friend and not Sarai's real official uncle exactly—so his daughter wouldn't be Sarai's real official cousin exactly either—just a sort-of cousin.

So what? Neither Mom nor Dad had any brothers or sisters, so Sarai had no real cousins anyway. She'd take what she could get.

Also, no one knew where Zarah was. Or even *if* she was, according to Mom and Dad and Grandpa. The adults had told Sarai about a million times there was no proof Zarah even existed. The only evidence of her existence was the fact that Sarai—and only Sarai—had heard Uncle Amir call Sarai "Zarah" a few times, and the adults had insisted that was almost certainly by mistake.

There are things you just know. Sarai knew with perfect faith Zarah was out there somewhere and that the adults needed to get cracking and look for her. What if Zarah was in some kind of trouble? With Uncle Amir dead, Zarah had no dad of her own to protect her.

There is only so much a nine-year-old can do in this world. If the grownups wouldn't do their jobs, if Mom couldn't fix herself and if the grownups couldn't or wouldn't find Zarah, Sarai wasn't going to just sit in her room and wait around. She had an idea how she could push things along.

Sarai took a black pen and sketched a Zarah looking a lot like herself, a girl about nine years old, olive skinned and dark haired and smiling. Maybe she had dark eyes and a strong nose like Sarai's. Sarai hoped she wasn't in any kind of trouble.

6 *Zarah's Fire*

Zarah had to escape tonight. What she'd fixed in her mind a few nights ago as an idea or a hope or a general plan was now a desperate immediate need—Jabali had come back and he scared her more than ever.

He called himself "Jabali" but sometimes he let a strange smile play on his lips when he said his own name, like he thought his name was a funny joke.

Zarah didn't see anything funny about Jabali. Maybe he grinned that ugly grin because he knew his name was a word for a kind of pig both in Arabic and in Spanish. Maybe he thought being a pig was funny. That would be just like him. She didn't know and she didn't care.

Jabali was a fat man even older than Ali. Jabali would rumble down the road to the Compound in a big black noisy SUV with huge black wheels that sprayed sand and gravel behind him. Then he jumped out of the SUV and slammed the door and shouted for Ali.

Jabali looked like that cartoon character she'd seen on television back home who was always trying to kill Bugs Bunny—not the bald one, but the one with a big greasy mustache that drooped down both sides of his thick lips like two scimitars. Jabali wore a black pistol with a squarish grip poking out of a stiff black plastic holster.

He always brought a big brown bottle of an alcohol drink and made a big show of swigging it down and offered it to Ali who always made a big show of refusing it and then they both laughed. Ali laughed a lot when Jabali came.

Twice in the past Jabali had delivered children younger than Zarah to live in the Compound and left them behind. One of these times Zarah saw Ali give him money. Another time he took a little boy away with him.

What scared Zarah this particular day was that for the first time Jabali fixed a long strange stare directly at her. He'd gone into Ali's tent with Ali and they stayed in there awhile and they came out and

Jabali looked at Zarah like he thought he could gobble her down for dinner the way he gobbled his food and then he winked at her and made a big slurping noise and Ali laughed and then the two men shook hands and went back into the tent.

Zarah had seen this kind of thing before in other places. She'd seen expressions like Jabali's on the faces of other men who'd taken other children.

She ran and hid among the stacks of tires on the edge of the Compound. Piles of big empty green and black garbage bags littered the ground. Zarah didn't know what the bags were for. She supposed somebody put things in them, but she didn't know what. She grabbed a bunch of the bags and covered herself with them like slippery green and black blankets. She crouched trembling under the bags for hours until Aida found her and pulled the bags off her.

This time Aida didn't beat Zarah. Aida just shook her finger at Zarah and then her shook her head and muttered something and ordered Zarah to go to training.

At first Zarah was glad Aida didn't beat her but then she thought about it and she wasn't glad after all.

Ali conducted two hours of training every day. He wanted each child to learn how to be a good jihadi and a good terrorist, even what he called a good "one-time terrorist." Zarah hated the idea of being a terrorist. She was especially suspicious of being a one-time terrorist. She knew what that meant—she'd seen it in her home country.

Today Ali showed all the children a picture of a school in a big city he said was north and east of them and explained that because they were small children they would have no trouble tricking their way into this school and mounting a good attack. He said it would be soon—very soon, in fact—and then made one of the smiles he made with his big teeth showing.

He said the school was full of people he called Khaffir, by which he meant non-Muslims.

This made no sense to Zarah. Back home there had always been a few people around who were not Muslim. A few times some of

29

them had come to her family's home for dinner. They seemed mistaken and confused, but her parents never talked about killing them.

Over the past few weeks, Ali had taught the children about choke points, ideal attack sites, and defense of safe havens. He said the Compound itself was a safe haven they should defend with their weapons and their lives and that was one reason he taught the children how to use different kinds of guns.

Zarah didn't like shooting pistols, which were heavy and hurt her hands when she fired them, but she didn't mind the bigger AR-15 rifle, which she could fire easily and didn't hurt her shoulder at all. Using the AR-15 to blow holes in big pieces of paper was about the only fun thing she did in the compound.

Today's lesson was about "perimeter rings". Ali explained what that was and how to escape through it. Then he made the children play a game. They took turns being part of a perimeter ring among the tire stacks surrounding the compound and being the one who tried to escape.

Since Zarah was actually planning to escape, she watched and listened closely, but she didn't think she learned much she hadn't already thought of on her own. When it was her turn to pretend to escape, she acted like a stupid little girl who didn't know what she was doing.

But of course she did know. Ali had emphasized over and over in their training that drills and rehearsals were essential to success in any struggle. Following his advice, she'd rehearsed her escape several nights in a row.

For example, she already knew about the tunnel where they were supposed to take cover if the Khaffir police or soldiers came. Of course, she wasn't going to try to escape through the tunnel—Ali would catch her in an instant.

And she'd already figured out how to use the piles of hundreds of old tires stacked around most of the perimeter. The stacks were big and black and higher than her head and they gave off a rubber smell. If she touched one it sometimes left black marks on her hands. But the tire stacks were good for hiding things and sometimes herself in secret places.

There were only three openings in the perimeter line of tire stacks. A narrow one opened on the nearby gravel road Jabali used to drive in and out. A huge sand dune blocked the second and largest gap on the opposite side of the compound in the direction of the hills and houses. And there was one tiny opening to and from the vegetable garden where all the girls worked.

After the perimeter training everyone went into the big tent and prayed and ate and then prayed again.

After sunset, Zarah went into the girls' tent and undressed and folded her gray abaya and laid it on the ground so that she was wearing only her jeans and tee shirt. She lay on her mattress and pulled her thin blanket over herself, covering even her head. She kept her socks and shoes on but was careful to keep her blanket covering them too so no one would see them.

She thought, Jabali wants me for that thing they do. But I won't be here.

By evening's end, the other girls had drifted in and lay down to sleep. Zarah stayed awake. A couple of girls chattered a while in the darkness, but Zarah pretended she was already asleep. She said nothing and fought off sleep and kept her eyes open and stared into the blackness under her blanket.

Late in the night, when all the other girls seemed asleep and the whole Compound was silent she rolled off her mattress onto the ground and stood and slipped her abaya on over her head and snuck out.

A billion stars shone down on her in the clear desert sky. The moon was full. It was the best kind of night she could hope for.

She crawled along the rocky uneven ground to the kitchen tent. Although the abaya slowed her progress it also cushioned her knees and elbows from the gravel and grit and sand. She pulled up the plastic lower edge of the tent and crawled under it. She crept across the tent floor to the table Aida and the older girls like Zarah used for cooking. In one quick deft movement Zarah straightened up and snatched the big chopping knife off the table and ducked down again.

Now she had almost all the equipment she needed: the knife and the cigarette lighter she'd swiped the previous week.

But she'd spotted something new on the table—a big bottle of the alcoholic drink she'd seen Jabali offer Ali. Jabali must have left it as a gift—another of his jokes. Of course, it was still sealed. Ali never opened the bottles to drink from them, but in training he'd shown the children some ways to use the brown liquor inside.

She straightened up again and grabbed the bottle and stuck it in the right pocket of her abaya and ducked down. She crawled out of the tent. She stopped to lower the flap behind her after she got outside.

She crawled to her favorite tire stack and lay the bottle on the ground and jumped up and grabbed the edge of the stack's topmost tire and pulled herself up. The top tires started to sway as if the whole stack might topple. She caught her breath and held still and used up precious seconds waiting for the stack to steady.

Now the hardest part—but also the most important. Once on top she lay on her belly across the tire and stuck her right hand down into the stack into its even deeper darkness.

She had hidden the end of a rope wedged between two tires near the top of the stack. But which side? She probed with her finger tips all around the inside of the tires but felt nothing.

Was this the wrong stack? No—this was the third stack in from the biggest pile of green plastic garbage bags, the stack against which she'd leaned the upright pallet. She was sure.

Urgency set Zarah's heart pounding. Her plan required a big head start before sunrise. If she couldn't find them she might as well give up and sneak back to her mattress.

She took out her cigarette lighter and with her feet hooked over the top tire she leaned head first down as far as she dared. With her left hand she gripped the inside of a tire to keep from falling in. With her right hand she flicked on the lighter. The flame blinded her for an instant but then her eyes got used to it and she saw the end of the rope. Somehow the rope had dislodged and fallen all the way to the ground on the bottom.

The flame flickered upward towards her face and licked at her hair. She pretended her mind was a camera and snapped a mental picture of the rope's location and flicked off the lighter.

With all the strength in her legs she pulled herself back up. She rearranged herself. She grabbed the topmost tire and lowered herself feet first down into the stack. Once her feet touched down, she crouched and felt around the ground with her right hand. She found the end of the rope where she pictured it in her mind and pulled it up. The two full canteens she'd hooked onto the rope earlier followed with it.

She looped the rope over her the back of her neck and her shoulders and adjusted the canteens so that the two balanced, one hanging on each side. She reached up and grabbed the top tire of the stack and climbed back up. Once at the top she swiveled her legs and lowered herself feet first down onto the ground outside.

When she hit the ground the two canteens clanked together. She grabbed them to cut the noise and dove onto the dirt and froze again.

No one came.

She retrieved the liquor bottle and stuck it in her pocket again and hugged the canteens to her chest to keep them silent. Just as Ali had trained her to crawl on her elbows and knees with a rifle in her hands, she crawled the thirty meters or so over the hard ground to the gap in the tires Jabali had driven through that very morning.

As she expected, John was sitting by the entrance, leaning against a tire. What he was doing was forbidden—smoking a stinking cigarette on guard.

She knew what came next. In every rehearsal, she'd practiced this same route out of her dorm tent to the kitchen tent and then to the tires and then to the Compound entrance by Jabali's road. At the end of each rehearsal she'd watched John smoke part of a single cigarette and then doze off.

It happened just like before. John tossed his half-smoked butt on the ground and lay back against his tire stack and in an instant fell asleep. She could just zip past him through the gap onto the road while John slept.

Zarah paused. She did not know where Jabali's gravel road led. All she knew was it led somewhere. She had planned to follow the road or tracks Jabali left in the desert to some place where there were other people. But who would these other people be? Others like Jabali?

Ali had said over and over that a good jihadi adjusts his plan to unexpected situations and unplanned opportunities.

Here was an expected situation—the sleeping guard and the burning cigarette on the ground. But she also had an unplanned opportunity—the bottle of alcohol.

Zarah tiptoed around and grabbed a bunch of plastic garbage bags and stuffed them under a tire stack about two meters from John. She lodged the bags in as firm as she could. She unscrewed the bottle cap and poured most of the alcohol from the bottle onto the bags until the liquid collected in small puddles in the bag's pockets and wrinkles and overflowed onto the ground.

Between thumb and finger she picked up John's still burning half-cigarette by its filter and dropped it on the ground about a meter away from the bags. She dribbled some of the remaining alcohol in a thin trail on the ground from the bags back to the cigarette and then a final couple of drops onto the burning tip of the cigarette.

The cigarette went out.

Zarah picked up the cigarette and stuck its filter into her mouth and took out her lighter and re-lit the cigarette and puffed with fury. The few drops of alcohol she'd soaked into the cigarette tip added even more stink, but they helped it flare up. Smoke and tears flooded her eyes. She took out the cigarette and clapped her free hand over her mouth to hold in the coughing fit that wracked her.

She puffed more and when the cigarette tip glowed bright red she dropped the cigarette into the alcohol trail she'd poured into the dirt. The alcohol started to flame. The flame race down the liquid path towards the plastic garbage bags she'd spread under and against the tires. The liquid caught fire and the bags began to fume a stinking black smoke. For a few instants Zarah watched to make sure the flames spread to the other garbage bags. When they did, she sprinted towards the big dune on the opposite side of the Compound.

7 *Mattie at The Vauxhall Arms*

When Hack got back from court and opened the door to their hotel room he found Mattie lying on her back in the big king bed, sheets pulled up to her chin, only her head and naked shoulders and arms poking out. She flashed him a big goofy grin like a small-town tourist in the big city. Which to Hack seemed about right.

He walked over and sat on the edge of the bed. "Comfy?"

"I napped. Couldn't help it. I'm a queen in a castle."

Hack made a show of inspecting the room: the wide desk with its large swivel chair, the cushy brown leather sofa, the big bureaus, the impressionist prints on the walls. "Not exactly the Ojibwa City Minnesota Motel Four."

She seemed to adjust herself under her sheets. "Are we really going to get to stay in this palace the whole week?"

"Longer maybe. Until the end of the trial. I told you, Sam's got some special thing he wants me to investigate."

"Don't you need some kind of license for that?"

"Probably. But he wrote me down as his computer consultant, which I'll do too. No license needed for that. Yet."

Her face turned serious. "And you haven't forgotten your promise to Sarai about finding Zarah."

He sighed. "I feel bad. But my sweet daughter didn't get around to telling me how. I've dug around all over the Internet and written emails and letters and submitted complicated forms to international agencies who take months to answer. It's a big planet with six billion people spread over two hundred countries. If Zarah even exists she could be anywhere on it."

"I know. I feel bad too. I've seen."

"Then you've also seen I can't get a job since first Gogol-Checkov and then ZNN did a number on my reputation. No one wants to hire a toxic racist Islamophobic white supremacist, even to code. And if Sam wins, SWASU pays his attorney's fees and his expenses, which includes me."

"And if he loses?"

"He's good for it."

Mattie had scattered empty snack packets and wrappers all over the room. Hack picked up an empty green plastic bag from her night stand next to the bed. A tiny cloud of peanut dust swooshed up. He said, "I see you raided the mini bar."

"I was hungry."

"By my estimate, that's about seventy-three dollars and eighty-four cents of snacks you scarfed."

"Worth every cent."

"Aren't you the teensiest bit repentant?"

"It's my birthday."

"You didn't tell me that."

"Now I have. But the truth is I thought free snacks came with the room. This is my first time in a classy hotel."

He said, "Well, don't worry about it. Sam won't. He won a ten-million-dollar contingency fee a few years ago suing some banks."

"Hmm…Worth knowing. So as long as we're here I plan to enjoy every minute of this hotel and you."

"How can I help?"

She seemed to wriggle. Even with her torso covered up Hack couldn't help noticing the outlines pressing up under the sheets. She said, "Well I have heard stories."

"What stories?"

"I've heard"—she pointed her index finger in his face—"the minute your typical horny male bastard traps a woman alone in a fancy hotel room, right away he's got nothing on his male pea brain but sex." She nodded. "They call it 'Hotel Sex'. He can't help it. It's hormones. Something to do with evolution."

"You think the African Savannah had hotel rooms?"

"They had bushes."

He said, "How'd you come by this anthropological insight?"

"Every woman any man ever suckered into a classy hotel room knows about it. From sad and bitter experience." She grabbed the top of her sheet and flung it away from herself with a flourish. Her grin turned out to be all she was wearing. "Is it true?"

8 Zarah's Inferno

Zarah sprinted through the darkness away from the fire and towards the sand dune and the gap it made in the Compound perimeter of tires. In the near darkness she collided hard with the dune. She leaned forward and clawed for purchase to pull herself up.

Grit sprayed through her fingers. Her sneakers splatted the sand behind her as she dug in and scrambled upwards. Every two steps up she slid down one. Once she slid back all the way down to the bottom. Only her abaya cushioned her knees as they slammed into the hard ground.

When she finally reached the top of the dune she sat and put her feet in front of her. She slid feet-first down the side of the dune until her sneakers hit firm ground. She sat on the ground and took off each shoe and shook the grit out and put the shoe on again, careful to tie its string in a perfect knot. She stood and wiped the debris off her abaya and started to walk into the open desert towards the hills to her east.

She'd covered at least a hundred meters when she heard the first yells from the compound behind her. She paused to glance back over her shoulder. A spreading red glow of flame punctuated the otherwise fathomless darkness. She listened a moment to the screaming and cursing voices and resumed her walk, lengthening her stride, but determined not to give in to her impulse to run. Instead, she picked her way with care along the rough dark ground.

She didn't trust the desert, especially at night. Many times she'd seen from the Compound that the surrounding terrain was uneven and full of rocks and holes and spiky vegetation. If she tripped and hurt herself she might slow down or even have to stop and it would be easier for Ali to find her and take her back to some new even more terrible punishment.

Thorny vegetation hid all around, eager to stick her. Thorns hurt a lot and could even make her sick. Huge cactuses with thick trunks and branches loomed over her in the darkness and stretched straight

39

up towards the sky like forked Arabic letter *alifs*. The big cactuses were scary, but the most dangerous might be the small ones that crouched low to the ground everywhere, hard to spot and easy to trip over in the night. She dodged among and around the plants.

New explosions thundered behind her. She stopped and turned completely around to look. She'd already reached a mild elevation of a few meters and she could see down and into the entire Compound.

The single small red glow of her original fire had multiplied into swarms of torches that spread towards one another until they coalesced into several blazes and finally into a single inferno. Brilliant detonations burst one after another, each with its own separate blinding blast and thunderous deafening roar.

And what were those four brilliant towers of flame that flared and soared up into the sky? Of course—trails from rockets Ali must have stored.

Small figures had fled the Compound and stood around it visible in the radiance. She counted. Were there only nine? Fear jabbed her in the chest and for a moment seemed to paralyze her breathing. She counted again. She spotted two children she'd missed the first time, standing in a small depression farther away, at first hidden in darkness but now revealed in the ever-greater incandescence. Eleven. She counted once more and then once more again. Eleven each time. So all the children she'd left behind had escaped, even John.

She saw no larger figures. So maybe Ali and Aida were nowhere around. She felt a twinge of regret about Aida, but for Ali, Zarah felt nothing at all.

What Zarah did feel was a shock that began to transform into a new terror. She'd meant the fire only the way Ali had taught—a way to distract an enemy. She'd hoped to trick Ali into thinking she'd escaped down Jabali's road so he would chase her in the wrong direction.

Zarah hadn't known Ali stored so many explosives. She hadn't realized her little fire could spread and blow them all skyward. She hadn't known about the rockets at all.

Though she was sweating in her abaya and from the warmth of the desert summer night and from her exertion, as the perspiration cooled her skin she began to tremble.

She reached under her garments and grabbed her amulet in both hands. This was no time to stand around shaking like a little girl. She had to get as far away as she could as fast as she could. She turned and took up her climb again, towards the peak of her hill and towards the town she hoped lay on the other side.

9 The Mujahid's Logical Questions

"What did you do with her?" the Mujahid asked Ali and Aida.

"Who do you mean?" Ali asked.

The Mujahid sat back relaxed in his easy chair and one at a time inspected each of the other three as they stood in front of him. At his command, Jabali and Ali and Aida had gathered in the sitting room of the Mujahid's safe house. He wanted to stay calm; in this very bad moment he very much needed to resist what he recognized as his own rage and occasional impetuosity.

Which was not easy. As politely as he could make himself, he asked again. "The little girl. Did you sell her on your own?"

Ali said, "Which little girl? We have six."

Ali watched the Mujahid. Aida's glance dart back and forth between Ali and the Mujahid. Jabali stood to one side and stared off into empty space.

"The one called Zarah. She was special to me. Did you sell her?"

Ali said, "No, of course not. Why would we do such a thing?"

"Money, of course," the Mujahid said.

Ali held his hands out in an imploring gesture. "What could that urchin possibly be worth?"

The Mujahid asked, "Did you ever wonder why I ordered you to give her a bigger ration of food?"

Ali said, "Because you cared about her?'"

The Mujahid snorted. "She's worth one million dollars American healthy," the Mujahid said.

"Really?" Ali said.

"Really."

Aida said, "Really?"

The Mujahid found this boring. "Really."

Ali said, "I had no idea."

"Nor I," Aida said.

Jabali said nothing.

The Mujahid said, "A Hollywood man offered me a million for

her."

"Why?" Ali asked.

"Who can explain the sick fancies of a man like that?" the Mujahid said. "A man who makes those movies that corrupt every thought and every yearning towards Allah any human being might feel? All the other children survived. So where is she?"

Aida said, "The fire must have burnt her up."

"I just said, all the other children survived. Why not her? And it's remarkably bad judgment for you to mention your fire, considering the damage it caused."

A few moments of silence while everyone thought. The Mujahid liked the silence. Maybe for a change silence would frighten the truth out of one of these idiots.

He gave up and broke the silence himself. "So how much did you charge Jabali when you tried to sell her to him?"

Ali said, "What?"

"What?" the Mujahid mocked. Then, "And don't lie."

Ali swallowed. "Five hundred dollars."

The Mujahid nodded, "Not only have you cost us a million dollars, you're a wretched businessman for yourself when you try to cheat me. Five hundred dollars. You lost our entire Compound. And do you imagine the Khaffir authorities didn't notice your little bonfire?"

Ali said nothing.

"Do you expect the authorities never heard or saw your inferno of explosions and rockets shooting into the air? From their local patrols or their outer space satellites? Any Khaffir astronaut they left behind on the moon must have seen them. Now huge stockpiles and inventories of weapons and drugs are blown up and the little girl is gone too. Your greed and incompetence have endangered ten years' work it has taken to build our networks and wasted tens of millions of our dollars. Do you understand?"

Ali said nothing.

"Yes," Aida said. "We understand."

"Jabali," the Mujahid said. He lifted his right hand.

With his left arm Jabali grabbed Ali from behind under Ali's left shoulder and across the top of his chest. With his right hand Jabali slashed his huge blade across the front of Ali's throat. Jabali dropped Ali and chased Aida the few feet she managed to scramble and repeated his efficient work with her.

Jabali turned to face the Mujahid over the bodies. He said, "I would not even have considered buying the girl if I'd known you had special plans for her. I would never deprive you of that kind of money."

"Not just money, but justice for an old enemy," the Mujahid said. "And I am certain you will not make the same mistake again."

"I will not," Jabali said.

"I want to know for sure if the little girl's dead. If she's not, I want to know where she is and I want her back."

"Of course," Jabali said.

"Now take care of the bodies." The Mujahid stood from his chair and walked around the bodies and then upstairs to bed. It had been a long night.

10 Lily's Salon

Lily sipped her coffee and stewed over her previous night's set-to with the ZNN reporter Lauren Goodwell. When she had awakened this morning, Lily still tasted the bitter metallic aftertaste that comes after violent emotion. Maybe it was time she cut back on the wine.

Today was going to be better. She was out of the house. She was lunching with four friends she hadn't seen in months.

Once a month Molly Caruthers hosted a Salon lunch at the Ojibwa Club in St. Paul. Molly was a poet and prestigious party host who'd come up with the Salon idea about eighteen months previous. Molly had called to invite Lily: "We'll gather smart creative people together, like they had in those nineteenth century Paris salons, you know, where George Sand read from her latest novels and Chopin and Liszt played their latest compositions and everyone had the most intelligent conversations. But this time women only."

"Sounds fun," Lily said. And it had also turned out to be good networking for her image consulting business. Molly invited only the kind of women who could hook Lily up with great clients. And Lily admitted to herself she felt flattered. She fit in with the other movers and shakers. She was one of them. She mattered.

Today four other women besides Lily sat at their favorite round table nestled in their special quiet cubbyhole of the Ojibwa Club's Sacagawea Room, where Molly's group had a standing monthly reservation.

Molly sat directly across from Lily. Molly was a warm plump blond woman out of whom flowed an apparently unlimited stream of kindness and understanding occasionally spiced with snark. To Lily's right sat the ultra-thin red-haired actress Sally Sue Boynton, who'd once starred in a network TV show and now acted in theaters around town when it suited her—her residuals meant she didn't need the money. On Molly's left sat Heather Hoyt, editor of "*Minnesota Happening Monthly*," her straight hair combed down her forehead in

45

brown bangs. Only the previous year she'd splashed Lily on her cover as the rising Minnesota businesswoman of the moment.

Today was special. Joleen Crowe had joined them. Joleen was the political powerhouse who'd served two terms as Minnesota Secretary of Education. Her graying hair was shaped in a short severe cut that didn't quite touch the collar of her black suit jacket.

Lily loved the Sacagawea Room. The Club founders had built the ceilings high with dark brown wood hewn from original old growth forests. From where Lily sat she could look through big bay windows directly onto a patio and beyond that down onto the banks of the Mississippi River, whose flowing blue surface sparkled in the sun with a myriad silver dimples.

The conversation was casual and pleasant. Everyone shared a bottle of Sauvignon Blanc except Lily, who feared a repeat of the previous night's debacle and stuck to her coffee. All five women feasted on delicious lightly dressed big salads and sweet oven-roasted carrots and crisp pea pods, followed of course by substantial chunks of the Ojibwa Club's renowned signature red cake.

Talk flowed free as the river below. The women chatted about their husbands if they had them or ex-husbands if they had those and various diets they'd failed at and politicians for whom they shared the required consensus visceral hatreds.

Lily found it pleasant just to listen, especially after her four months' isolation and the previous night. She contributed to the conversation only an occasional "that's so true" or "for sure" when someone hit on the right clever phrase and she made a point of laughing when someone made a witty remark.

After a while, hostess Molly noticed Lily's reserve and asked, "It's wonderful to see you again, Lily. Though you are quiet today. Everything all right with you?"

"Of course."

The editor Heather Hoyt asked, "How's business?"

"Fine."

"Getting new clients?"

"You bet."

"Anyone I know?"

Lily faked a smile. "You'll find out when the time comes."

"The reason I'm asking is I'd gotten the impression you're not giving your business as much attention since that incident of yours."

"No. Business is business. Attention must be paid, so I pay it. But I'm not really in the market for new clients. I'm full up."

Heather wasn't giving up. "But you did lose one, didn't you?"

"You could say that."

The actress Sally Sue asked, "What's that about, Heather?"

The politico Joleen said, "Heather's referring to the fact that a few months ago Lily ran over her own client Tariq Daghestani in her car and killed him. I knew him, of course—a good friend, I thought. He seemed such a distinguished and impressive man."

Heather said, "Yes. And so cultured too."

Sally Sue said, "Oh yes, that's right."

Molly put in, "Well, the man was driving a van loaded with explosives."

"I read that," Joleen said. "But when I read it I wondered."

"Wondered what?" Lily asked.

"Oh, it's probably not a good time."

Lily looked at her. "For what?"

Joleen said, "Never mind."

Lily said, "No. Go ahead, please. Mind. It's time I talked with friends. Until now I've talked only with the authorities."

Joleen said, "Well, I wondered, and I've seen some questions asked here and there on many news sources, how could you have known at the time, Lily?"

"Known what?"

"That van had explosives in it."

"I didn't," Lily said.

"I don't understand," Sally Sue said. "But you ran him over anyway?"

Molly said, "He was standing in the street pointing a gun at her

47

husband."

"Ex-husband," Heather said. "That's true, isn't it, Lily?"

"Oh," Sally Sue said. "Now I remember."

Heather said, "But what I don't understand—and I hope you'll forgive me, for asking this, Lily, but I guess it's the journalist in me—wasn't your ex-husband on the run from the police at the time? For murder? I mean, how'd you know he wasn't the one in the wrong? Maybe Doctor Daghestani had good reason to be pointing a gun at him."

"But no good reason for the van full of explosives," Molly said. "And do we really have to talk about all this?"

Lily said. "It's fine. Remember, I'd just seen Nat—the ex-husband you're all talking about—stop this man Khaled—who I knew was close to Daghestani—from shooting up a school bus full of Jewish kids."

Sally Sue asked, "So your ex seemed to know what he was doing? I mean, somehow?"

"Somehow." Lily nodded.

"Why does it matter what religion the kids were?" Sally Sue asked.

Lily said, "Well, it doesn't, as far as stopping the attack. I'd do that for any kids. But it obviously mattered to Khaled. He and Daghestani chose Jewish kids. First at the school bus and then at the JCC."

"So it has to do with Israel?" Joleen asked.

"Sure." Heather nodded. "Israel."

"Now I understand," Sally Sue said.

"I don't," Lily said. "Israel? Why Israel?"

"Well," Joleen said. "That's where the Jews have been having so many problems so many years with Muslims. So it's not surprising that something like this could happen. I mean, it is terrible, and I'm the last person to support this kind of thing, but you've got to admit—"

"No, I don't," Lily interrupted. "I don't admit whatever you're going to say next." Lily could feel the heat rising in her, but she couldn't stop herself.

Joleen shrugged. She made eye contact with Heather, who shrugged back at her. Their shared message: obviously Lily wasn't going to be reasonable. Probably best to let it go.

Lily thought, but should she let it go? These were her friends. Or were they? As good a time as any to find out. "There is no legitimate connection between whatever you think is going on between Israelis and Arabs and someone trying to blow my daughter and her friends to pieces."

"Of course not," Molly said. "No one said that."

"I certainly didn't," Joleen said. "But the point isn't whether the Muslim response is legitimate—no one says it is—but that this kind of thing wouldn't happen in the first place if the Israelis could make peace with the Arabs, who after all, were there first and are indigenous to the land."

"I don't buy that. Assuming for the sake of argument your version of what happened is true, which it's not."

"How can you say that?" Joleen asked.

"For starters, Jews are the indigenous people of that land," Lily said. "People call us Jews because we came from the ancient kingdom of Judea that existed three thousand years ago."

"Of course, you'd think that," Joleen said, "being Jewish yourself. And that's what's the Old Testament says. But there's no evidence outside that sexist old religious book that any such kingdom ever existed."

"I say it because it's true. Not just the Hebrew Scriptures. All western history says it. Two thousand years ago and more. The ancient Greek historians and philosophers and Roman historians too."

Joleen said, "Of course you'd say so."

"The Assyrians said so. In writing. In a version that squares with the Bible's version, King Sennacherib bragged how he'd cooped up a king he called 'Hezekiah the Jew' in Hezekiah's royal city

49

Jerusalem like a bird in a cage. In 700 B.C. Hundreds of years
before the Greeks and Romans came around and fourteen hundred
years before the Arabs took over."

"Assuming some of that's true," Joleen said. "Does it justify
what Zionists do?"

Sally Sue said, "That's another thing I don't understand. People
I know are always talking about these terrible Zionists. Who are
these Zionists?"

"Me. I'm a Zionist," Lily said. She looked around. She was a
Zionist? She repeated it slowly, as if she were revealing and
discovering something at the same time. "I am a Zionist. And even
if I hadn't been a Zionist before I had to run down Daghestani—that
fucking monster—I am now."

There. She'd done it. She'd dropped the Big One—the F-
Bomb—a definite nuclear turd—into the previously semi-polite
conversation.

Molly said, "Lily's upset. She doesn't necessarily mean
everything she's saying."

Why stop now? "Of course I mean it. The Jews have as much
right to our own country as anyone else. Arabs have twenty
countries. Muslims have fifty. All we want is one tiny Jewish
country on one percent of the land from that corrupt old Muslim
Turkish empire, where a million Jews suffered as second-class
citizens under the Muslim version of Jim Crow. Then came 1918
when the British broke up the Turkish empire and said we could live
in our own country again—if we can keep it."

Lily began to run out of gas. She added, "Which we will." She
nodded. "Keep it, I mean." She felt the warm flush in her neck and
face.

She looked around the table. The other women were staring at
her, Molly in sympathy and Sally Sue in confusion. Heather and
Joleen were shaking their heads in apparent pitying sadness: poor
Lily—she used to be one of us—an educated progressive person
who would never dream of running a man over in her car, now

ranting like a religious fanatic.

Yes, her rant complete with its F-Bomb was a definite conversation stopper.

And a Salon stopper too, it turned out. The other women all split the bill and got up and left and muttered polite goodbyes and Molly took Lily's hand in both of hers and said, "We'll talk soon, Lily. In the meantime, take care of yourself" and patted Lily's hand and followed the others out.

Lily wandered alone out of the now-empty Sacagawea Room through the halls of the Ojibwa Club and out the door to the parking lot and her BMW. She stopped by the driver side door and looked back at the building. What had she been doing for an entire year in that place with those women?

She got in her car and drove home, immersed in even more misery than she'd felt after her ZNN fiasco. And this time she'd been completely sober, although probably jacked up from all the coffee.

Had she entered some strange Alice-in-Wonderland world? Where everybody else knew facts Lily knew were lies? Where Lily herself knew in her soul things few of the people in her world seemed to fathom?

Could the others imagine what it felt like to hit a human being with your car? To drive your four-thousand-pound machine at him intending to hit him? To hear the thud of metal against flesh? To follow through and plow under him and see the man fly through the air and land and splatter against the pavement like a broken doll?

No, of course not.

But did they also really understand in their souls about men like Khaled and Daghestani who'd shoot up a bus full of children or blow up a building full of human beings just because their targets were Jews?

No, of course not.

If they come to kill you, you have the right to kill them first. If they come to kill your children, it's not just a right, it's an obligation. Every mother knows that.

And what about the Zionism thing? She'd always dismissed her father's tedious prattling about the Jewish state as sentimental gibberish which made sense only to Sam's older generation, still stuck in its tribal past of primitive loyalties.

Lily and her friends were nothing like her father and his friends. She attached to no tribe. She was on the right side of history, part of a great universal human community emerging with greater extent and force each day, a consensus that would do away with nationalisms and borders and the horribly destructive wars that those regressive relics inflicted on humanity.

Sure, she sent Sarai to a Jewish school. Partly it was to make Sam happy, but mostly because it boasted a high academic record, and maybe as a side benefit to expose Sarai to ideas Sarai would naturally reject as she grew older and wiser as Lily had grown.

But she'd just heard herself parrot every argument from her father she'd ever ignored. She'd heard her own voice out loud calling herself a Zionist. It was like discovering she'd been a Mississippi Delta blues singer her entire life and hadn't known it. Or a Chinese woman. Or a woman trapped in the brain of a man.

She was a Zionist trapped in the brain of a Progressive.

11 Grandmother

Zarah had been on the move uphill about two hours when she decided it was time to rest and plan. The rising sun was about to pile its additional blistering heat on top of the nighttime mugginess. She needed shelter.

She sat on the ground and looked back downward towards the ruin of the compound, only a small black blister in the distance. She was now too far away to see the people she knew must be there.

She lifted one of her canteens and unscrewed the lid and took several big gulps—the first water of her trek.

Zarah fingered Grandmother's amulet through her abaya and tee shirt. When Zarah was much younger and smaller than now Zarah's parents had sent her on a two-week visit with her Bedouin Grandmother.

Everybody called the woman "Grandmother." Later, Zarah had decided she couldn't be Zarah's actual grandmother, so maybe she was something like Zarah's grandmother's grandmother. She was the oldest person Zarah had ever known and looked it. Ravines corrugated her dark brown cheeks like the deepest wadis of the desert.

She could walk, but barely, and so slowly Zarah felt like a puppy dancing around her when Grandmother teetered her way across her home camp.

The women in the camp cared for Grandmother. Even the men treated her with respect. The women brought Grandmother food and water once early every evening, which was the only time she ate. Since her teeth had long ago vanished they fed her only figs and other soft food she could gum.

Grandmother taught Zarah to sit on the ground and eat only with the three fingers of her right hand from the camp meals, which gave off aromas different from those in Zarah's city home but were still wonderful.

Grandmother's skin was wrinkled like an old date dried too long in the desert sun. She even smelled sort of like an old date. But Zarah loved dates and she loved this ancient woman, so it was a happy smell. Grandmother could also be demanding and forgetful and distracted, but she was always kind and sweet to Zarah whenever she showed awareness of Zarah, which sadly wasn't always.

Grandmother wore an amulet about her neck she declared protected her. She took it off once or twice and let Zarah hold and admire it. It didn't look like much—only some cheap looking silvery beads hung on a small string. The strings looped through a small clasp to where they bunched together. Even at that young age Zarah could tell it couldn't be as expensive as some of the necklaces and rings she'd seen on women in her home city. But the idea fascinated Zarah—that a bauble could keep a woman alive a hundred years or more.

Grandmother didn't just give Zarah occasional treats and pet and kiss her. Grandmother worried that growing up in the city, Zarah wasn't learning everything she needed to know in order to grow into a proper woman. So she asked Zarah hard questions about things Zarah had never thought of.

Once Grandmother said, "So, tender city blossom, if you were out in that desert all alone and you didn't bring water with you, what would you do?"

It was early evening. The two sat cross-legged next to each other on the edge of Grandmother's fragrant tent. They looked out into the desert beyond the green Jericho rose plants and the low yucca bushes with their bright scarlet flowers strung on thin green stalks and the two gum Arabic trees with their spiny branches. To Zarah the desert looked like nothing but empty sand dunes, barren, grim and hopeless.

Zarah said, "Find some water, I guess."

"You guess. But how?"

"I don't know, Grandmother."

"How could you, growing up so far from your proper home?

What do they teach you in that school you go to?" She shook her head with sadness. "But I will tell you." She nodded her head up and down and sang this last phrase three times like it was part of some old song. "I will tell you, I will tell you, I will tell you."

Then in the same tune, she sang, "You will remember, you will remember, you will remember." Then in a more normal speaking voice, "Water flows down. Do you understand?"

"I'm not sure."

"If you see hills, head toward them. The likeliest place to find water is at the bottom of a hill. Will you remember?"

"Yes, Grandmother."

"Or maybe you will see some damp sand. You can dig there. There might be water under the dampness. Will you remember?"

"Yes, Grandmother. I will remember."

"Animals need water too. And they know things we don't. So if you see an animal trail, the trail may lead you to water."

"Yes. I see."

"Now answer me: If you come upon an animal trail on a hill and if the trail goes both up and down which way will you go? Uphill or downhill?"

Zarah thought for a moment. "Downhill, Grandmother."

"Why?"

"You just said water flows down and not up."

Grandmother kissed Zarah on her forehead. "You do listen. And you are smart. You will remember, won't you?"

"Yes, Grandmother."

And Zarah did remember, which was one more reason she'd headed towards the hills in the eastern distance instead of going down Jabali's road towards whatever foul hole Jabali had come out of. She knew she was going to need water, and of course where there was water there might also be food. The lack of food worried her. The two canteens would last awhile, but she carried no food— only the knife and the lighter. And of course, Grandmother's final gift.

She clutched the amulet with both hands and more of Grandmother's advice came back. In the day, Zarah could look and listen for birds because the birds could see from the air where there was water and fly there. Or just before sunrise, Zarah could dig up cool stones and lick the dew that collected on them.

When Grandmother had mentioned licking dew off stones the ancient woman had burst into laughter. It was kind of a cackle really, but it was beautiful anyway.

Zarah laughed too. The idea of water from stones seemed funny. After a while she stopped laughing but Grandmother shook her head and kept laughing until tears ran down the grooves in her dry furrowed cheeks like rain down dry stream beds.

Zarah asked, "What's so funny?"

"I just remembered how during one of the really big wars many years ago when I was a young girl only ten or twenty years older than you are now, we found the wreck of a British jeep. All made of cold metal. So much water collected on the silvery ribs and in little sockets and dripped off, it was like discovering a new well."

She laughed again and muttered something about human skeletons Zarah didn't catch and stared off into a past Zarah couldn't imagine. Then she sighed and fell asleep. Zarah leaned against her and napped too.

The last day of Zarah's visit, when Zarah's father came to pick up Zarah and take her home, Grandmother said, "Very soon I won't need this anymore." She was no taller than Zarah and she didn't have to bend down. She lifted the amulet from around her own neck and placed it around Zarah's and kissed Zarah's forehead one last time.

As Zarah made her way through the night over the rough ground away from the compound and towards the distant hills, every so often she felt through the fabric for her amulet to reassure herself it was still there. She sang to Grandmother and to herself in Grandmother's old tune: "I remember, I remember, I remember."

12 *Mattie's Birthday Dinner*

Mattie stared down at her plate. Tuna on toast. Mattie hated fish and she especially hated tuna. It reminded her of growing up poor, not merely deprived poor but ravenous go-to-bed-hungry poor, the kind of poor that came from having a father too sick to work but too proud to take welfare, when they never ate fresh meat and when frozen fish sticks were close as they got. And tuna? Self-respecting alley cats who happened on it ought to sniff once and hop off their garbage can lids and stalk away.

The Hedgehog Barrel Bar and Grill had seemed the natural choice for her birthday dinner. It was only a short walk from the Vauxhall Arms, and the website promised honking big platters of beef and live country music, both of which Hack and Mattie loved.

The waitress who dumped the tuna on Mattie's plate was terrible. Mattie had waitressed ten years and she knew bad waitressing when she saw it—Mattie had run into the worst waitress ever.

The Hedgehog Barrel hostess who'd led Hack and Mattie to their table had been professional and friendly. When she saw Hack and Mattie push through the old-fashioned saloon-style double swinging doors she smiled in welcome from behind her podium. Then she conducted them past the huge hardwood bar that stretched along the left front side of the restaurant to their table near the stage.

The stage was on the back right, an empty cube carved out of the Hedgehog Barrel's red brick back wall. The stage was about eight feet high and twelve feet wide and twelve feet deep. The brown planks of its polyurethane-coated hardwood floor gleamed in the light flooding down from its ceiling.

When the hostess left Mattie and Hack at their table Mattie saw Hack eye the stage and in an instant knew what he was thinking.

Mattie like the smell and look of the Hedgehog Barrel. Its smell was the old-fashioned beer smell she associated with the good times she'd spent with her two aunts as a kid when they'd let her hang out with them in local bars. That had been her first chance to sing in public. She'd hop onto a table and sing for quarters. Everyone, even the drunks—especially the drunks, actually—treated her like a princess.

The Hedgehog Barrel had an old-west look, but it was clean and modern, with high gray metal ceilings, a wide dark brown floor and lots of wooden tables and chairs. She figured the big space could handle at least a hundred fifty customers.

Fun pictures decorated the walls on all sides. Some were old sepia photos of long-dead tough desert Indians and dusty cavalrymen glaring into the camera. Newer and bigger vivid colorful paintings of wild west scenes hung here and there: cowboys with bright red or green scarves and huge domed hats roping steers or breaking broncs, grizzled cooks dispensing heaping helpings from chuck wagons, and dogged prospectors up to their knees in mountain streams panning for gold.

Of course, there was the obligatory photo of the actor Val Kilmer as Doc Holiday in the movie "Tombstone," smirking at the camera, the famous caption beneath him: "I'm your huckleberry."

She'd never quite figured out what a huckleberry was, but everyone knew it was cool. She also knew that her new guy Hack had turned out to be a huckleberry when he needed to.

Then Jennifer showed up. The waitress. She was shapely enough—although Mattie thought her plumper than she needed to be—and she piled her blond hair in a big bouffant on top of her head. In the single brief glimpse Mattie got of Jennifer's big blue eyes before Jennifer turned her back on Mattie to face Hack, those eyes seemed to gleam. "Hi, I'm Jennifer and I'll be taking care of you," Jennifer announced to Hack. "Would you like a beverage, sir?"

"Water, please," Hack said. "And a beer—whatever comes in a cold bottle."

"Of course," Jennifer said and sashayed away.

A rare opportunity: Mattie'd never been personally on the spot to watch some bitch seduce her ex-husband Rennie. Too late after the fact, she'd come to realize it'd been happening plenty. She was curious to watch the process unfold with Hack.

An instant later, Jennifer returned with a sixteen-ounce glass and a pitcher of ice water and with a flourish set it on the table directly in front of him and poured him a glass. "I'll have your beer out in a minute. Have you decided what you want to eat, sir?"

Hack said, "A burger and fries, please."

"No problem," Jennifer said, and turned to leave.

"Just a second, please," Hack said. "Let's not forget my friend."

"Yes, let's not," Mattie put in. "I'd like the same, please."

Jennifer kept her eyes on Hack. She nodded and smiled at him. "No problem." She left. If anything she enhanced the arc and swath of her sashay.

A heavy-set man with a gray beard and big black cowboy hat pulled a clattering metal hand cart loaded with music gear past their table. He stopped his cart next to the stage. One by one he lifted drums and stands and cymbals up. He grunted as he hoisted his big barrel body onto the stage. Piece by piece he moved his gear to the middle of the back and began assembling the components into a drum kit.

Mattie watched Hack watch the man. Hack said, "A fourteen-inch bass drum. Interesting."

Mattie wasn't sure what was interesting about the measurement of a bass drum. On the job singing she'd never paid much attention to the particulars of the instrumentalists playing behind her. They just made sounds she liked or didn't like and helped her along or got in her way.

Jennifer popped up again. With no connection to anything Mattie knew about Jennifer's actual job, Jennifer asked Hack, "New to Phoenix?"

"That's right," Hack said. "How'd you guess?"

"Oh, I can always spot a newbie," Jennifer said. "Tip: drink lots of water. That's why I brought the big glass and the pitcher."

"It is hot out there."

"A hundred and eight right now. And that's after sunset. I think it hit a hundred fifteen today."

"You don't say."

Behind Jennifer, a man at another table was making ever more extravagant arm waving movements, obviously trying for Jennifer's attention. Mattie said, "Jennifer, I think one of your other customers might need something."

"Really?" Jennifer glanced over her shoulder.

Hack smiled. "He looks desperate and we're fine. Maybe you should take care of him."

Jennifer shrugged. "Okay," and strolled in the man's direction. She tossed a smile over her shoulder at Hack as she headed away.

Mattie watched Hack watch two more heavy set bearded men in big hats climb onto the stage with instruments and amps and begin to set up. Hack really couldn't take his eyes off them.

Mattie leaned close to Hack and whispered, "Notice anything about Jennifer?"

"Huh?" His eyes were innocent. "No. What?"

"She's coming on to you."

"No way."

"You didn't notice she's fawning all over you?"

"She's a waitress. Fawning's her job."

Mattie shrugged and leaned back again. "Watch and see."

Jennifer popped back at their table. With an even greater flourish than before she set a heaping plate before Hack. "Here you are, sir. Will there be anything else?"

"Mustard and ketchup would be nice. And my lady friend's meal as well, please."

"No problem." As Jennifer leaned forward as if to impart a deep secret her breasts seemed to bulge through her uniform. "And there's something else I can do for you."

"I'll bite."

"Really?" Mattie could have sworn Jennifer simpered, "I'll bet."

Mattie helped out. "It's an expression."

"Sure." She gave Mattie a cursory nod. "Well, two gay guys—well I don't know they're gay, but"—she shrugged—"they ordered a six-hundred-dollar bottle of wine and they only drank one glass each. Then they left. Our rules say now we've got to throw out the whole bottle. But they left a lot more in the bottle. I can bring it for you."

"How much?" Hack asked.

"Oh, for you it's free." She dimpled.

"That would be great," Hack said. "And my friend's meal as well, please. It's her birthday."

"No problem." Jennifer disappeared a moment and reappeared with the wine bottle and a glass.

"Two glasses, please," Hack said.

"No problem." Jennifer left again.

Mattie propped her elbow on the table and her chin in her hand. She smiled at Hack. "Your food's getting cold."

"I'll start after yours comes."

Rennie never waited to eat. Rennie approached food like he approached sex—grab and go. And he'd been the least bad in a long series of bad choices. What an odd dude, this new Huckleberry.

Jennifer brought Mattie a plate and another wine glass and with a thin smile set them both in front of Mattie. "See? A meal for the birthday girl." Then she left.

Mattie stared down at her plate. "Tuna."

Hack grabbed her plate in his right hand and his plate in his left hand and with one swift move double-switched them. "I love tuna."

"No you don't."

"Yes I do."

"No you don't."

"I do. I long for tuna. I yearn for tuna, especially when the tuna-less nights grow long and dark and cold." He made a mournful face. "I hide under the blankets and wait for the morning and each day's new meager promised portion of tuna."

"Please stop saying that stuff."

"I can't say I love tuna?"

"No."

"It's a free country and I'm a free man."

"And you're lying. Believe me, I've had a lot of experience in that department and I know when a man's lying."

"Well as it happens, despite your harsh and hurtful aspersions, tuna happens to be a delicacy I cherish."

That was another thing. Neither Rennie nor any of the dimwits before him had ever used words like "aspersion" or "cherish." She said, "I don't believe you."

"Your call. But if I can't love tuna, can I at least eat it? I'm starving here."

Mattie picked up her burger in both hands—it was too big for just one hand. It bulged with tomatoes and lettuce and pickles. Mustard and ketchup dripped onto her hands and onto the plate. She took a small bite. She almost moaned in ecstasy. "Okay. You can eat the tuna. It's my birthday, after all. But you can't say you love it."

Hack took a bite of his sandwich and followed with an immediate gulp of his wine.

"If you love that tuna so much, why'd you have to wash it down with six-hundred-dollar wine?"

"They serve this tuna here exactly the way they serve it in Paris. They call it—he intoned through his nose like a B-movie Frenchman—'Thon à la Catalane'."

Mattie felt tears brim in her eyes.

"What's the matter? Something wrong with your hamburger?"

"It's your French accent," she lied. "It's awful."

"I didn't know you know French," he said.

"I don't." She grabbed the wine bottle herself and poured a glassful and gulped it down. The wine hit Mattie with about a million different fruity delicious flavors all at once—maybe worth six hundred dollars, she supposed—though she distinctly remembered buying her first car for three-fifty.

One loud electric guitar chord boomed from the stage. Then another. That turned out to be the band's entire sound check and tune-up. The drummer counted, "One…two, two two three, four!" and they roared into the Toby Keith song "I Love This Bar."

Mattie followed Hack's eyes up to the stage and to the drummer and bass player, who were locked in a nice tight groove. She thought, that's where he really wants to be. Up there with them. But who am I to complain? I'm bad as he is.

The guitarist doubled as lead singer. He groaned out a guttural throaty rumble that ricocheted around and near the notes without ever quite hitting any.

The band finished to a smattering of applause from the tables around Mattie and Hack. The leader said, "Good evening, ladies and gentlemen. We're Dudley and Friends and we'll be helping you dance and enjoy yourselves the rest of the evening."

In the quiet moment that followed, Mattie leaned over and said to Hack, "The band is tight, but the singer's terrible."

"I agree."

"You know what that band could use?"

"I bet I do."

"A girl singer."

Hack popped one of her fries in his mouth and sucked on it—perfect crispy texture and just the right amount of salt. Since he'd gotten back from court to their hotel room, this had become a perfect day and now a perfect evening with the perfect woman. He carried Sam's credit card in his wallet and in the next day or two he'd be stuffing the wallet with a big wad of Sam's cash. He hadn't felt this good since the first time Sarai called him "Daddy." He asked, "Any particular girl singer in mind?"

"While you're wandering around investigating for Sam, what'll I be doing?"

"Good move there—answering a question with a question."

Hack luxuriated in the satisfaction that came with his accurate read of Mattie. He'd finally gotten one right. Mattie had kept him off guard right from their beginning as a couple, when to his amazement she'd hid him in her house from the cops and the FBI and the terrorists who'd framed him.

Since that wild couple of nights he'd been chasing after her always at least two steps and two emotions behind. He'd given up imagining he'd ever catch up. But for just this one moment he might almost have pulled up alongside. Of course, it was kind of a cheat, since he'd always known she lived to sing.

Well if Hack had to chase Mattie from behind, at least he'd get a good view. He leaned back and viewed her jeans-covered butt and savored his fruity six-hundred-dollar wine with its big bold insouciant varietal fruity flavors as she rose from the table and strode to stand in front of the stage waiting to be noticed.

Which of course didn't take long. The three musicians were conferring about something. Two of them were facing down stage but the drummer was facing stage front. He said something and pointed to Mattie. Dudley turned and sauntered to the edge of the stage and leaned down with his eyebrows up in a congenial but non-committal questioning expression, like he was expecting her to request "Sweet Caroline" or some other non-country tune he'd have to refuse.

Although professional musicians were always reluctant to let random strangers sit in, Hack knew Mattie would get her way and sing. Men didn't ignore her. Mattie smiled up at the man and within a few moments he was grinning his big bearded face off right back at her. The man held out his arm and she grabbed it to hoist herself onto the stage—although Hack knew with iron certainty that from where Mattie stood she could have mounted the stage like an Olympic gymnast.

Dudley strolled to the microphone. "Ladies and gentlemen, we have a special guest vocalist tonight. She's going to favor us with a song we all love. So let's give a warm welcome to"—he glanced at her and she said something—"Mattie, who's going to perform that very old favorite 'Careless Love'." He waved his left arm towards the microphone to welcome her. Then he said into the mike, "Here's Mattie," and stepped back and picked up his guitar.

Mattie stepped to the microphone. She lowered it down on the stand with practiced hand. She gazed from table to table around the room with a calm and confident expression.

Hack knew Mattie had sung thousands of songs in bars. After all, back in Ojibwa City, he'd played keyboards behind her for hundreds. But he thought he detected a little nervous crinkle around her eyes.

If it was there, the crinkle disappeared. And Mattie caught him off guard one more time. Instead of the big tremulous contralto she used to belt and wail rock and R&B standards, she crooned in a higher, gentler, almost wispy part of her voice he'd never heard from her:

"...Love oh love oh careless love..."

The ambient crowd noise at the tables around him began to fade.

"...Love oh love oh careless love..."

The bartenders and waitresses stifled their clatter of plates and glasses and silverware.

..."You made me weep, you made me moan,
Careless love you wrecked my happy home...

By now even the waitress Jennifer was facing the stage.

The three players behind Mattie were trading glances—first surprise and then pleasure.

Mattie's sweet voice was the only presence in the room. And she knew it. Her eyes tracked around the room to every table and one by one to every person in the room before she settled her look on Hack alone.

More perfection for an already perfect day?

Mattie finished her song and mumbled into the mike "Thank you" the pretend-shy way singers do. Applause came. Someone whistled. With exaggerated deliberation Mattie placed the microphone back in its slot on the stand. She stepped to the edge of the stage and with a single move hopped down onto the floor. Facing straight ahead like a soldier she marched the few steps towards Hack and their table. Without a glance at Hack she plopped back down in her chair and sighed a big sigh and crossed her arms in front of her and stared straight ahead. The applause trailed off. She shook her head and finally looked at Hack with a timidity he'd rarely seen in her. "Well?"

He said nothing—just laid his hand on hers.

A loud clearing of a throat followed by an "Excuse me" made Hack glance up. The band leader Dudley was standing by their table.

Mattie said, "Yes?"

The man spoke and sang with pretty much the same voice. He rumbled, "The boys and I were wondering if you're available so this could be a regular thing."

Mattie said, "If what could be?"

"You singing with us."

Mattie gave Dudley her sweetest killer smile and stood. "Let's talk," she said. The two went off into a corner. Hack poured himself the last drops of his wine and watched them—a better show than anything on TV. Hard bargaining. Dudley said something and Mattie nodded and said something back and Dudley shook his head and said something and then Mattie shook her head.

Jennifer came up and handed him the bill. "Will that be all, sir? Or may I get you and your companion some dessert?" Her voice had become cool and distant and professional.

Hack smiled up at her. "No, thanks." He handed her Sam's credit card.

"Very well." She took the card and left.

Mattie and Dudley were still going back and forth. This went on at least five more minutes. Finally, Dudley shrugged and threw his hands up in the air. Mattie grinned and stuck out her own right hand and he stuck out his and the two shook.

Dudley went back to the stage and Mattie came back and slipped into her chair. She said, "Well."

"You got the gig?"

"Naturally."

"What's the deal?"

"At least five nights a week. Plus lots of special events. And decent money. Better than decent."

"That's great for you."

"But?"

"I'll be missing you all those nights."

"No you won't."

"No?" But Hack knew what was coming. After all, he was now only one step behind.

"I told him he can't have me without getting you too. We're a team. So you'll be there too. You heard—they're tight and you'll fit in great. They need a good keyboard player anyway."

"Well happy birthday to you." He laid his hand over hers on the table. "You do know how to get what you want."

"Yeah," she said. She squeezed his hand and half-stood and leaned forward and grabbed him by the shoulder and smooched him a big sloppy wet mouth-to-mouth kiss and fell back into her chair. "Happy birthday to me. And you're right. I do know how to get what I want."

She added, "And what you want too."

13 Zarah's Cave

The morning sun poured its blistering white heat down on Zarah and the desert around her. As she trudged uphill she kept an eye out for daytime shelter.

She spotted a small opening about five meters to her right. She walked around the hillside to inspect it. The opening was about one meter across. It looked safe as far as she could see into its darkness, but that was only a meter or two.

She'd be cooler in there than out in the desert sun, but what if dangerous creatures already had the same idea? She didn't want to meet any of them on their own territory.

The hillside was a patchwork of sand dotted with clusters of small green plants rarely taller than Zarah. She scouted around until she found a dead black branch about a meter and a half long. She picked it up and stuck it into the cave entrance and waved it around. A few dry twigs snapped off it against the cave walls and fell. Nothing else happened.

Zarah wasn't satisfied. She laid the branch on the ground. A small bush crouched nearby. It was about a meter high. It sprouted some live green branches and some dead leafless ones. She broke off a few of the dead ones and laid several handfuls on the ground besides by the bigger dead tree branch. She took out her kitchen knife and cut the branches she'd snapped off the bush into smaller twigs and laid them in a pile. She inserted some dead leaves under it. She took out her cigarette lighter and lit the leaves. The leaves and dry twigs on top of them flamed. She stuck the end of the longest and greenest branch into the burning pile and lifted the pile and tossed the the clump of burning debris into the cave opening far as she could.

It happened too fast for Zarah to react: a black meter-long snake wriggled out of the cave between her legs and disappeared like a living narrow bullet into the desert behind her. By the time she had jumped back and looked around it was already gone from sight.

She shuddered. She'd also heard a quick high-pitched shriek from the cave. She used the branch to broom the burnt pile of debris out of the cave onto the space in front of it. Along with the cluster of ashes and cinders rolled a small animal, burnt gray and obviously dead.

She poked at it with a stick. It was a rat or other kind of vermin—forbidden to eat. She knocked the little corpse down the hill with her stick and returned to her cleaning.

She cut some living branches still bearing green leaves as a makeshift broom to brush off the ground just inside the cave as clean and bare as she could. She removed her abaya and laid it on the clean bare spot. Then she lay down on the cloth with her canteens next to her and her knife clutched in her right hand. It did seem cooler in the shade of the cave lip. She closed her left hand through her shirt around her amulet and in a few moments she slept.

She woke to the tickle of something crawling on up her jeans. Grandmother's voice in her head warned, "Just don't move."

Zarah ignored Grandmother and jumped up and brushed down the side of her leg with the dull spine of her knife. She felt her knife nick against something and heard a click. She grabbed her canteens and jumped out onto the worn dirt space in front of the cave and ran a few meters away and turned to look back into the spot she'd vacated.

It was near sundown, but enough light remained to show a huge scorpion, orange as the sun just now setting in the west. The scorpion squatted on her abaya like an insectoid dragon guarding its treasure, its huge stinger coiled forward and poised over its back like a spear.

She wanted her abaya—if only for the journey ahead, to protect herself from the fierce desert sun. A tee shirt and jeans could never provide the cover she needed. Besides, the abaya was hers. She couldn't let any creature no matter how scary steal even a single one of her few possessions. Not anymore. That part of her life was over.

A memory—something she'd seen Jabali do in the Compound.

Children had come upon a huge orange scorpion like this one and had run squealing away. She and John heard them and ran towards the scorpion. Zarah remembered her first sight of the ugly orange monster hunkered on the sand with its huge stinger curled over its head. John started to throw rocks at it and Zarah joined him, but the thing was hard to hit or hurt, especially from the safe distance John and Zarah kept.

This was one of the days Jabali came. He must have heard the racket. He appeared out of nowhere and stooped and with a single swipe of a big shiny steel knife he cut off the scorpion's stinger. The stinger flew half meter away and lay useless in the sand.

"This soldier's disarmed. Harmless now." He grinned his foul grin and sauntered back into the tent with Ali. John and Zarah grabbed long sticks and wacked the stinger-less scorpion past the tires out into the desert road.

Could Zarah do what Jabali did? She stepped closer to the scorpion. She couldn't tell if it saw or heard her. She couldn't tell what it was thinking or if it was thinking.

She wanted her abaya. She laid her canteens down on the ground and stepped close enough to make a feeble wave of her knife a few inches above the scorpion. The thing moved only a few inches to another spot on the cloth. She waved her knife again and it moved a few inches back.

Zarah took a deep breath and closed her eyes. No—she had to keep her eyes open. Despite the thing's ugliness she focused her gaze on every detail and stepped forward with her right foot. She knelt with a single quick bend in her right knee and with her right hand swept her blade through the bottom of its stinger. The stinger flew off and fell on the ground nearby.

She could do what Jabali did. Zarah stuck the knife in her belt and grabbed the edge of her abaya with both hand and lifted it straight up. The scorpion flew off into the cave. She shook out her abaya and felt it through to make sure nothing else disgusting lingered there and slipped the cloth over her head. She picked up her canteens and began a new night's trudge up the hill.

14 The Dream Palace of the Mujahid

The Mujahid woke from one of his dreams that was not a dream. He pretended to himself they were only dreams, but in the temporary self-awareness that lasted only through the first moments of wakefulness he recognized this was not a dream at all but in fact a memory.

He was six years old. His father was beating his mother. He didn't know why his father was beating her. Maybe it was something she said or did. Maybe it was something his father only thought she did. Or maybe something his father thought she thought. It didn't matter. There was nothing he could do. His father held all the power in his hard arms with their corded muscles and pale skin sprouting frightening hairs like thick black wires.

His older brother was crying too and tried to get between his father and mother, but the brother was only ten years old and helpless. Their father tossed the slender older boy against the wall and the boy crumpled there like a piece of cardboard.

His mother was shouting something, but there was no understanding what. Her crying choked her voice and garbled her words. The blood and tears smeared together on her face.

The Mujahid remembered this particular event as one that marked a new life for him. Up until then, he had spent almost all his time with his mother and older sisters and with the other women.

Now he entered an all-male world where he eventually learned he belonged. Right away he noticed that his older brother did not belong, although at the time he didn't know why. His father ignored the boy who had tried to get in the way of a man and focused his attention on teaching the younger brother, who accompanied his father and uncles to the places they went and listened hard to their conversations and learned from them how to think and talk and eventually to act like a man.

The Mujahid developed the correct healthy contempt any strong man must feel for the pointless nattering of women and the

72

poisonous evil of the Jews and the suicidal weakness of the West. He recognized the necessity of the Crusaders' inevitable downfall and their replacement by the generous and just rule of Allah and his people.

The dream troubled the Mujahid only briefly. As he awakened fully, he put it out of his mind. He didn't know why he dreamed this single dream so often. He supposed it was important but he couldn't imagine why.

15 *Professor Groucho*

The anonymous phone caller to Sam's office had specified ten A.M. sharp. Five minutes early, Hack pulled the Ford Fusion sedan he'd rented with Sam's magic card into Lot A2B on the SWASU Campus.

Hack stayed in the cool comfort of the car. The caller had said not to get out. Hack didn't even need to turn off the engine, which was fine with him. The rental was blessed with a powerful Arizona-capable air conditioner. On the forty-mile trip over State Highway 13 from the Vauxhall Arms to SWASU, the dashboard had recorded an outside temperature of 116 degrees Fahrenheit. The horrific number alarmed Hack, so he switched the display to Celsius. Now the dash displayed only 46 degrees, which was at least psychologically tolerable.

The engine idled in near-perfect silence, so Hack could keep his nice groove going with Charles Mingus on the car's Sirius Satellite radio. The Sirius was a treat. Back in Minnesota, Hack's friend Gus Dropo had equipped the 1973 Audi Fox he rebuilt for Hack with only a period-appropriate AM-FM radio and an 8-track tape player. Hack had run through his ancient collection of two dozen 8-track tapes until they'd worn down to soup. Only half played at all. And new tapes in the obsolete format cost at least fifteen bucks—way out of his recent price range.

Hack had driven to the campus because earlier that morning Sam had handed Hack a little pink message slip and said, "Check this out, will you?"

"What is it?"

The two were sitting across the desk from each other in the icy cool of the Phoenix office Sam had borrowed from a lawyer friend for the trial.

Sam said, "Surely you recognize it. It's called a message. It's the reason I brought you to Phoenix. Last week a man phoned and claimed to be a professor from SWASU and said he's got information we can use. The trial takes all my time and Laghdaf's time and we can't chase down every crackpot."

"Is he a crackpot?"

"It's your job to tell me that. So get out there, please."

"And do what?"

"Investigate. Talk to him. If he's got a story, listen to it. If he's got documents, grab them. That sort of thing."

"They expelled Amos almost two years ago. The trial's almost over. Where's this guy been all this time?"

"You're asking the right questions but the wrong man." Without another word Sam grabbed a handful of documents off his desk into his arms and hopped up and dashed out of the room.

Sam's abrupt exit didn't offend Hack. Sam was always walking off in the middle of conversations—sometimes conversations he himself started. You'd be at a party or in a meeting smack in the middle of telling Sam what you thought was the most fascinating tale and you'd be just about to arrive at its stunning climax when Sam would think of something or remember something or simply lose interest and without a word wander off.

Sam often hurt the feelings of people new to him, but Hack was used to him. Hack wondered if Sam had ever pulled his trademark routine on a judge in chambers or on a jury in trial. Hack would love to see that.

With Sam out of the room and their conversation apparently finished, Hack phoned the professor. The professor spoke in a near whisper Hack could hardly make out. "Can we make it…*garble*…?"

Hack said, "Sorry. I didn't quite catch that."

"I said…*garble*…"

"I still can't understand you. Sorry."

In a slightly louder hoarse croak with an obviously fake pseudo-Russian accent: "Is ten A.M. a time beneficial for your consideration?"

"Very beneficial. What building's your office in?"

"What your automobile make and model?"

A curve ball. "I'm not sure. I rented something. I can check."

A pause. "I see."

"Do you really need my make and model?"

"Call me after check and give me then."

"If you say so."

"And the license plate number too, I think." A pause. "Da, the license plate."

Obviously a crackpot. "Whatever you say."

"And park in Lot AB2. No different lot. It is on west side of campus. They have gotten good signs."

"After I park, which building should I go to?"

"Nyet! Do not go to building."

"How can we meet?"

"Just wait in car in Lot AB2 as instructed and you I will find. Is summer break and there will not be so many peoples. You understand?

"Yes, I understand."

"You sure?"

"Yes. I understand."

"You had better for help of mine." The call clicked off.

So Hack drove to SWASU and parked in Lot A2B and sat relishing the cool air conditioning and the music while he waited. Nothing happened for a while. Quite a while.

He must have dozed, because the sound of knuckles rapping on window glass woke him. He opened his eyes and saw a face peeking in through the passenger-side window. What looked through the curvature of the glass like black horizontal stripes marred the face. Words floated from the face in the same pseudo-Russian accent Hack had heard over the phone. "May I have the permission to enter into the vehicle of yours, please?"

Hack clicked the door locks open. "Be my guest."

The man yanked the passenger door open and slipped in and slammed the door and turned his head to stare at Hack.

Hack saw why the man had looked weird through the car

window. "Are those Groucho glasses?"

"Please not to concern yourself with details."

"I've always been a Harpo man myself. The dude could really play his instrument."

The man paused. "As did Chico. He performed on decent piano."

"True. But he played mostly comic gimmicks."

The man turned his head and looked at Hack—maybe. With the man's eyes hidden behind the big black plastic frames and under the fake black eyebrows, it was hard to be sure.

Hack said, "Can you see through those?"

The man said, "Groucho had better singing voice."

"We don't know that. I mean, Harpo never even spoke. For all we know under that wig he was another Pavarotti."

"A point." The man breathed out a sigh and looked forward and said in a regular Midwestern American accent, "I suppose you think I'm crazy."

"The thought occurred."

"There's a cult controlling this campus you wouldn't believe. And the high priestess—this Sterns-Marquardt woman—she's a demon—you can't ever let her find out you've talked to me."

Hack decided on the therapeutic approach. "Go on."

"I can't afford to be connected to you or your lawsuit. In any way, shape or form. I come up for tenure next year."

"Tenure in what?"

"Mathematics. If I don't get tenure I'm out of here and maybe my wife throws in the towel and I go back to coding or my children go hungry."

"Go on."

The man sighed again. He took off his Groucho glasses and let Hack see his face. He had a thin face with a thin nose and thin lips. Everything about his face was pale—even his hair, which seemed almost translucent. "So this is me."

"Go on."

"And I've been following your case. They put me on the Bias Response Committee and the Diversity Committee."

"Why?"

"No choice."

"What's mathematics got to do with diversity?"

"My question exactly. The question I dare not ask out loud."

"I understand."

"You do?"

"Been there myself." As a software developer, Hack had lived through his own identity politics nightmare at his employer Gogol-Chekhov before they canned him.

"Then you know." He said it the way a teenage hero in a zombie movie says it when the town cop finally believes him.

"I know."

"But there's things especially rotten about the Bias Response Committee. I can't say what. I can't even say for sure I know what. I can only say it's something dangerous."

Hack gave a nod he hoped was encouraging. "For example."

"I just said I can't say what."

"Why?"

"Because I don't actually understand it." The man held up a brown fifteen-inch wallet swollen thick with documents. "I'm smart with numbers, but the gobbledygook these people use for language makes no sense to me. Maybe you can figure it out."

The man pushed the wallet into Hack's lap and put on his Groucho glasses and shoved the passenger door open and jumped out. He turned. "Remember, you don't know me."

"Can't argue with that."

The man disappeared. He left behind a wide-open passenger door which might as well have been the door to an oven. The heat smacked Hack in his face. In an instant sweat flooded his eyes.

Hack scooted across the bucket seats to close the door, but the shifter mount between the bucket seats blocked his way and he couldn't reach far enough. He hurtled himself left out the driver side and raced around behind the car and slammed the door shut. He raced back around and jumped into the driver's seat and pulled the driver door shut.

Too late. Now he was all sweaty. And the hellish heat in the car matched the hellish heat outside. The air conditioner was going to have to start all over. But at least he'd never turned off the car.

He realized he was sitting on the document wallet. He contorted to lift his butt and with his right hand reached under and grabbed the wallet and tossed it onto the passenger seat. He sat down straight again and pulled out of his parking space and drove back to Phoenix.

16 I Accuse

Hack took an empty seat at the back of the mostly empty courtroom to watch Sam cross-examine SWASU Dean Robert Stamp.

Sam saved histrionics for special moments. He began this cross-examination like most of his others, in the same quiet voice Hack had heard him use to argue with Lily—all calm, reason and endless patience.

Sam: Dean Stamp, you are familiar with the idea of due process, are you not?

Stamp: Well, I'm not a lawyer. My field is Philosophy. I hold the Maximilian Goldstone Chair in Philosophy.

Sam: In your capacity as Dean of Students you also assumed the duty of overseeing discipline of students, correct?

Stamp: Yes.

Sam: As part of your job as Dean, you familiarized yourself with SWASU Disciplinary Policies and Procedures?

Stamp: Yes.

Sam: In fact, you were required to, is that right?

Stamp: That is right.

Sam: Because that document and the principles upon which it is based provide the blueprint for the disciplinary process you are charged with carrying out?

Stamp: Yes.

Sam: And the principles include principles of fairness?

Stamp: I don't know that.

Sam: You don't know what fairness is?

Stamp: I don't know the precise lawyer definition. From what I've seen, few non-lawyers do. Or lawyers for that matter.

Sam: Touché, Dean Stamp. Let me try again. From your understanding of the SWASU Policies you are charged with enforcing, would you agree that SWASU intended the Policies to require fairness towards students facing potential discipline?

Stamp: And to their victims as well.

Sam: Assuming the existence of victims. When you met for the first time with Amos Owens, you consulted the Policies document, did you not? To see how you should proceed?

Stamp: No.

Sam: You didn't?

Stamp: No need. As you say, I'm very familiar with it.

Sam: Actually, Dean Stamp, I say nothing here. I'm just asking questions. If something gets said, it's you who says it.

Stamp: Fair enough.

Sam: Yes. Fairness. Exactly what we're after.

Attorney for SWASU: Objection.

Judge: Sustained.

Sam: The first time you met with Amos Owens, a student facing potential discipline, you did not inform him of the nature of the accusation against him, did you?

Stamp: That would have been premature.

Sam: Would you like me to quote from the SWASU Policies and Procedures on that?

Stamp: No need. I know the part you're going to read.

Sam: What part am I going to read?

Stamp: That the student facing potential discipline must be informed of the nature of the allegation against him.

Sam: Is that all?

Stamp: And the potential action to be taken.

Sam: You met with Amos Owens a total of three times, is that right?

Stamp: Correct.

Sam: The first time you met with him you did not inform him of the allegation against him, did you?

Stamp: No.

Sam: That first time you also did not tell him he might be expelled?

Stamp: It was a question of discretion.

Sam: The SWASU Policies do not give you discretion whether to tell him, do they?

Stamp: Not in so many words.

Sam: Not in any words, isn't that right?

Stamp: I can't point to any specific language, no.

Sam: You can't point to any vague language, can you?

Stamp: Not as I sit here.

Hack watched Sam spend two painstaking hours eliciting from Stamp one "no" after another: no, Stamp didn't tell Owens the charges against him or the risk of expulsion the second time they met; or the third time; no, he never gave Owens the chance to present facts or arguments in his defense; no, he never told Owens who had made the decision to expel him; no, he never identified to Owens the witnesses against him or gave Owens the chance to cross-examine those witnesses; no, he never gave Owens a chance to appeal to any University body higher than the body that had made the decision if there was such a higher body. And so on. And on.

After Hack's beery night with Mattie at the Hedgehog Barrel and his early rise to meet Professor Groucho, Hack fell into a near stupor. But when Sam started repeating one particular question over and over, Hack sat upright and caught the last part of the series.

Sam: Once again, who made the decision to expel Amos Owens from SWASU?

Stamp: SWASU itself, of course.

Sam: Which particular people at SWASU?

Stamp: You want names?

Sam: I said so.

Stamp: It was no particular individual. It was a group decision.

Sam: What group?

Stamp: The Bias Response Committee.

Sam: Do you serve on that Committee?

Stamp: No.

Sam: And your role is just to rubber stamp it? In keeping with your name, Dean Stamp?

Attorney for SWASU: Objection, Your Honor!

Judge: Sustained. Keep your bad puns to a minimum, Counselor—and your personal aspersions.

Sam: I apologize, Your Honor. But there is a serious underlying point. Dean Stamp never told my client Amos Owens who made the decision to expel him.

Judge: You've established that. Move on.

Sam: Let's try another approach.

Hack watched Sam go back to his table, where Laghdaf handed him a document and Sam spouted what Hack recognized as formulaic language to get it on the record as Plaintiff's Exhibit P00025. Stamp authenticated it as a copy of an article he'd written for the SWASU school paper and the SWASU attorney Macklin did not object to its admission. Sam handed Dean Stamp the document and asked him to read the underlined part.

Stamp (reading): "An essential component of any disciplinary process is the personal affirmation that can come only when the victim feels vindicated. Victims of bias incidents often come to our University as outsiders. They do not see their own cultures in the histories we assign them or hear their own voices in the novels and plays we tell them to read or recognize their own faces in the paintings we tell them to look at. Naturally, they feel excluded. The University can play a valuable social justice role by paying close attention to their concerns and by vindicating them as members of previously under-represented identity groups. I will always remember the satisfaction I felt after a successful disciplinary decision in response to one student's encounter with repeated microaggressions led the student to tell me that the student no longer felt invisible. He truly existed within our community.

Sam: You wrote that?

Stamp: Yes.

Sam: You have been a Professor of Philosophy?

Stamp: Head of the Department.

Sam: You no doubt recognize the saying of the famous French philosopher René Descartes: "Cogito, ergo sum." Latin for "I think, therefore I am."

Stamp: Actually, he wrote it originally in French: "Je pense, donc je suis." Descartes was answering challenging questions. How do I know the world is even real? Or that I myself really exist?

Sam: And the fact I think answers questions like that?

Stamp: So Descartes said. More precisely, the fact I question my own existence proves I do in fact exist.

Sam: But now you have replaced his answer with your own answer?

Stamp: I don't know what you're asking.

Sam: I'm asking whether you and the rest of the SWASU administration have worked up something new to put in the place of "Cogito, ergo sum—I think, therefore I am." In this new scheme of yours, students don't have to exercise any thought at all to prove to themselves they exist.

Stamp: I still don't understand what you're getting at.

Judge: Counselor, neither do I.

Sam: In your article, haven't you laid out a handy path for one to affirm one's existence? Instead of Descartes' "Cogito, ergo sum," you've got "Accuso, ergo sum—I accuse, therefore I am."

Defendant's attorney: Objection! Move to strike.

Judge: Motion granted. Please, Mr. Lapidos. You know better.

Sam: With all respect, Your Honor, I don't think I do. I'm quite serious.

Judge: And it happens I attended a Catholic high school, Counselor—back in the dark ages when they still forced us to study Latin. And I remember enough Latin to tell you that yours is terrible. That is not how an ancient Roman or a medieval churchman would have said "I accuse." But we can take that up in chambers.

Sam: Your Honor, I look forward to the instruction.

17 Lily and Julia

"I've run out of steam," Lily told Julia. "I'm on my last leg. At wit's end. Beat. I'm every cliché you can think of and I don't know what to do."

It was the day after Lily's Salon disaster and two days after her ZNN interview. Lily was sitting in Barry's Grill in St. Paul on the opposite side of a booth from Julia Delacroix.

Except for her father and her daughter and a husband she'd now divorced, Lily had never known any human being she felt closer to or trusted more than Julia. And when Gogol-Chekhov had fired Nat and he'd turned depressed and unavailable, it was Julia to whom Lily had turned for solace.

From the moment two years ago when Lily had first conceived her image consulting business, Lily had called Julia nearly every night. They spit-balled and shot down crackpot business ideas, poked fun at Lily's déclassé competition, and giggled like teenagers when Lily defiled the confidences of her most image-challenged clients.

The two had shared the entire experience of Lily's rise to local fame and financial success. Lily counted Julia almost as a business partner, although Julia had turned down Lily's offer to share her profits. Julia had invested part of a large inheritance in her own hip business, a trendy restaurant called "The Golden Goose." She didn't need the money.

Julia gazed across the table with concerned brown eyes behind her black framed glasses. "How can I help?"

"I'm ten minutes from going out of business. I've lost half my clients and I've stopped answering any phone calls from the few clients I still have."

"Why don't you answer?"

"I don't want to."

Julia laughed. "A Lily answer. It's the same answer you gave that time at Camp Rosenfeld when you refused to go in swimming and Counselor Whitten wanted to know why you hadn't put on your swimsuit and you announced, 'I don't want to', and sat down on the lake shore and just watched the rest of us—and that was the end of it."

Lily smiled a weak smile of acknowledgment. "I remember."

During the pause that followed, Julia looked down and toyed with a tea spoon. Then, "You know, I spoke with Joleen Crowe this morning."

"Really? I just had lunch with her yesterday at Molly's Salon."

"I know."

Of course—friend conferring with friend: what are we going to do about Lily? Poor Lily. Sad little Lily.

Lily asked, "And what was your conclusion?"

"Conclusion? There was no conclusion."

Lily said nothing.

Julia snuck a peek from her spoon to glance up at Lily. "Of course, we're all concerned."

"Did you and she share any theories?"

"About what?"

"About what happened in January."

"We might have touched on the subject."

"You know what happened. You know what I did."

"Not really. It's odd, but you've never shared that day with me. All I know is what I've gotten from the media."

"Like ZNN?" Lily couldn't keep a taint of bitterness out of her voice.

"Not just ZNN. The Star-Tribune. Online media. Social Media. It's everywhere. But you've never told me."

"And what did you learn?"

"What do you mean?"

"Let me help. I'm a racist who ran over my client because he was dark skinned—though now that I think about it, his skin was no darker than mine. Or I'm an Islamophobe who killed Tariq because I hate Muslims. Or I'm part of a Zionist plot. Or he was my forbidden

87

lover and I ran over him because I was mad with jealousy or I was terrified the other Jews would find out."

Julia regarded Lily without speaking.

Lily said, "Or maybe Nat and I were in on it."

"In on what?"

"You got me. It's not my"—Lily nearly spat out the word—'narrative'. I'm sure the usual people have come up with the usual theories. I've stopped paying attention."

"That's good. You should."

"Right."

"Look, I wasn't there. But whatever your reasons, whether justified or unjustified, you committed an act of profound violence. You killed a man. That's got to have a psychological effect on you."

"It didn't seem to affect Nat."

"What do you mean?"

"Ten minutes before I ran down Tariq in my car, I'd seen Nat run down another guy right next to a stalled school bus full of Jewish kids. I almost lost my mind. I thought Nat must be a monster. Then Nat showed me the rifle the man had under his coat. It was black and bulbous and the single ugliest thing I ever saw."

"Okay." Julia's face was expressionless.

Lily said, "So an old yellow van drove by, and Nat jumped away and drove off without me, and I ran and got my own car and drove towards the JCC to get Sarai, and when I got near it there was Tariq standing in front of the van pointing another ugly black gun at Nat. I reacted in the moment and did to Tariq what Nat had done to Khaled."

Julia said, "Okay."

"So I got out and looked at Tariq and froze in terror and I've been completely frozen ever since."

"That's natural."

"Maybe. But Nat's reaction was different. He just cracked jokes, even when we were standing in the street practically on top of Tariq's body and all the cops were pointing their guns at us. If it ever affected him, he didn't show it."

"Then there's something wrong with him. You were right to divorce him."

"Later I asked him. Nat says he surprised himself by what he did and by how he reacted. But then the more he thought about it, the more he realized there's been violence since the beginning of time. And through all those generations of violence, there have always been some decent people who managed to live decent lives. His theory is that if the decent people couldn't be violent, the others would make the world uninhabitable for the rest of us, and we wouldn't even have a civilization we could live in."

"Do you buy that?"

"Maybe."

"Well I don't. We don't need to sink to that level. And doing what you did—it should—it must—affect you."

Lily thought back in the conversation. "A few minutes ago you said something."

"I did?"

"You said 'whether justified or unjustified' when you talked about what I did. What did you mean by that?"

"Did I say that?"

"Yes."

"Well, just that I wasn't there."

"So?"

"I don't know the exact circumstances."

"I just told you the circumstances."

Julia said nothing.

Julia too? Lily said, "What?"

Julia said, "I'm not really comfortable having this conversation."

"You don't believe me?"

"It's not that."

"It sounds like that."

Julia said, "Look, I wasn't there and I don't personally know what happened. And I'm not saying what you're saying isn't at least subjectively true. Memory is tricky. But even if you remember everything that happened that day exactly the way it really happened, there's a larger context."

"A context."

Again with "I'm not really comfortable having this conversation."

"I'm not comfortable not having this conversation."

Julia sighed. "Okay. Yes. There's a context."

"Which is?"

"The entire history of imperialism and oppression and misery Muslims have suffered at the hands of the West, including America and Israel."

Lily said. "Go on."

"Well, that's just it. It's hardly surprising they get frustrated and desperate and react and act out in ways that are hard for us Westerners to understand. And we do have to understand. I'm not saying what you say Tariq did was right, of course—"

"Of course," Lily muttered.

Evidently Julia heard her. "Of course. But there's punching up and punching down. The West is on top. The Muslims are on the bottom. When Tariq and this other guy did what you say they did, they were punching up. You see?"

"And that's the big context? Punching?"

"Don't trivialize what I'm saying. There is such a thing as social justice. And non-white people have definitely been getting the short end of the social justice stick for centuries."

"My dad says there's no such thing as social justice—only justice. Justice and sometimes mercy."

"Bullshit. If being a Jew is about anything, it's about social justice. It's not about Israel or avoiding pork chops or any of that God crap. I mean, you don't take any of that God crap seriously, do you?"

Lily asked, "What makes you say this?"

Julia said, "You know I've always thought that way."

"Of course, but why just now? This instant?"

"Since what happened I've been worried you might go over to the other side."

"What other side?"

"The 'Jews are God's chosen people' side. You know, 'God gave Israel to us'. 'Kill for peace'. That side."

"What's Israel got to do with it?"

"Everything, of course. What do you think Tariq and those other men were so frustrated about that they'd be driven to do such a terrible thing?"

"You tell me."

"At this point in history, the whole idea of starting yet another new country is strictly nineteenth century. Just another tribe of toxic males staking its claim to some real estate so they can battle other testosterone-driven males over it. The idea of Israel is depressing and backward and reactionary. The world doesn't need more countries. We'd all be better off without any."

"Julia, in case you haven't noticed, you live in a country."

"No choice for now."

"You don't consider yourself an American?"

"I don't consider myself particularly American. I don't consider myself Jewish. I prefer to see myself as a citizen of the world."

"Where do you pay taxes and vote?"

"Right here in the good old U.S. of A. For now."

"So if there's one country in the Mideast where there's free speech and freedom of religion, that has no value?"

"Israel gets no credit from me. A peaceful and united world will do better for everyone."

"But the Arabs have countries too. And you'd be the first to shout it from the rooftops if even one of them protected civil rights and civil liberties the way Israel does."

Julia shrugged.

Lily said, "And it means nothing if two gay men can walk down the street hand in hand and no one kills them for it?"

Julia made a dismissive gesture with her right hand. "Pink-washing."

Lily hadn't heard that one. "Pink-washing"?

"Image building. To make themselves look good."

"So these tricky Jews don't care about freedom for gay people or respect for human life? They just do token good deeds to cover up their basic evil? Not because they believe in it?"

"I never said tricky Jews."

"Yes you did."

Julia's expression turned sour.

Lily said, "You know, I saw just the other day in the news that those tricky Israeli Jews have taken thousands of people wounded horribly in the Syrian civil war and snuck them into Israel at night to treat in Israeli hospitals. The doctors and nurses are Arabic-speaking Jews or Israeli Arabs or Druze. They speak only Arabic to the patients, who start out terrified to be surrounded by Jews— especially the children. After the doctors treat these patients, the Israeli Army has to smuggle them back to Syria at night. The people can't tell anyone who treated them or where for fear they'll be murdered."

Julia said, "Yeah. I read that too."

Lily said, "I admit it makes me proud that Israelis are treating enemies who hate them the way human beings should treat other human beings, even if those enemies don't return the favor." She paused and looked into Julia's eyes. "Proud to be a Jew."

Julia said, "If it gives you the warm-and-fuzzies, that's nice for you."

In Lily's experience, there was no way to convince another person to feel different feelings, so she let Julia slide the conversation onto her restaurant and her problems finding reliable help. Thirty minutes later the lunch ended. Lily never ate. She just stirred her steamed vegetables around on her plate. The two women hugged and promised to call each other soon and Lily went out to the parking lot and got in to her BMW and drove home.

While she drove, she wondered. Through all the summer camps and Hebrew School and Brandeis University, Lily had felt only indifference at anything Jewish. She went through the motions of Hebrew School and a Bat Mitzvah out of a mild curiosity and a desire to please her mother and satisfy her father and maybe because the other kids did.

This entire Jew business was a business for rabbis. Anything more passionate than a friendly tolerance towards some ancient religion was old-fashioned and disrespectable, like her father's relentless passion for the state of Israel, or even geeky, like Jonah Friedlander with his thick glasses and outdated clothes and clumsy manner.

What ever happened to Jonah Friedlander? Oh, right. He became a doctor. The last time she'd seen him he'd grown a thick black beard. Then she'd heard he moved to Jerusalem and married a Jewish girl there. Or married the girl first and then moved.

Lily herself had married a gentile. Nat had no interest in religion. What originally attracted her to him was—what? Well, he was kind and funny and smart and okay looking. He'd turned out to be a great father and a decent human being—although she now knew he didn't seem to blink an eye about killing a man.

Julia had been hostile to anything Jewish. Julia paraded her open scorn in Hebrew School. She came because her parents made her. She scribbled nasty notes about Mr. Margolis and snuck them behind her back to Lily in the desk behind her. Mr. Margolis had been some kind of refugee from some horrendous persecution somewhere in Eastern Europe. His English was clumsy and thickly accented and his clothes too large and too slovenly and too out of fashion. He was bald and smelled like he ate weird foreign food and he had bad breath. Nothing this pathetic refugee said carried any relevance to the American kids who paid more rapt attention to Madonna or Cyndi Lauper than to whatever gobbledygook Mr. Margolis stuttered on about. Lily couldn't remember a single word of it, just the vaguely embarrassing way he said whatever he said.

And just like with the summer camp swimming, she'd finally told her parents, "I don't want to" and didn't go any more.

These days, when Lily drove Sarai to Friday night synagogue services—always at Sarai's begging—Lily could stumble through the prayer book Hebrew phonetically, but she had no idea what a single word of any of the prayers meant, except for the English translations, which Sarai giggled at and told her were all wrong.

Of all the kids who tormented Mr. Margolis the most aggressive and relentless had been Julia. At first, Julia's bad-girl open mockery was part of the fun of being her friend. But at some point Lily had started to feel embarrassed by her friend's seemingly pointless cruelty.

Now finally, driving home alone in her BMW, she remembered her puerile brattiness and felt a warm flush of shame. Ridiculously too late, she was indignant at the other kids and at Julia and most of all at herself. What way was that for a bunch of ignorant American princes and princesses to treat a man who'd suffered so much and who'd only been trying to tell them something important about things that mattered so much to him, that for all these snotty spoiled punks knew were what gave the man his reasons and sources of strength to survive?

Could she look up Mr. Margolis? She envisioned herself finding him and throwing herself at his feet to apologize and maybe even finding some way to make it up to him.

Then she remembered. He'd moved to Israel.

18 It Ain't Gamblin'

Hack has always been obsessively punctual. He was determined to make it on time for their first rehearsal and gig with Dudley. Hack raced on foot from the federal court house to the Vauxhall Arms parking lot. He jumped in the Ford and pulled it out to the loading zone in front of the hotel and texted Mattie. In a few minutes she came through the big revolving doors and got in the car. She wore jeans and a tee shirt but carried a slinky looking red dress on a hanger. The price tag still hung on it. She laid the dress flat on the back seat with care. Her new cowboy hat was so wide-brimmed that to fit into the front passenger seat she had to remove it and hold it in her lap.

He glanced over. "Nice Stetson."

"Tom Mix style," she said. "Like the cowboy in the silent movies. Got to look the part tonight."

"Picked all that up in the Hotel Shop?" he asked.

"That's right."

"How much?"

She shrugged. "Didn't look. It's my birthday."

"Almost forgot."

Hack drove them to the Hedgehog Barrel and they made it for their first band rehearsal at 5:55 P.M. The gig was at eight-thirty.

Dudley and Friends were already in the basement green room tuning up for rehearsal. A Yamaha P-125 portable digital piano was already set up on a black metal stand. A little portable bench sat in front of it. The bench was just a black plastic cushion on top of two crossed metal legs.

Dudley asked, "Is this rig okay? Borrowed it from a friend."

"It's fine," Hack said.

The drummer's name turned out to be Marty and the bass player was Bob. As he shook hands with them, Hack couldn't help noticing their powerful resemblance.

"Identical twins," Dudley explained. Then, all about business, he asked, "Do you know the Brooks and Dunn song 'Neon Moon'?"

"Not really, but play it and I'll join in."

Dudley raised an eyebrow but shrugged and counted off and the three other instrumentalists started. After listening one time through, Hack identified the key and the changes and joined in. Perfect pitch is a handy tool for a gigging musician and Hack had relied on his freak gift to cheat his way through many a gig.

They played through a few more tunes and Dudley seemed satisfied. Two or three times he suggested keyboard riffs from recordings people would recognize and Hack did as asked. Two hours later, Dudley and Marty and Bob all seemed happy and satisfied, especially when Mattie crooned not only with the tenderness they'd heard from her the night before but also belted out like the big-voiced singer Hack was used to. And unlike Hack, she already knew all the songs.

Mattie said, "Well Dudley, you satisfied?"

"Indeed I am," he answered and looked around to check with Marty and Bob who returned brief nods. "Well," Dudley said, "Looks like we got us a thing."

"That's right," Marty said, and stood up and shook Hack's hand. Bob followed suit.

"So we got a name for this new configuration?" Dudley asked.

Marty said, "Dudley and the Do-rights"?

"Truly lame," Bob said. "How about Dudley and the Play-rights?"

"Even worse," Marty said. "Besides, it sounds like we write plays."

Bob nodded. "And we don't."

Marty said, "We don't even go to plays."

Bob said, "Never been."

"Don't never want to," Marty said, affecting an exaggerated mock-southern drawl. "You don't never go to no plays, do you, buddy?"

"Actually, I have seen a few," Hack said.

Bob asked, "What kind?"

"All kinds."

Marty said, "Like that Shakespeare feller?"

"He's the best."

Bob said, "You mean, you enjoy that?"

"Yeah. A lot."

Bob and Marty exchanged glances. Marty said, "Well, that could change the situation. I don't know if I'd ever even want to associate with anyone enjoys those there uppity Shakespeare plays."

"Me neither," Bob said.

Were they serious? Hack glanced back and forth between the two men and saw four identical pale blue eyes peering at him from two nearly identical faces wearing two exactly identical bland expressions. If their tongues were stuck in their black furry cheeks, the beards hid the bulge.

Bob stroked his beard. "Say, Marty, do we want to share the stage with this dude?"

"Well, when you think about it, all the world's a stage anyway."

Bob said, "True. And all the men and women merely players."

Marty: "They have their exits and their entrances."

Bob: "And one man in his time plays many parts."

Marty: "Now that's odd, isn't it?"

Bob: "You mean the hetero normative sexism—leaving out women—like women get to play only one biologically determined cisnormative part and only men are allowed to play many parts?"

Marty: "All that goes without saying. But that one line—'they have their exits and their entrances'—makes no sense. Don't you think the poet Sweet Swan of Avon should have put the word 'entrances' first and then the word 'exits'? It's not logical. Don't you have to enter the stage first before you exit?"

Bob: "Sure. You have to live before you die."

"You've never lived in Minnesota," Hack said.

Bob and Marty both beamed. Bob said, "You'll do fine," and Marty stepped forward to shake Hack's hand again.

Dudley sighed. "Glad that's settled. Why not just 'Dudley and Mattie and Friends'?"

Mattie said, "Seriously?"

"Seriously," Dudley said. "You're the singer, so your name's there. Of course I'm still boss."

"Of course. And Hack's on keyboards."

Dudley gave a single emphatic nod. "Absolutely."

"Great. Well, there's something else," Mattie said.

"What's that?"

"To really get somewhere we need our own songs," Mattie said. "And Hack writes too."

Hack said, "I didn't know we want to get anywhere."

Mattie said, "Of course we do. Otherwise, why bother?"

"This is the first I've heard." Hack looked at Mattie and she stared back with a placid expression.

Dudley glanced back and forth between them. "I'll let you two settle that between yourselves."

"We will," Mattie smiled. "Anyway, Hack here writes good songs."

"You don't say." Dudley looked at Hack. "That right?"

Hack gave what he hoped was a modest shrug. "Not country songs. Now that I think about it, I did write one that might fit this band. But I wasn't thinking about it as a country song. I wrote it to be a sort of world-weary bluesy thing—comic, though—but not especially country."

Dudley said, "You sure there's a difference?"

Hack said, "Maybe none, I suppose. Except maybe the way the band plays behind the singer."

"Then show us the song and we'll play behind it the country way and see if we like it."

They ran the song and Hack sang it and the men seemed to like it. Hack hadn't yet gotten around to showing this one to Mattie and she seemed to react with less enthusiasm than she usually expressed for the odd little pairings of words to tunes he came up with. She just smiled a thin little smile.

Eight thirty arrived. The band cooked and Mattie killed and the decent-sized crowd two-stepped and occasionally waltzed through it all. Dudley covered newer tunes like George Strait and Brad Paisley, but he favored songs from the older country tradition of Waylon and Willie and back to Hank Williams and even before that to Jimmie Rodgers the Singing Brakeman. Mattie knew all the words to all the songs. And though Hack had never actually played them, he could fake them.

By twelve-thirty A.M., a couple of beers and the fun of playing live music in front of real people put Hack in a frisky mood. He had half a bottle of cold beer set on the floor by his right foot. He'd spread three beers over four hours, so he felt like it didn't affect his playing.

Dudley touched Hack on the left shoulder. "Well, Buddy," Dudley said, "Time for our second-to-last tune. Let's give yours a chance."

Hack peered over his keyboard into the darkness. A few hours ago, at least a hundred customers had clogged the place, but only about fifteen had stuck around, all of them men. No one was dancing anymore. The few not half-crocked looked completely crocked. Most had laid their heads down on the tables scattered around the big room, so that Hack saw not their faces but crowns of hats and tops of heads.

Mattie said nothing. She just moved out of the lights and leaned against the wall to watch from the dimness there.

Dudley spoke into the mike, "Ladies and gentlemen, we have a treat. Our new keyboard player Hack Wilder will now perform the world premiere of his own new comical bluesy and country and western song, "It Ain't Gamblin' When You Know You're Gonna Lose."

Out in the darkness, one someone barked out a short laugh—a wobbly beginning for a world premiere.

Hack took comfort in remembering he sang at least as well as

Dudley. Hack hit the opening piano chords and the band joined him
in its country way. He sang:

Like a fool you bet the ranch,
But he's beat you just with the aces he's showing.
Hole cards don't matter,
You know exactly where this is going.
    You raise anyway
    Just to see what he'll say
    And hope you can get him confused—
But it ain't gamblin' when you know you're gonna lose.

    A few snickers came out of the darkness. Encouraged, Hack
sang the second episode of his tale to a repeat of the same tune:

The wrong part of town
No earthly idea what you're there for.
This muscle-bound bozo
Makes a comment you prob'ly shouldn't care for.
    You can act like a clown
    And simply back down
    But sometimes you just got to choose—
And it ain't gamblin' when you know you're gonna lose.

Marty and Bob shifted to a funkier groove as Hack launched into the
bridge:

No, it ain't gamblin'
When there's just no way to win.
You see his fist by his ear
He'll lay it smack dab on your chin.
You've run out of luck
Don't bother to duck
Just pray it leaves only a bruise—
And it ain't gamblin' when you know you're gonna lose.

Dudley twanged out a gamy instrumental on his guitar. Then Hack
spun out the final chapter of his melancholy story in another repeat

of the original tune:

You met her in some barroom
Don't rightly recall all you said there.
She's got a lot of miles on her
But she's still pretty light on the tread wear.
      You think you know why
      She's got that look in her eye--
      Or maybe it's only the booze--
And it ain't gamblin' when you know you're gonna lose.

One final bridge:

No, it ain't gamblin'
When you know you got no chance.
Say so long to your pride,
You're roped up and tied,
And like her puppet you're gonna dance.

She's gonna break your heart
And that's just the start
Of a lifetime of singin' the blues—
No it ain't gamblin' when you know you're gonna lose,
It ain't gamblin' when you know you're gonna lose.

A smattering of tepid applause fluttered from the few still conscious. The noise seemed to disturb one man, who lifted his bald head and shot a brief bleary glance around the room and laid his head down again.

Dudley gave Hack a friendly smack on the back. He said, "Good job. Too long and complicated for a hit record. But we'll keep it in the band book."

A lot of world premieres had gone worse. At least there was no riot like with Stravinsky in Paris a hundred years before.

Mattie stepped in front of the keyboard and looked down at him with an expression Hack thought he recognized.

"Trouble?" he said.

"No, not really," she said. She grabbed the mike and turned her back on him to face the mostly empty tables and sang out "Someday I'm gonna be famous, do I have talent, well no"—the opening line of the Brad Paisley song "Celebrity." The boys jumped in to catch up and she belted her way through the song and all five managed to finish—or at least stop—at the same time, just like they had for most of the previous thirty songs or so.

By that standard, musically speaking, it was a pretty good night for Hack.

19 Lily Comes Home

Lily had eaten nothing at lunch with Julia. She went into the kitchen to make a sandwich. She looked in the bread box and found a bag with three stale slices. She looked in the refrigerator: no mayo, no mustard, no meat. No orange juice. One half-empty half-gallon of milk, a few half packs of Gouda cheese, and a few carrots and tomatoes.

Unacceptable. How had her beautiful darling Sarai been sustaining herself? Lily steeled herself and went out again and got back in her car and zipped over to Trader Joe's and parked in the lot. When she passed the stringy-haired grad student type in the parking lot holding up a "Boycott Israel" sign she shot him a dirty look but said nothing. But the sight of him sparked an anger that led to some thinking which in turn led to a decision.

She pushed her cart up and down the aisles and scoured every section for Israeli products and loaded her cart with them. She bought cheese from Israel and hummus from Israel and wine from Israel. Much to her pleasant surprise she found kosher chicken and frozen ground beef packages in the meat department and bought a package of two fresh chicken breasts and two frozen chickens and five individually wrapped one-pound packages of ground beef.

Lily wasn't alone. A lot of other Minnesotans—most of them clearly not Jewish—were buying the same items from the same shelves.

She came out of the store with two hefty bags she could barely carry. She crooked one in each arm and balanced them against her chest. She couldn't see over the tops of the bags; she had to peek between them to see where she was going. She trundled past the "Boycott Israel" guy and stopped and turned to face him.

With great care she placed each bag on the parking lot pavement. He looked at her with mild curiosity. She reached into one of the bags.

"I'm sorry," she said.

"About what?"

"I couldn't find any Israeli eggs. I guess Minnesota's too far to ship them here fresh. But I did find these." She reached into one of the bags and pulled out three packages of feta cheese and laid it on the asphalt. "And these," and laid out the hummus. She kept on layering the assorted cheeses and other items on the pavement until they formed a nice pile.

The "Boycott Israel" guy stood stiff. With each item she displayed, the red in his face progressed one or two additional quanta towards the ultraviolet end of the electro-magnetic spectrum.

When she finished she crossed her arms and smiled at him.

He said, "You know you're giving aid and comfort to apartheid."

"Have you ever been to Israel?"

"No. I went to Palestine. I met a lot of Arabs. They explained it all to me."

"Talk to any Israelis?"

"The ones they had me meet all side with the Palestinians."

"Any who don't?"

"Why should I listen to them?"

"To hear their side."

"They don't have a side."

"That's sad. In fact, you're sad." She remembered the apartheid of South Africa, where blacks were locked out of spaces and schools and occupations reserved for whites, and then she remembered her own single journey to Israel: Arabs working and shopping in the stores and working and eating in the restaurants, Arab women in hijabs at the University, women in chadors strolling on the roads, women in burkinis on the beaches, Arabs on the professional sports teams, Arabs in the parliament and on the Supreme Court, Arabs here, Arabs there, Arabs nearly everywhere.

Whatever was going on, it wasn't apartheid. But how she could explain to this smug young zealot standing in a parking lot waving a sign?

Instead all she said was, "I recommend you do go and see for yourself. In any argument, anybody who takes one side's word for anything is an idiot. You don't want to be an idiot, do you?"

Apparently he did. He turned his back on her and waved his sign in the opposite direction.

She repacked her groceries and took her bags and drove home and loaded up her kitchen pantry and refrigerator with all the goodies. She laid one of the packages of fresh chicken breasts on the counter. She went to the front window and stood watching for Sarai to come home from summer camp.

The June lawn was small and tidy and very green. She wondered who'd been mowing it. The last time she remembered noticing her lawn white heaps of snow had covered it. When she and Nat had moved in, the maple in the front yard had stood only about thirty feet high. Now it seemed to tower over the house.

She sat in quiet peace for about forty minutes, her mind empty and clear. After some time in that pleasant state, she came back to awareness of herself. She remembered a month or two right out of college when she'd tried meditation. The goal was to empty your mind. But she'd been cursed with incurable monkey-mind and couldn't stop thinking. She realized that just now she'd finally achieved her original goal. Empty mind. It just happened, with no effort or plan or intention at all.

In about thirty minutes Nancy Terrel's SUV stopped in front of the house and Sarai hopped out and sprinted up the walk to the door and through it. Nancy drove away.

"Hola, Mamacita," Sarai said as she breezed past Lily and up the stairs. It was a special three-week Spanish immersion camp.

Lily smiled to herself and walked up the stairs after Sarai. She knocked on Sarai's door.

From behind the door came, "What is it, Mom? Or should I say, Que es?"

"Either is fine. I'm making dinner tonight. Please be ready at five-thirty."

The door came cracked open to a slit and revealed a sliver of Sarai's little round face. "Really?"

"Of course. Why?"

"It's been a few months since you cooked."

"I'm pretty good, if you remember."

"I do."

"And all that's over. I'll be cooking most nights again."

"Really?"

Lily bent and kissed her daughter's cheek. "Yes. Five-thirty sharp, please."

Sarai said, "Okay." She shut the door and Lily went back down stairs and plopped down on the sofa. She picked up her Norman Mailer "Armies of the Night" book and started reading.

Half an hour later she threw it down. It bounced off the sofa and fell to the floor. Suddenly all his fine prose seemed like so much crap. Wasn't Norman Mailer a Jew? You'd never know it from his writing. Should that matter? Time to cook, anyway.

Lily went into the kitchen and put on her apron and went to work. She would resume her cooking career with something easy. She remembered a simple Martha Stewart recipe. She started the brown rice in a small pot of water on the stove. She cut off about two ounces of the feta cheese and crumbled it up in a small bowl and mixed in half a teaspoon of dried oregano. Thank goodness she still had her spices. Spices last pretty much forever, right?

She made pockets in the chicken breasts by holding each one flat in her palm and making an incision in its thicker side with a paring knife. She stuffed the pockets with the cheese-oregano mixture. Then she heated olive oil to medium-high in a skillet and browned the chicken breasts.

She covered the skillet and cooked until the chicken looked done, which took about fifteen minutes. She put the platter in the oven to keep it warm. She stirred a butter and lemon-juice sauce in the skillet.

At five-twenty-five, Sarai showed up and without being asked set the kitchen table for two. Lily served the rice and the two chicken breasts. She drizzled some sauce onto the chicken and put the remainder of the sauce in a small bowl on the table.

Lily asked, "Ready?"

Sarai mumbled something.

"What was that, sweetheart?"

"A blessing we learned in school."

"Oh. That's nice."

The two ate in quiet for two or three minutes.

Lily said, "I should probably tell you, that's kosher chicken. From Trader Joe's."

"Really?"

"And the cheese is from Israel."

"Cool."

"It's an old recipe from Martha Stewart."

"It's delicious." Sarai nodded and resumed eating.

Lil paused her own eating to watch Sarai. Sarai ate with a quiet measured dignity, like a genuine little princess. Not spoiled at all. Where did she come from? From Bea, my own mother. Sarai takes after her. Sometimes she even tilts her head at that odd angle just like Bea did. I'm glad her grandmother got to see her before dying.

Sarai looked up and caught Lily watching her and stopped chewing and smiled.

Lily asked, "Is everything okay?"

"Oh yeah. And it's great you're cooking again. Thanks."

"I said I'll be cooking a lot. What do you think of the kosher chicken?"

"Oh, it's actually better than the other chicken, I think. I heard in school a lot of foodies prefer kosher chicken because of the way it's butchered and drained of blood. Only…"

Lily said, "Only what, sweetheart? You don't like the sauce? I don't have to make that particular sauce next time."

"It's not the sauce, Mom. Well, it's partly the sauce. Even though it's delicious."

"Okay…"

"Sarai said, "Well…it's just that we kind of lose the point of cooking a kosher chicken if we put cheese in it. If we're trying to make a kosher meal, I mean. You know, mixing meat and dairy."

"Really? Are you sure? I thought that meat-and-dairy thing only applied to beef and lamb. Like cheeseburgers."

"Chicken counts as meat, Mom."

"Are you sure?"

"You're paying for a Jewish school, Mom. I'm completely sure. We're not supposed to boil a kid in its mother's milk."

Lily thought for a moment. "But chicken mothers—I mean, hens—don't give milk. They're birds. Only mammals give milk."

Sarai nodded. "I know. I asked that very question in class." She shrugged her little shoulders in almost a stereotypical Yiddish inflected gesture—again evocative to Lily of her Bea. Sarai said, "I don't make the rules. I'm just telling you. But thanks for cooking. It's delicious anyway."

"I'll remember that next time."

Sarai said, "I'll do the dishes."

"We'll do them together," her mother said.

Later that evening, Lily knocked on Sarai's bedroom door.

Sarai's voice piped through the door, "Hola, Madre."

"Hola, cariña."

Sarai opened her door wide. "You speak Spanish?"

"I'm afraid only high school Spanish."

"We can practice together. Señora Hernandez said use it or lose it."

"I'd love that. Though like she says, I've lost a lot."

"I'll help you remember. Or—" She furrowed her brow and enunciated: "Te ayudaré a recordar."

"Gracias. In the meantime, may I come in?"

"Sure, Mom." Sarai stepped back from her door.

Lily walked in. How long had it been since she'd been in Sarai's room? But unlike the unholy mess she remembered from her own childhood Sarai's room was neat, organized and orderly.

A few crumpled sheets lay near the waste basket. Sarai followed her mother's glance towards them and dashed over and picked them up and dropped them in the basket.

Sarai had two bookcases. One seemed to be all fiction. The other was nonfiction. Sarai had alphabetized the fiction bookcase by author's last name. Sarai had organized her non-fiction bookcase by topic. Her Spanish books stood neat and prim adjacent to her Hebrew books in what must be a foreign language section.

Sarai had the bedroom of a tiny adult. Not just any regular adult either, but a college professor or a lawyer. Was that good? Probably. But maybe she's started taking care of herself because I haven't been taking good care of her lately.

Lily took a Spanish book from the shelf and inspected it. "Can you read this?"

"Some. A lot of Spanish words are related to English words. But sometimes they fool you. They look the same but they're not."

Lily put the Spanish book back and took out a Hebrew book with its strange alphabet. "And this?"

"That's even harder," Sarai said. "But I'm working on it. And thanks again for dinner, Mom."

Lily smiled. "Even though I kind of messed up the kosher chicken?"

Sarai grabbed Lily and hugged her hard around the waist. "You didn't mess up anything."

Lily caressed Sarai's hair and thought, now she's not only taking care of herself; she wants to take care of me too. But get hold of yourself. Say something normal. Ask a follow-up question. "So besides studying languages, what do you do in here so much of your time?"

Sarai let go and stepped back. "Promise you won't get mad?"

"That's the easiest promise I ever made."

"I've been trying to do it on my own. Dad and Grandpa think it's sort of crazy."

"What's crazy?"

"Trying to find Zarah."

"Zarah?"

"Uncle Amir's daughter. Don't you remember?"

"I remember. You asked your father and grandfather to do it. Aren't they?"

"Dad's gotten nowhere. Grandpa's been too busy preparing for his trial. And now he's hired Dad to help him with that. I think they're both too busy. Or maybe they secretly think it's pointless."

"I see."

The little adult said, "It is what it is."

Lily said, "But you're nine years old."

"I'm aware of that, Mom."

"How can you hunt all over this big planet for Zarah from this little room in St. Paul?"

Sarai smiled. "The Internet. My computer."

"Show me."

Later, after Lily had put Sarai to bed, Lily propped herself against her big pillow in her own bed thinking about a paragraph she'd just read about the old-time Hebrews in the Adin Steinsaltz essay "On Being Free". She'd discovered it in the same bookcase where she'd replaced the Norman Mailer book after tiring of him and his voice. Lily vaguely remembered sticking the Steinsaltz book there after Sam had given it to her for some long ago birthday:

> "The real tragedy of the exile in Egypt was that the slaves became more and more like their masters, thinking like them and even dreaming the same dreams."

Lily's phone rang. She answered. It was Sam.

He said, "Sorry to return your call so late."

"No need to apologize, Dad. I know what it's like for you in trial. How's that going, anyway?"

He said, "We'll know when we know. What's up?"

"You may not realize what an amazing granddaughter you have."

"I realize. You didn't call just to tell me that."

"You remember Zarah?"

"I remember the name."

"Since you've been too busy and Nat got nowhere and I've been preoccupied with my own so very precious self, Sarai decided to take direct action and find Zarah on her own."

"From St. Paul?"

"Yes. From her little girl bedroom in our little old house in little old St. Paul."

"How's she going about it?"

"The Internet. There are a lot of resources on missing children."

"For instance?"

"For instance, The FBI has a website just for missing children. And a lot of police authorities keep all kinds of data. And there are private organizations. Sarai's been hunting through all these databases and emailing all of these organizations asking for information about Zarah."

"Do they respond to a nine-year-old?"

"She's cagey enough to leave out that part."

"Of course. Any luck?"

"No."

Sam said, "We've never had any reason to think Zarah is in the U.S., assuming she exists at all."

"That's what I told Sarai. She showed me how she's also contacted The International Centre for Missing and Exploited Children. They run a Global Missing Children's Network."

"And no luck there, right?"

"I'm sure they do their best, but no."

Lily heard the phone clatter onto something hard like a desk top or table and there was a pause at his end of the line. The pause didn't bother Lily. It meant Sam was thinking. She'd seen it often in childhood. She pictured him. He had put the phone down and was pacing whatever room he was in and he'd go in his little circles two or three times and then he'd freeze and stare at the wall in a trance that might last two minutes or twenty. Then he'd do some more circles. Eventually, he'd come back to the conversation and say something. Sometimes it was something obvious—although not always obvious till Sam said it. Sometimes it was wacky. Sometimes it was both obvious and wacky—and the more of both the better.

Lily could wait. She leaned her head back on her pillow and stared at the ceiling and thought about putting the phone on her bed table and picking up her book again but decided it wasn't worth the risk she'd miss her father's return to this world.

There was some clicking and clattering at his end as he picked up the phone again. He said, "I've thought it through."

"Okay."

"Let's assume Zarah is real and she's alive."

"Why?

"Because assuming the opposite is a dead end. It leads nowhere. But the idea she's out there at least theoretically could lead to finding her. If it turns out she's not, the only harm will be a little wasted effort and frustration."

Lily said nothing.

Sam said, "But I guarantee sometime or somewhere in the process the world will show you something new. Maybe something wonderful."

"Me?"

Father and daughter shared a familiar uncomfortable silence over the phone. Then he said, "When you visited Israel that time, did you go to Jerusalem?"

"Sure. Like every tourist."

"What'd you see?

She said, "The usual. A lot of Israelis. Some of the non-religious men came on to me. A lot of religious men who didn't. The religious men wore beards and the women wore beautiful headgear. And

112

Muslims. Some of them got a little grabby too. And I ate some
wonderful food and I heard some great music."

"See any history?"

"The Western Wall, like everyone else. The scale model of the
Second Temple. That sort of thing."

He nodded. "Did you visit the Siloam Tunnel?

"Doesn't sound familiar."

"It's also called Hezekiah's Tunnel."

"Still nope."

"You'd remember. Go there next time. You can walk nearly the
entire passage underground. I did that myself a few years ago."

"Okay."

, His voice warmed with enthusiasm. "The Second Book of Kings
records the history. The Jews—of course I mean we—built the
tunnel in the time of King Hezekiah in the late eighth or early
seventh century B.C.E.. That's twenty-eight hundred years ago."

"I remember the name Hezekiah." Of course—she herself had
just said Hezekiah's name at the Salon the day before. She asked,
"What did they built it for?"

"To protect the Jerusalem water supply. We anticipated a siege
from the Assyrians under King Sennacherib, so we connected the
upstream Gihon Spring which was outside the city walls to the Pool
of Siloam within the walls. The tunnel was almost six hundred yards
long—six football fields."

"And we know this happened?"

"The builders left an inscription in Hebrew. About a hundred
thirty years ago a kid found it swimming in the Siloam pool. The
inscription confirms the biblical story. As does the existence of the
tunnel, of course, since it's right where our book says it was."

She said, "Sounds fascinating. I'll make a point to visit if I ever
get back to Jerusalem. But what's your point?"

Sam went on. "They had no modern equipment. To build the
tunnel, two separate teams started from both ends and by the light of
their torches cut with hand tools through hard bedrock towards each

other trying to meet in the middle. Remember, the tunnel was six hundred yards long."

"So how did the two teams meet?"

"Great question. The inscription says that as the two teams got closer they began to hear each other. I suppose at first they heard at most each other's scritching and scratching in the rock. Later they heard louder pounding and digging and eventually voices. So each team tunneled towards the noise. And that's how the two teams broke through and found each other."

Lily said, "I see where you're headed."

Sam, "We assume Zarah is alive because that potentially leads us somewhere. We and Zarah are two teams tunneling through darkness trying to find each other. Neither of us knows where the other is or even if we're headed in the right direction. But if Zarah is alive and she's looking for help, she's looking for us."

She asked, "So what do we do to connect up?"

"Listen. Listen hard."

Another pause, this time much longer. "Assuming I could help, how would I start?"

He said, "I might have a way. But you'll have to fly to Phoenix."

She swallowed. "Please don't ask me to do that."

"It's necessary."

"Dad, are your sure this isn't just your way to get me out of this house and out of town?"

"That would be a good thing. But the truth is, if you want to do this, you'll really have to come where I am."

"Why?"

"Can't say over the phone."

She said, "That's conveniently mysterious."

"Yes, it is."

A long pause. She listened to his silence at the other end of the line, implacable but patient. She said, "I don't know."

He said, "It's your choice, Sweetheart."

"But what if Zarah's out there all alone, right?"

"I didn't say that."

"You don't need to. You know I'll say it to myself."

In a gentle voice he said, "When you come, bring your computer."

20 Zarah's Hunger

The hunger which Zarah had ignored when it was a mere craving was now a fierce agony. She guessed it was past midnight, which meant it had been more than thirty hours since she'd eaten. The occasional sips she rationed herself from the limited water supply in her canteens helped, but only a little.

As Zarah worked her way uphill in darkness, the way got steeper, and. as the way got steeper her earlier confident strides got shorter. Harsher terrain forced her to change to short mincing steps and stingy watchful care.

Instead of tiny pebbles she was treading more often over big rocks that bumped and bruised feet shielded only by thin socks and worn sneakers. Several times she stumbled. Once she tripped onto rough ground that scraped and stung her palms as she broke her fall.

She was confronting abrupt grades her child's legs felt too short and too tired to mount. She had to hunt around for smoother paths uphill. The relentless effort was consuming her time and burning her energy.

A sudden wave of dizziness caught her off guard as it washed over and seemed to douse for a moment whatever fire still burned within. The white of a nearby nearly waist-high stone caught her eye and she sat on it. The hard surface cooled and refreshed even through her jeans. She wondered whether come morning she'd find water to lick as Grandmother had promised—should she stay on the rock until then?

All kinds of scents drifted her way on the suffocating night air. Many were fragrant and sweet. Some were pungent. A few reminded her of home. All added to her misery.

Against her will—to the extent she still controlled the drift of her thoughts—the aromas sent Zarah's mind wandering back a few years to home. Mother was teaching her how to prepare for Ramadan. "We shop now, before Ramadan," Mother explained. "It can wear out a woman to shop in the daytime heat during Ramadan, when we should be fasting and resting."

They were shopping in the bazaar to stock the *moona* where they kept the food at home. Mother led her past stalls and at each stall she stopped to explain the produce. The mountains of rice and flour and mounds of raisins and prunes enthralled Zarah, as did the immense heaps of nuts and legumes along with the stockpiles of all the various spices and the special *Baharat* spice mixture.

Zarah loved to watch Mother haggle with the merchants. At first Zarah had been a little shocked to watch this normally mild peaceful woman take such staunch positions, fists by her side, as if the fate of the entire world rose or fell on the price of a lentil. But after a time she grew proud of Mother's tenacity. After one particularly dogged session with a grizzled seller of dried apricot and tamarind, a debate conducted with mutual mad displays of shouting and eye-rolling and arm-waving, Mother took Zarah aside and laughed. "He always raises his prices just before Ramadan. But I'm on to him and he knows it and we have a good time."

Then Mother and Zarah went home and Mother showed Zarah how to make juice out of the dried apricots and tamarind she'd pried out of the dealer. Mother let Zarah help mix the meat and pine nuts and roll them into *kubba* meat balls and roll thin sheets of dough into the *boureg* and run all her little kitchen errands and clean up afterwards.

Zarah's mind strayed naturally to the *Iftar* feast that came at the end of the Ramadan fast.

She shook herself and told herself to block the memories. Stop thinking about Mother. Think about getting food here and now. And it doesn't have to be delicious. It just has to be something you can eat.

Zarah rose from her stone and resumed her trek uphill. Now that she hiked through the desert she did see all around the green she'd anticipated, but the green turned out to be mostly thin brush and spiny grasses and low spiky cactuses. She saw no way to use Grandmother's teachings about finding water or food. Yet so much

117

life ranging all around her must include something to eat—if only she could recognize it and take advantage.

Then the nighttime breeze picked up and infected the air with a new odor—the stench of rotten meat—the stink of death.

She knew it from the wars she'd wandered through at home and from her hard journeys since. You smelled it before you saw it. You smelled dead people and dead animals and then you saw corpses rotting in the sun all mingled together like there was no difference between human and animal. Sometimes if you got too close you saw a man or a woman or a child turned into nothing more than a dark pile of rotten rags and decaying flesh and feasting maggots and flies.

You smelled it and you didn't want to see it, but there it was.

A flash of memory: Mother trying to stay between Zarah and some uglier-even-than-usual sight as they trudged through some more-wasted-than-usual town.

The ache of her loneliness flared in her heart again.

Zarah shifted direction towards the source of the smell. In a few minutes she found a kind of wolf stretched out on its side on the ground. It looked smaller than the wolves she remembered back home. Maybe it was a cub. No, it was a fully formed adult. It was just small.

It would have been gaunt except that its neck and jaw were swollen to twice normal size. The skin around its dead eyes was red and puffed and bloated under the gray fur. She leaned down and examined the corpse. Something had embedded hundreds of tiny thorn-like things in the skin around the animal's head.

A closer look showed they weren't thorns; they were stingers. She'd seen this before in Africa. At the time she'd known she was in Africa because almost everyone she saw had black skin like Ali and John, not olive or brown like her own or Jabali's or paler like a few of the other children in the Compound. And she'd learned in Africa to watch out for the bees who flared to fury in an instant and swarmed and killed any creature that drew their rage.

She cocked her head to listen. She didn't hear any of the buzzing she'd expect if a hive were nearby. She remembered that bees mostly slept at night. So the bees must have killed this small wolf during the day.

Hadn't Grandmother said where there were bees there might be water? And didn't bees mean flowers? And didn't water and flowers mean fruit?

And the small wolf too. Where's there's a wolf there must be animals for it to hunt. But animals permitted to eat? Not likely. Though the animals the wolf ate must themselves eat, and their food could be food fit for Zarah.

She started her slow trek uphill again, watching for more of the wolves and listening for bees just in case. Out of the corner of her eye she sensed a shadow move uphill past her on her right. She stopped still. Had she seen something real or was it just a nighttime phantom?

This time she'd follow Grandmother's instruction: "In the desert, sometimes the right way is to stay completely still. Just don't move."

The breeze came down the hill and brushed her face. It brought a pungent dog smell. Another of the wolves. Upwind. So maybe it wouldn't smell her.

Just don't move.

The shadow was slinking around in the near darkness up ahead. What was it doing?

She heard grunts. A wild pig ran downhill past her just a few meters to her right.

At least she thought it was a pig. In the moonlight it was hard to be sure. It seemed nearly a meter high and pig-shaped with a long snout. She thought she glimpsed a gleam of long canines or tusks protruding from its lower jaws. As it sprinted by it grunted pig-like grunts and made strange clacking noises.

The small wolf prowled downhill on her left in the same direction downhill, like it was stalking the pig.

She was caught in the middle of some deadly struggle between wild animals. Just don't move.

Behind her she heard more grunts and then some dog-like yips. The small wolf sprinted up hill on her left and then a herd of the pig-like animals came clacking uphill after it.

Zarah wondered for a moment if she should move to her right and away from the creatures. No—too early to know. Just don't move.

The right choice: there was a sudden explosion of clacking and yipping and howling from the darkening terrain uphill and to her right. Grunts and squeals and one violent scream told her a big fight was happening—the pig-like animals against the wolf.

The wolf tore down the hill to her right and the pigs followed hard after. The racket trailed off downhill and disappeared.

For the long moments it took for the sounds to die away Zarah stayed put. She wondered how long she should wait. Grandmother hadn't mentioned that part.

Eventually she could stand still no longer. She resumed her hike up the hill.

Maybe the pigs had been eating something she could eat. When she first heard them they'd been uphill on the right. She moved in that direction through the bushes and bunches of grass. The footing here seemed less rugged anyway.

Low to the ground close just past the bushes grew several bunches of strange short plants. Each one sprouted clusters of thick flat thorny leaves. The leaves were flat-shaped and about the size of *atayef*—a pancake Zarah's family had eaten to break the Ramadan fast.

She pictured herself in the kitchen, helping her mother stuff the atayef with delicious cheese or nut filling. In her memory, Mother and she were laughing about something, she couldn't remember what. It didn't matter. It was the laughter that mattered.

And now it wasn't the thick flat leaves that mattered. It was the fruit that shone among them.

Even in the near total darkness, Zarah saw hundreds of the fruit all around, each about the size of her little girl's fist, dark and plump and luscious.

Grandmother had said, "Look before you eat." Zarah couldn't afford to let her ravenous hunger lead her to a dangerous mistake. She scooted close to one of the plants and knelt. Careful not to touch any pad or fruit, she took out her lighter and lit it and held it over the plant to inspect the fruit.

Each fruit had a hollow concave top mounted with a crown from which sprouted long thin thorns like skinny spears. Out of the reddish skin below the top poked small bumps, each with its own personal wide stubby thorn.

These desert mothers protected their children.

She flicked off the lighter. The fruit might be delicious or it might taste terrible. And she'd have to risk the possibility it was poison. But what about the thorns?

Zarah straightened up and walked over to a bush. It was alive, and its branches bent springy and flexible. She took her knife from her waistband under her abaya and sawed through a few.

She stuck her knife back and went back to the cactuses. She knelt down and bent one of the green branches double and with both hands used it as a tong to grip one of the fruit.

The smooth ends of the branch kept slipping off. She moved her hands closer up to the gripping end. The movement brought her hand directly over a pad and too close to it. Its thorn nicked the underside of her wrist.

She shrank away from the pain and licked the spot a few moments. When the anguish dwindled to a mere ache she placed her hands at the ends of the bent green branch directly over the fruit and squeezed.

The fruit hit the ground and bounced three little bounces about a meter along the ground. Zarah left it there and repeated the process again and again until she'd knocked off two dozen or more of the fruit, all spread out on the ground. Careful never to touch any of fruit with her hands, she collected more of the green branches into both hands and broomed most of the fruit together into a single jumble.

She settled down on the ground on her haunches and stared at her haul. She had the fruit but she still didn't dare eat them.

She tried using her bunch of branches to scrape the thorns off one of the fruit, but she lit her lighter for a moment and saw she was getting nowhere and gave up.

She took a canteen and poured some of her precious water over one of the fruit, hoping to wash off or at least soften the thorns. She lit her lighter again and examined the fruit. No change.

She flicked off her lighter and sat some more.

After a few minutes Zarah gathered some of the smallest dry twigs and branches and stacked a small pile near her hoard. On top of the pile she put a few pieces of slightly bigger brush as thick as her fingers. She scouted around and gathered what the meager supply of small fuel she could manage and put it all on top.

She got down on her knees and knelt close to the pile and took out her lighter and lit some of the dry leaves under one of the smallest twigs at the bottom. First the leaves and then her small twig flamed. The larger twigs and brush on top caught. She blew on the pile until she had a small but genuine fire. She grabbed her tongs and picked up one of the fruit and held it just above the flames and dipped it down and held it there. The tongs crisped in the flame and broke apart. The fruit fell into the fire and bounced and rolled away.

She made another pair of tongs and picked up the burnt fruit and inspected it in the light of the fire. It was a little blackened, but the thorns and bumps were gone. She'd burned them off.

She touched the fruit. It was still a little hot, but she no longer cared. She cut off a tiny chunk with her knife and brought it up and took it into her mouth.

No thorns. Just fruit. Juicy and pulpy and syrupy and sweet. Delicious.

She sat cross-legged and poured a few drops of onto her fingertips and said a small pre-meal blessing, "Bismillah."

She took another bite and then another until she'd eaten one entire fruit. She gazed with satisfaction at her hoard and the feast she was about to enjoy.

Within an hour, Zarah had prepared and eaten a dozen fruit. The sticky juice had dribbled onto her lips and chin. Some had dripped all the way down to her neck. Tiny seeds stuck in her teeth. She didn't care.

As taught to say after eating, she said the word "Alhamdulillah" and gathered a bunch more fruit. But how to carry them?

She took off her abaya and tied it into a kind of sack and piled another two dozen of the de-thorned fruit into it and laid it across her left shoulder. Dressed only in jeans and tee shirt and sneakers, she resumed her trek up the dark hill.

Grandmother was proud tonight.

21 Hack and Mattie Back at the Ranch

In total darkness Hack inched from the hotel room bathroom towards their bed. "You in there?"

Mattie had maintained complete radio silence through the entire drive home from the Hedgehog Barrel gig. She grunted noncommittal rebuffs at his conversational openings and stared straight out the passenger window.

Once they'd finished their elevator ride up and their short walk down the hall, she slammed open the door of their room. She sailed her Tom Mix hat into the Vauxhall Arms' gilt-trimmed chair in the corner and sat on the bed and tore off her boots and wriggled out of her jeans. She threw the jeans on top of her hat—denting the tip of its dome—and rolled over onto the middle of the bed and pulled the sheets and blankets over her.

Stumped, Hack stayed wary and said nothing. He followed her in and shut the door and pulled off his own boots and took his jeans and folded them neatly into a bureau drawer. He went into the bathroom and brushed his teeth. When he came out of the bathroom Mattie had already turned out the lights.

He inched in the total darkness towards their bed. "You in there?" he asked again.

"There's only one bed in this hole." Then, after a pause, "Lucky for you."

"I see," he said. "Or more accurately, I don't see." From the direction her voice came from he guessed Mattie had moved to the right side of the bed—the side closest to the bathroom. Hack probed down and found the soft mattress with the fingertips of his right hand. He started inching backwards towards the bottom of the bed. When he got there he switched to navigating left-handed and made a sharp left turn. A hard projection he'd failed to notice earlier banged the side of his knee, but he was moving slow, so it smarted no more than your average kick to the shins.

Keeping his left hand on the bed's edge, he maneuvered the rest of the way along its bottom and took another sharp left turn to the top. He leaned down and with his right hand felt for the bedspread and blankets and top sheet and lifted them all and slid under them into bed. He turned onto his left side and scrooched backward to the far side of the king bed until he brushed up against her back.

Which felt different from ever before. He said, "In Minnesota, you told me you always sleep naked."

"Not tonight."

"I didn't know you even owned pajamas."

"Add that to the long list of things you don't know."

He felt behind him with his fingertips. "It's like a burka. You're covered top to bottom."

She wriggled away from him so they no longer touched.

He said, "And they're flannel."

"Arizonans over-air-condition."

"Not possible."

She said nothing.

He said, "It's a hundred degrees outside."

She said nothing.

"Did I do something?"

"No. What could you ever do?"

"I don't know. That's why I asked."

"If you did do something and you were paying attention, you'd know."

"Do I get a hint?"

"No."

"So be it." He sidled back to the opposite edge of the bed and shifted himself to face away from her. After yesterday's apparently premature burst of over-confidence, it turned out he was two steps behind after all.

But at two-thirty in the morning after a day that had started at six, Hack wasn't going to waste precious sleep time repeating with Mattie the kind of guessing game cycles he'd been through when married to Lily. In a few moments he settled into sleep.

125

22 Memories Are Made of This

The Mujahid woke up from another of his dreams that wasn't a dream.

This time he didn't mind; the memory was a fond one. He'd turned fourteen. His father and uncles let him help execute two men caught having sex with each other.

A crowd of several hundred gathered in the street. The two men stood facing the wall blindfolded with their hands tied behind their backs. For the trial, Father accused the men of sodomy and other disgusting acts while the two men stood trembling but silent.

Father ignored calls from the mob to shoot the criminals where they stood. Instead Father let his son follow along as Father and his brothers pushed the criminals up the concrete stairs to the top of the old building.

Once on the roof, they led the criminals to the edge.

"I have something to show you," Father said to everyone.

Then Father grabbed one of the men by the thick strong bonds that tied his arms and hands behind him and pushed. But Father didn't let go. He held on to the bonds so that the bound and blindfolded criminal dangled over the street, his feet propped against the wall. Father laughed, "Do you feel the fire beneath you? That is the pit of Hell waiting for you."

The criminal made no sound.

Father used his immense strength to pull the criminal back up close to him and said, "I want to hear you scream," and dangled him again.

The man still made no sound.

Father yelled "Scream" and the criminal finally screamed but it was a curse. Father cursed him back and he said, "Use the knife" and the boy who would grow up to become the Mujahid cut the bonds. The criminal fell and broke on the hard ground below.

The mob surged towards the body and screamed curses and picked up pebbles and rocks and big stones and hurled them down on the criminal's broken body until they crushed his head.

Then they calmed for a few moments and stepped back and waited for Father and his brothers to do the same thing with the other criminal, but this one screamed the first time Father dangled him, so Father simply dropped him.

It was good memory. The Mujahid had learned much about justice and he had demonstrated his courage.

That the first of the two criminals was his older brother was an odd strange thing.

23 The Scout On The Hill

Another day was coming and Zarah needed shelter again. The higher she went up the hill, the sparser became the vegetation. By the time she neared the top, it was almost morning, and the pre-dawn light revealed only a few spots of green here and there spread over the mostly dark hard ground. And no cave in sight.

Here the most common plants were the scattered individual cactuses which looked like straight upright Arabic *alifs*. Some were little green spiny pencils that came only to her knees, but there were many others that rose past twice her height. Wide-spaced vertical rows of sharp thorns ran up and down their trunks.

The tallest one towered at least fifteen meters above her. It sprouted thick branches that grew out of its sides in tubes thicker than Zarah's body and somehow reminded her of big green thumbs. Some of its branches curled out and then bent straight up. A few curved through the air and bent towards the ground like massive green snakes eager to strike down on her.

Although she saw no cave, she did spot a thicket of green bushes, many of them grown taller than her head. She squirmed her way in among the branches, taking care to avoid any that might surprise her with painful thorns. In the middle of the thicket she found a bare spot under the tallest and leafiest bush. She laid her canteens and her hoard of fruit on the ground and lay down next to them and curled up and fell asleep.

Much later Zarah woke in darkness to the sound of a man talking in a loud commanding voice from the far side of her thicket.

She must have slept through the entire fifteen-hour summer day. As she'd hoped, the thicket had sheltered her from the sun's fiery direct heat in relatively cool comfort. She felt fresh and rested, despite a growing queasiness in her stomach.

The man was giving directions. She heard him say in Spanish, "You're on the right track. Stay on the path you're on and you'll be fine."

Who was he? And who was he talking with?

She crept to the edge of the bushes and peered out. He was standing on the crest of the hill, silhouetted against the last light of a darkening sky.

He wore a dark blue bandanna on his head. From under the cloth a thick scruff of black hair poked down the back of his neck. The square black handle of a big pistol like Jabali's Glock jutted from a holster at his side. He had high cheekbones and a nose like Jabali's but his face was thinner and not as ugly. He was talking into a black phone from which protruded a short unusually thick antenna—a satellite phone like Ali's.

The man said something and clicked off his phone and moved down the over the hill out of her sight to the other side.

A wave of pain struck her insides. She felt like she was going to explode. She grabbed one of her canteens and scampered back down the hill at least fifty meters away from the man and crouched by a thick rock. She yanked off her pants.

Too much fruit too soon?

After a few minutes she felt better. She waited to make sure she had finished and cleaned herself with some of the precious water from her canteen and a few handfuls of small green leaves she plucked from nearby. She rested awhile on the rock. Then she pulled up her jeans and crouched low to the ground as she crept back up the hill again.

What now?

Her plan had been to cross over the hilltop and eventually down to the town she'd seen on Ali's computer screen that day in the Compound. With enough fruit and water and the fact she'd be headed downhill, she'd been sure she could finish her journey with relative ease.

But a man blocked her way. A man with a gun.

Zarah felt sick and frustrated and frightened, and she knew she'd be famished again very soon. The fruit she'd so carefully gathered was dangerous, at least if it was all she ate. She needed something else to eat—bread or meat or something solid. And her water was running low.

What was the man doing there? Why did he have to stand in that spot when she'd taken so many chances and worked so hard to get this far? And who'd he been giving directions to?

Maybe she could sneak past him. It was still pretty dark and she was small and nimble.

She snuck back to her temporary home in the bush. She dumped the rest of the fruit onto the ground from her abaya and pulled the garment on over her head. She grabbed the second canteen and slung it over her shoulder. It clanked almost empty against the first one.

She crept on hands and feet out of the bush. She lowered herself to the ground and crawled up the hill. She slowed as she got close to the spot where she'd seen him before. She didn't see the man or hear him.

But she did smell something. Something wonderful. Melted cheese and a fragrant sauce. Exotic spices. It was coming from the thicket of bushes nearby on the hill, only a few dozen meters away.

Zarah hesitated. Tiny in the distance far down below glowed blurry little lights where there must be homes and people. She could head their way.

But the aroma tantalized. She'd eaten nothing for more than two days but a few small fruit, and her body had rejected those. One canteen was empty and the other one almost empty. How far could she get on an empty stomach and a few swallows of water—even downhill?

She turned towards the thicket and its promise of food.

24 ZNN Reports

Hack woke lying on his back in his hotel bed. The hotel clock radio read 5:12 A.M.. Had he slept even two hours? He looked upwards into the darkness and thought about getting back to sleep, but he still felt too wired from the gig.

Now what?

As quietly as he could he lifted his covers a few inches and pulled his legs out from under them and pivoted to place his bare feet on the floor. He felt around the dark to grab his jeans off the floor like he would have at home, but then remembered he'd put them in a bureau drawer. He tiptoed to the bureau and opened the drawer and slipped his jeans out and then on. He remembered his shoes were next to the chair. He grabbed them and sat long enough on a chair to slip them on. He didn't bother with socks. He snatched the top paperback from the little stack he kept on his end table and slipped out the door to the hallway and then rode down the elevator to the main floor.

The hotel bar was open and empty—not even a bartender. Hack took a chair at a low table in back and opened his book. It turned out to be "Darker Than Amber," by John D. Macdonald—a novel he'd read only twice before. Travis McGee had come up against a gang of homicidal con artists who lured naive lonely men into steamy relationships on ocean cruise ships, sucked them dry of money and threw them overboard.

Like so many other TVs in airports and hotel lobbies, the one hung behind the bar was tuned to ZNN, which was blaring something about someone—apparently someone truly awful. Every time Hack happened to glance up from his novel he saw a different story with a different angle about the awful doings of this awful man all ZNN contributors seemed to hate with an all-consuming hatred. He was all they could talk about. Nothing newsworthy didn't involve this awful man.

Hack enjoyed a couple of hours absorbed in his novel and

131

ignoring the TV when Mattie sat beside him in the other chair at his table.

"Bad sleep?" she asked.

"No, I slept fine," he said. "But only an hour or two."

"Don't let me stop your reading."

"It's okay." He glanced up and recognized Lauren Goodwell's face on the television screen. "Hey. There's that news-babe who slimed me on ZNN," he said. "This past January when I was hiding out."

"I remember her." Mattie looked over at the screen. "Who do you suppose she's lying about today?"

"I think she just reported on an ambush interview she did with Lily."

"Our Lily? Why?"

Hack shook his head. "Sorry. I was too engrossed in my book. Caught just the tail end."

Lauren Goodwell said, "And in this morning's top headline, Arizona and federal authorities raided a rural compound overnight. In a place where life off the grid is common, these were folks who struggled to make do."

The ZNN camera panned across a swath of debris burned black beyond recognition.

"Looks like a war zone," Mattie said. "In Syria or someplace like that."

Mattie seemed friendly enough. Or biding her time to waylay him later. Hack decided not to trouble temporarily smooth waters. He'd find out soon enough what had bugged her the previous night.

Lauren said, "This trailer is all that's left of these pathetic peoples' paltry personal possessions."

"Nice alliteration there," Hack said. "Pretty piquant."

"Shh," Mattie said. "I want to hear."

Lauren Goodwell spoke. "This trailer contained a large part of the Compound dwellers' meager world—a world bereft of luxury or even basic creature comforts."

The camera showed the messy inside of a small trailer with a bunk bed with two bare mattresses, towels hung from racks nailed into its sides and a heap of filthy-looking clothing.

Mattie said. "I wonder where in Arizona? Near here? And why'd the cops raid it?"

Hack said, "And who burned it out like that?"

Mattie said, "When the camera panned past that pile of dirty clothes, did you notice the bulletproof vests?"

Lauren Goodwell's voice over continued as the camera changed to an aerial shot. The blackened area was surrounded by stacks of black tires. "The Compound is located in an area just south and west of Phoenix where unconventional people often flee to live undisturbed in their unconventional ways. Locals make it a point of pride to be tolerant of those who choose to live according to their own ideas. And with the raid, locals now worry."

The screen showed Lauren Goodwell standing in a desert. She said, "Many are quick to distance the area's pleasant counter cultural vibe from the compound and the unusual people who dwelt there."

Hack began to suspect something. "Wait for it," he said.

Lauren Goodwell said, "Authorities allege the tenants were a cult preparing for wrongdoing. And locals fear that publicity around a case infused with allegations of terrorism, child abuse and faith healing might contribute to a rise in racism and Islamophobia. They fear that white supremacist and the alt-right will pounce on these events to advance an Islamophobic narrative."

"Aha," Hack said.

Lauren Goodwell said, "Anonymous sources say authorities have known about the compound for some time, but a jurisdictional dispute between federal and state authorities delayed the raid. But the fire set by someone inside the Compound accelerated their timetable. No one knows who set the fire or why."

"Authorities say they found the dead body of a three-year-old boy buried in hills just outside the compound, as well as a tunnel with a cache of military small arms and chemical traces from used high explosives. They have made no arrests, but Child Protective Services has taken eleven children under protection. Authorities say adults were training the children to commit a terrorist attack on a Phoenix school."

"A dead baby and a terrorist attack on a school," Mattie said. "You think she'd have started her story with that."

The TV showed on a high built-up berm of tires filled in with rocks and sand and debris.

Lauren Goodwell explained, "A neighbor says that the Compound leader—a now missing Arizona man named Ali—told the neighbor he planned to build an 'earth ship', which is an ecofriendly self-sustaining home using tires packed with upcycled materials as bricks. I'm no expert, but this looks like potential material for an earth ship."

"She's right about one thing," Hack said. "She's no expert. That's a sand-butt backstop for a firing range."

25 The Groucho Papers

"The Court calls Alyssa Sterns-Marquardt."

From his usual spot in the back of the courtroom, Hack watched Professor Sterns-Marquardt stride to the witness stand and seat herself for Sam's cross-examination. She was slightly and pleasantly rounded. She wore a dark blue suit and short hair and big dark framed glasses through which she stared around the court room with a self-confident expression Hack hoped hid at least a little discomfort.

Hack admitted to himself Sterns-Marquardt had handled herself well on direct. The SWASU attorney Macklin led her step by step through the Amos Owens disciplinary process. Sam and Laghdaf sat quietly and made no objections as she explained the general purposes of the Bias Response Committee and how its disciplinary process worked. When the unidentified student "Jane Doe" reported Amos Owens' hate speech about Muslim-governed countries, the rules required her Committee to take immediate action. A review of the facts showed that the words Amos Owens used satisfied the SWASU definition of hate speech: it was speech that might insult or offend a person because of some trait, in this case, because the person was a Muslim.

SWASU guidelines for disciplinary action then required her Bias Response Committee to recommend to Dean Stamp that Owens be expelled. Owens had offended Muslims and made Muslims and other marginalized groups on campus feel unsafe. The law and University policies required the University not only to be safe and welcoming to all students from all backgrounds but also to present the appearance of being safe and welcoming. Simple as that.

Sam and Laghdaf had spent the night before at their office poring over "The Groucho Papers," which is what they nicknamed the treasure trove of incriminating documents Hack had brought back from SWASU.

After arriving in the morning, the already exhausted Hack had become irate and frustrated when Sam and Laghdaf told him they couldn't enter into evidence a single page of the Groucho Papers. He didn't understand it any better than he understood why Sam and Laghdaf had chosen a trial with the judge as fact-finder instead of a having a jury. To the extent Hack understood—or didn't understand—their lawyer explanations, the means by which Hack had gotten hold of the stolen documents and the lack of a witness to authenticate them ruled out their use as evidence. Or something like that.

Hack asked, "So she can just get on the stand and lie and then skate away?"

"Like Wayne Gretzky," Laghdaf said.

Hack asked Laghdaf, "You played hockey growing up?"

Laghdaf said, "In Mauritania? You do know that's in the Sahara, right?"

Sam fixed Hack with a sad hound dog look and said, "It happens every day. Get used to it."

So today Sam rose from his chair with a different plan for his cross-examination.

Sam: The student Jane Doe who reported Amos Owens was an employee of the Bias Response Team?

Sterns-Marquardt: I wouldn't use the word 'employee.' She was a volunteer.

Sam: A volunteer who was paid twenty dollars an hour—more than the prevailing minimum wage?

Sterns-Marquardt: But much less than you get.

Sam: Not always, Professor. Depends on the case. And the job for which you pay her twenty dollars an hour is to haunt the campus looking for what you've taught her to label hate speech?

Sterns-Marquardt: I reject your use of the word "haunt."

Sam: You'd prefer "hunt"?

Sterns-Marquardt: I reject any such loaded word. If she happens on an instance of hate speech, she is to report it. She happened on one. She reported it.

Sam: Isn't there an extra benefit for those who report more cases?

Sterns-Marquardt: If you're suggesting an incentive to invent bias cases, not at all. And there's no need. Sadly, there's plenty of hate speech out there.

Sam: You regard the SWASU campus as awash in hate speech?

Sterns-Marquardt: As I explained before, much of it is unconscious, of course.

Sam: Of course. But isn't it true that Jane Doe who reported Amos Owens is also a student of yours in one of your upper level seminars? One called "Interdisciplinary Intersectionality Studies," I believe?

Sterns-Marquardt: A fine student, actually.

Sam: I'm sure she is. And zealous too?

Sterns-Marquardt: I don't know what you mean when say "zealous."

Sam: You give her not only money but extra academic credit for her work on behalf of the Bias Response Committee, do you not?

Sterns-Marquardt: You mean, course credits?

Sam: Yes. Towards graduation.

Sterns-Marquardt: Yes.

Sam: And other less tangible forms of credit?

Sterns-Marquardt: Once again, I don't know what you mean.

Sam: You've recommended her for a prestigious scholarship and for acceptance into a highly regarded program of graduate studies?

Sterns-Marquardt: Because she's a fine student.

Sam: But she's not a member of the men's basketball team herself, is she?

Sterns-Marquardt: No.

Sam: She was not actually present when Amos Owens asked the fatal question you regard as biased enough to justify throwing him out of the University?

Sterns-Marquardt: I don't believe so.

Sam: You relied on her word for something that she did not witness herself?

Sterns-Marquardt: Mr. Owens doesn't deny he said it.

Sam: Yes, Amos is an honest young man. And of course, you regard his merely asking his question he asked as sufficiently Islamophobic to justify his expulsion?

Sterns-Marquardt: No one made him say it.

Sam: And you relied on whom to arrive at your definition of Islamophobia?

Sterns-Marquardt: I don't know what you've read, but there is in the bias response community a generally accepted definition of Islamophobia.

Sam: You have never relied on any outside organization in framing your Committee's definition of Islamophobia?

Sterns-Marquardt: Whatever you may have seen, I assure you the Committee takes into account all points of view.

Sam: And you never relied on any outside organization in handling the Amos Owens case in particular?

Sterns-Marquardt: I don't what documents you've been looking at, but I can say emphatically no.

From his seat in the back Hack wondered, why does she keep talking about what Sam's seen or read? Does she know about the Groucho Papers? Is she trying to cover herself?

Sam must have been wondering the same thing. He stopped and looked at the wall above and behind Judge Zernial a long moment. He clasped his hands in front of him and swiveled to his right and walked across the courtroom a few steps towards the defense table. Then as abruptly as a swimmer making his turn at pool's end, he pivoted and walked back to his original spot and turned to face Sterns-Marquardt again. Then he stood there.

The courtroom was silent through Sam's exhibition. All eyes followed him in one direction and then back again.

Judge Zernial broke the silence. She said, "Counselor? Do you have more questions for this witness?"

Sam: Sorry, Your Honor. Yes. Professor, isn't that the third consecutive time in three consecutive answers you have spoken of some document you think I may have read?

Sterns-Marquardt: I don't know what you're talking about. And I don't recall any such documents.

Sam: Are you in fact personally aware of any document anywhere that indicates you did consult with some person or organization outside SWASU in handling the Amos Owens case?

Defense Attorney: Objection!

Sam: Your Honor, I'm only asking a follow-up question to clarify Professor Sterns-Marquardt's own testimony.

Judge: Overruled. Professor, please answer the question.

Sterns-Marquardt: I don't quite understand the question.

Sam: Let me help. Have you at any time ever looked at any document tending to indicate you or your committee consulted with any outside organization concerning what to do about Amos Owens?

Sterns-Marquardt: I don't remember for sure.

Sam turned and looked towards Laghdaf sitting at the table with Amos Owens and said to Laghdaf, "Mr. Laghdaf, please."

At first Laghdaf looked puzzled as he looked up towards Sam. Then recognition seemed to pass across Laghdaf's face. He reached into a stack of documents on the table and extracted a thin tan manila folder and handed it up to Sam. Sam took it. He opened it and stared at something inside for a moment. He shook his head in apparent sadness. He slapped the folder shut and then snapped it against his thigh with a report that echoed through the courtroom.

Sam turned to face Sterns-Marquardt. He waved the folder around in the air with his right hand and said, "Professor, as you sit here right now, do you have some personal recollection of having read any document of the type you just mentioned three times? For example, a letter from an outside organization instructing you how to decide the Owens case?"

Sterns-Marquardt was staring at Sam's waving folder like a bird hypnotized by the moving head of a snake. Her answer was simultaneous with the response of her lawyer. She said, "Now that you remind me, yes," just as the SWASU lawyer Macklin leapt to his feet and shouted "Objection!"

Judge Zernial said, "The objection is overruled. Counselor, the barn door is wide open and the horse is loose."

Sam *(continuing to wave the folder):* You are familiar with an organization called the 'Anti Islamophobia League', are you not? Sometimes called by the acronym 'AIL'?

Sterns-Marquardt: I've heard of that group, of course. A very prestigious organization critical in our struggle against Islamophobia.

Sam: Have you ever read an email addressed to you personally from AIL, in which AIL specifically instructs you to recommend expulsion of Amos Owens?

Sterns-Marquardt: I recall an email touching on that issue. But I entirely reject your using the word "instructs." They did not instruct. They just gave an advisory opinion.

Sam: An advisory opinion in which they used the expression "set an example."

Sterns-Marquardt: If you say so.

Sam: How about the phrase "our common struggle against common oppressors and those like Owens who serve oppression by promulgating Islamophobia." That ring a bell?

Sterns-Marquardt: Perhaps.

Sam: "And the word 'faggot' applied to Amos Owens?

Sterns-Marquardt (just looking at Sam)

Sam: Until contradicted, I'll take that as a "yes." How about "dupe of Zionism?"

Sterns-Marquardt: Anti-Zionism is not anti-Semitism, Mr. Lapidos—if that's what you're suggesting.

Sam: How about "satanic Jews who have hypnotized the world." Does that count?

Defense Attorney (standing): Objection! Your Honor, we have the right beforehand to see any document used to refresh the recollection of a witness.

Judge: I was wondering what took you so long, Counselor. You are correct. Mr. Lapidos?

Sam took the folder over to Macklin and handed it to him. The man opened it and read it. He looked up and said, "This is just a check list of possible evidentiary objections."

Sam said, "A tool for my colleague and myself during trial. Our own recollection is not always perfect."

The Judge said, "Mr. Lapidos, in what possible way are you using that cheat sheet to refresh the recollection of this witness?"

Sam said, "I never said anything about refreshing witness recollection, Your Honor. I am asking about extraordinarily relevant documents which the witness has testified she read during the process by which she decided to recommend Mr. Owens' expulsion and which the defense never produced."

The Judge looked at Macklin. "Counselor?"

Macklin shot Sterns-Marquardt a poisonous glance, then sighed. "If so, Your Honor, it is because I was not aware of them."

Sam said, "Your Honor, I know Mr. Macklin and I know his integrity and I believe him. But we are nevertheless entitled to those documents."

Judge Zernial said, "Yes, Counselor, you are."

26 Reunion In Phoenix

Mattie saw by the big clocks hanging behind the Vauxhall Arms front desk it was six P.M in Phoenix. And, as it happened, already two A.M. tomorrow in London. In Tokyo, ten A.M.. But tomorrow or yesterday? Mattie wasn't too sure how that International Date Line thing worked.

Hack sat next to her on the plush sofa by the natural gas fireplace. Mattie was sipping her incredibly delicious cold Café Borgia while Hack took occasional tastes from a frosty glass of some Czech beer whose name he admitted he couldn't pronounce. Mattie was wearing her best jeans and Tony Lama boots and the new Tom Mix hat she loved. Hack still wore the courtroom-appropriate suit Sam had sprung for, although he'd loosened his collar and tie.

Mattie thought he looked sexy in his fancy clothes, but she wasn't going to admit it just that moment.

Lily and Sarai walked in through the revolving door. Tiny Sarai gazed in wonder at the huge space with its vaulted roof and luxurious furniture and elegant strolling businesspeople. Almost-as-tiny Lily was just looking around—obviously for Hack and Mattie.

Mattie and Hack both stood and waved.

Mattie heard Lily say to Sarai "It's the hottest I've ever been," and Sarai answer, "I warned you, Mom." Then Sarai spotted Hack and ran across the vast lobby and jumped into his arms. Lily trailed Sarai tugging a small wheeled suitcase behind her. She saw Mattie and waved and smiled. "Hi, Mattie."

Mattie smiled and said "Hi" back. For some reason, what could have been an awkward moment wasn't. Maybe because Lily was so classy. She even looked classy in her blue Patagonia Lattice Back dress, identical to the one in the photo Mattie had seen in the glossy *Phoenix Today* Magazine on the coffee table in her room upstairs.

Lily crossed her hands onto her bare upper arms in the frigid air conditioning of the lobby. Mattie thought, maybe I should have warned her. If she didn't bring a sweater, she can buy a nice one in the Hotel shop. Maybe we'll shop together. She could show me things.

"This is so Sam," Hack had explained to Mattie while they waited for Lily and Sarai. "I mean, putting the ex-wife and ex-husband and current woman friend in the same hotel. He's oblivious to that stuff, or at least he pretends to be. He'd never connect up with the idea that might be uncomfortable."

"It isn't for me if it isn't for her," Mattie said.

"Good. But it shows you how Sam thinks—or doesn't think."

"It's fine," Mattie told him. "I like Lily fine. She did me a big favor by dumping you."

"You have the nicest way of putting things," Hack said.

Mattie said, "And Sarai's a sweetheart and a treat and a hoot all rolled into one."

"I can't disagree with that." Hack leaned forward to kiss her but she turned her head so his lips landed on her cheek.

"We're in a classy place," she said. "Act classy."

"I'd only be acting."

"Fake it like you fake those country songs."

He fingered the jade bangle on her wrist. "What's that you got on? I don't think I've seen it before."

"Just something I picked up."

"In the Hotel Shop?"

"Where else?"

"Using Sam's card?"

"What else?"

"I think I finally got it figured out—your birthday's not a one-day thing—it's like the Twelve Days of Christmas."

"Totally."

"Let me know when you get to five Golden rings."

Mattie stood up from the couch and Sarai jumped down from Hack's arms and ran to Mattie and gave her a quick hug around the waist. She said, "Hi, Mattie."

"Hello, Sarai." Mattie bent down and kissed Sarai's cheek.
Mattie felt a little self-conscious and out of the corner of her eye she
saw Lily still smiling. What a nice woman. Sarai stepped back and
looked at each of the three adults left to right in turn, then back
again the opposite way.

There was a long pause. Hack said, "Well, we're all here
together in one place again. Just like home."

"Yes, we are," Lily said. Another pause.

Sarai said, "Am I the only one hungry? I bet the restaurant here
is great."

Sarai was right. After Lily and Sarai checked in to the hotel and
put their stuff in their room, all four met in the Vauxhall Bistro.
After Hack's steak and Mattie's burger and Lily's salmon bisque
and Sarai's vegetarian Pasta Primavera, the four strolled to the lobby
again.

"Well, what now?" Mattie asked.

Lily said, "I'll have to check in with Sam. He has something I
need."

Hack said, "He gave it to me. I can pass it on to you. but only in
private."

Mattie said, "Really?"

"I'm serious," Hack said. "I need to give it to her in private."

Lily said, "How private?"

"As private as we can get in a hotel" Hack said.

Lily said, "Come on up to my room," and shrugged at Mattie
and walked over to the elevator. Hack trailed her.

Mattie and Sarai stood smiling at each other in the high-
ceilinged lobby. Mattie said, "So, Sarai? Want to check out the
Hotel Shop?"

27 *Discovery Discovery*

Lily and Hack stood side by side facing the door as they rode up the elevator. Neither spoke.

Lily sneaked a peek at her ex-husband. He looked the same physically, short and square and solid, with dark hair and a small dark beard, but he had changed in some indefinable way. She was sure the changes had something to do with the violent things both he and she had each done that terrible January day.

As far as any husband-wife connection, there wasn't one. She felt no sexual feeling towards him at all. That was dead. Nor did he give any sign he felt any current sexual interest in her—and she was confident she could detect that signal in any man, no matter how hard he tried to hide it.

The elevator door opened and she left first and walked down to her room and he followed her. She opened the door. She went in and turned to face him. He followed her in and closed the door behind them.

She spoke. "Nat—"

He held up his left hand. "Please, I'm 'Hack'. We're not married anymore."

"That's going to feel strange to me."

"Not as strange as calling me 'Nat' feels to me. You and Sam are the only people who've called me 'Nat' since Mrs. Prynne in high school. Even Sam has stopped. You're the holdout."

"Okay," she said, "Hack." The word tasted strange and sour on her tongue. She'd always hated that nickname. For reasons obvious to her and all of her friends—her former friends, evidently—she hadn't wanted to be married to a 'Hack'. But now that he wasn't her husband, it seemed to suit him. She repeated "Hack" and smiled.

He smiled back. "Thanks."

She said, "What did Sam give you for me?"

"You brought your computer, right?"

She nodded.

145

He said, "Let's boot it up."

Lily took her laptop out of its case and placed it in on the hotel room desk and plugged it into outlet on the base of the table lamp. She pulled up the swivel chair and got the laptop up and running.

Hack grabbed a kitchen table chair and pulled it up next to her and sat. He handed her a small card.

"What's that for?"

"A secure encrypted satellite Internet connection. Plug it in that slot."

She did as asked and asked, "Now what?"

"Now I have something for you." He reached into his pocket and pulled out a flash drive and held it out.

She took the flash drive and looked her question at him. He nodded. She stuck the drive into the USB port on the side of the laptop. A message flashed on the screen:

"You need to format this drive first.
Press 'Yes' to format or Press 'Cancel'"

He said, "Click the 'cancel' button."

She did. "Now what?"

"Let me explain. This flash drive is encrypted. There's material there you can't let anyone else see. Ever. Not even Sarai. Especially not Sarai."

"But my whole reason for being in Phoenix is to help Sarai find Zarah."

"And maybe this can help. Sam's not sure. But what he is sure of is that only you can see it. He made a big point of this. Sarai can never see it. Not ever. Aside from everything else, it might put her at risk. Promise?"

"Of course. What's on it?

Hack shook his head. "Haven't looked. Sam told me not to. Only Sam's seen it. And maybe Laghdaf, I suppose."

"Who's Laghdaf?

"He helps Sam with this stuff.'

"What stuff?"

Hack nodded toward the flash drive. "The stuff that's on the drive. Whatever that is. Laghdaf's also second-chairing the trial. You'll meet him."

Lily asked, "So what do I do next?"

"Learn the decryption key and use it to get onto the drive. I'll show you how."

"Okay." She grabbed a hotel pen and stationery pad on the desk. "What's the key?"

Hack shook his head. "You can't write it down. You have to memorize it."

"How long is it?"

"Just fifteen characters: numbers, both upper and lower-case letters and special characters, in a randomly generated sequence."

"Fifteen?"

"He wanted to use twenty-eight, but for your sake I bargained him down to fifteen."

"Thanks." Lily couldn't help noticing Hack's smirk. "You don't think I can do it, do you?"

"I'm sure you can," he said. "But it's going to take a while."

She said. "So let's get going. Without us Mattie and Sarai might be getting bored downstairs."

"Unless Mattie's showing her the Hotel Shop," Hack said. "In which case they're both doing fine."

Lily said, "I hope this new Hack guy doesn't turn out to be a cheapskate party-pooper like that Nat was. That Nat was no fun at all for a lot of years. Let Mattie have some fun. I don't know Mattie very well, but I get the impression she's had a tough life up to now."

Hack said, "It's all on Sam's card anyway."

Lily said, "And he'll never notice or care. Why should he? Mattie helped save Sarai's life." Then, "Here's a question. Why is Sam entrusting me with all this secret material?"

Hack said, "It can't be a surprise to you that your father has a high opinion of your abilities."

"He doesn't say so very often."

"He does to me." Hack paused. "I've gotten nowhere with this thing and you can look at this fresh material with fresh eyes. Plus you're our only available resource, what with the trial and everything. As soon as the trial ends, I promise I'll come back to it and help you if I can."

"Makes sense," Lily said.

"Let's just focus on your memorization for now."

So Lily focused, and after thirty minutes, she could recite the fifteen-character decryption sequence not only forward but also at Hack's insistence backwards.

Hack showed her the steps for entering the key into the laptop and open the drive. She followed his instructions and saw icons representing hundreds—no, thousands—of files and folders with all kinds of names. "Good grief," she said. "Where'd Sam get all this?"

"It's discovery Sam still has from the time he defended Gus Dropo—plus more."

"Because your friend Amir was the murder victim?"

"Right."

"Why all the secrecy? The feds already have it, since they provided the discovery in the first place."

"Well, the way Sam explained, there's regular discovery and there's discovery discovery."

"Discovery discovery?"

"Regular discovery is things the other side has to give you to satisfy its obligations under the rules of discovery which are part of the law. That's on this drive."

"I know about regular discovery."

"Then there's other discovery, which is things you discover on your own."

"Normally called investigation."

Hack said, "Yes. That's on this drive too. Then there's a third kind of discovery where you know things you maybe shouldn't know at all. And nobody else knows you know. And you don't want anybody else to know you know or especially how you know. That's on this drive too—discovery discovery."

"And Dad kept it."

"Sam keeps everything. You know that."

She nodded. "And some part of this can help find Zarah?"

Hack said, "If she exists, she's Amir's daughter, right? And this is all information about Amir that Sam or his many friends or some other less-than-friends could find."

"Like there was maybe somebody else besides Gus or you with a motive to kill Amir."

"Which there was."

"Okay," she said. "Thanks. I'll read it all. But this is a lot. It's going to take a lot of time. What about Sarai?"

"I love to spend as much time with her as possible."

"I thought you were too busy helping Sam with the trial."

"Tomorrow's Friday, right? Judge Zernial ordered a break in the trial. She's got other business. So for sure I can take Sarai tomorrow. Anyway, I'll make time."

"Make all the time you want," Lily said.

"Thanks."

"Of course." Lily smiled. "And she might as well get to know Mattie too."

"She might as well." Then, "So now—"

She interrupted. "Now you want me to repeat the encryption key again." So she did. Backwards.

28 *Zarah the Lotus Eater*

Zarah darted to the farther thicket and bent and ducked into its maze of stalks. A canopy of branches blocked the moonlight and she picked her way more by feel than by sight.

She reached the thicket's edge and peered out from its cover into an open moonlit space about ten meters by ten. Big boulders bordered the other side.

Except for the lack of tires, the Spanish-speaking man's little domain reminded her of Ali's forbidden corner of the Compound. Like Ali, the man kept a disorderly stronghold. Big green canvas tarps covered stacks of wooden crates. Dirt blotches smeared the canvas. Strange metal equipment and small boxes lay all about.

The man was standing with his back to her. He was cooking something delicious-smelling in a frying pan on a single burner propane stove. He hummed a little rhythmic tune as he dropped peppers and onions and little white chunks of chicken that sizzled and crackled as they hit the grease in the pan. Zarah sat back on her haunches. She wondered if the mingled aromas were going to make her faint.

A small shelf of rock projected out over the stove. An AR15 leaned barrel-upward against the shelf in easy reach of the man. She recognized the AR15 from its distinctive shape and butt stock and pistol grip and the hand guard over its muzzle.

The man had propped two solar panels just like Ali's facing south and upwards at forty-five-degree angles to capture energy from the daytime sun. Each panel was a rectangle about one and one-half meters across. Of course, at night the panels gathered no energy. But Zarah knew he could use the big truck batteries on the wooden pallet nearby to store plenty of electricity to run the radio and other equipment strewn about his camp.

On Zarah's side of the clearing only a few feet away sat a cardboard box, the four brown flaps of its lid torn up and open. Zarah couldn't read the western alphabet of the words on its side.

But the pictures were clear: bars.

Although the man seemed absorbed in his cooking, she couldn't chance a dash for the bars. She stayed where she was.

The right choice. Just that moment the man lifted his pan with his right hand and with his left rotated the knob to turn off the stove. He turned away and carried the pan to the middle of the space and sat cross-legged on a low flat rock so that he faced towards the town and distant houses. Zarah followed his gaze and realized that looking east from his camp the man had a perfect unobscured view of the entire valley below.

He ate with a shiny steel fork directly from his skillet. He was a slow methodical eater who chewed with great thoroughness and a kind of stolid unrushed dignity. Every so often he took a swig from a giant black water bottle he kept on the ground by his feet.

The man took about half an hour to finish his meal. He removed a rag from his pocket and wiped his mouth and face. He stood and walked away from Zarah back to the edge of the space near his stove and dumped the remnant of morsels and grease from his pan onto the ground. Then he knelt down and spooned a little sand from the ground onto the pan. He took his rag and rubbed the sand around in the pan. He held the pan up in the moonlight and inspected it and gave it a few more rubs with the rag and set it back on the stove.

As the man stood facing away, Zarah dashed to the cardboard box and reached in and grabbed two handfuls of bars. She spied a carton with a picture of fruit on it and snatched that up too. She darted back into the bushes and picked her way back through her thicket and out the other side and ran down the back of the hill.

She examined her haul: four bars, each in its own separate green paper-like wrapping. Pictures on the wrapping showed brown oat bars covered in chocolate. She tore the wrapping off a package and bit into a bar. Delicious. A little piece fell off the edge of her mouth. She snatched the chunk out of the air with her left hand before it could hit the ground and stuck it back in her mouth. Grainy crumbs and chocolate flakes flecked her lips. She licked around them to capture every morsel.

She sat and thought. Before, when she'd eaten too fast, she'd gotten sick. This time she'd be careful. Worse, she realized that in her greed she'd forgotten to say the required pre-meal blessing.

She said it now and opened another package. She made herself eat slowly and thoroughly as she downed the next bar. The crunchy bars were hard to chew without water, but she let the inside of her mouth moisten each bite and chewed a long time before she swallowed.

Then she pried open the top of the little carton. It was some kind of fruity beverage. She swigged it all down. Wet and sweet.

She took the other two packages and slid them into the pockets of her abaya, one bar on each side. She slipped back up the hill again and through her bushes to watch the man again. Maybe she could grab more food.

When she reached her spy spot on the edge of the thicket and took a kneeling position to check on him again, the man was standing on the lip of the hill looking down and east into the valley below. Night vision binoculars hung around his neck.

The man's phone gave a quiet buzz and he thumbed it and said, "Pedro." He listened a moment and said in Spanish, "Just a second." He set the phone in a black plastic holster at his left side and lifted his binoculars and looked through them. He kept his binoculars to his eyes with his right hand and with his left took up his phone again. "I think I've got you. How many in your team?"

He paused for his caller to answer. Then, "Ten? Really?" He grunted. "That's a lot of dope."

Another pause to listen.

"Yeah?"

Pause to listen.

"I see you. You're off-track. About half a kilometer too far east."

Pause to listen.

"Okay. Go to mile marker 158. That's another two hours' hike from you. Then wait there."

Pause to listen.

"I'll make sure there are two cars."

Pause to listen.

"Okay." He clicked his phone off. He pressed another button and it must have been a speed dial because in a moment he spoke again. "Pedro here. I got a pick up for you. At 158 in about two hours or maybe a little more."

Pause.

"Yes. But one thing. This team's bigger than usual. There's ten. Each carrying fifty or sixty pounds—though I think there's three women so some loads will be smaller. But no matter what you'll still need two cars."

Pause, this time with a grunt of obvious impatience.

"I'm just a scout. I just watch and guide. Pick-up and delivery is your job and your problem." He clicked off.

Pedro went back to his white rock and sat in the dirt in front of it. He picked headphones off the dirt and put them on and leaned back against the rock and closed his eyes.

Zarah watched Pedro awhile. From where he sat, if he happened to open his eyes, he'd have a clear view of the cardboard box full of goodies.

The people he was guiding and ordering around were traveling by night. So maybe he'd sleep through the heat of the day like she'd been doing. If she timed it right maybe she could come back at end of day before he woke up and grab a lot more food.

She picked her way back through the thicket and along the side of the hill and to her own bush and crawled in and settled there for a long day's nap.

29 Uncle Amir

Nine-thirty sharp in the morning. Lily heard the expected knock at their hotel room door and opened it. Hack and Mattie stepped in.

Sarai was sitting poised on the front edge of a plush chair staring at the door like a pointer at a waterfowl. She'd planted herself there two hours ago. She had to bend forwards a little because of the colorful new Vauxhall Arms pack she'd already strapped on her back. Maui Jim sunglasses—also from the hotel shop, of course— poked out from under the blue bill of her new Arizona Diamondbacks cap. She wore shorts and a white tee shirt.

Sarai jumped up and ran to Hack and hugged him. He tried to hoist her into his arms but she slid down in his hands.

Hack said, "You're all slathered up. You slither down."

"Slather and slither," Sarai giggled. "Mom ordered me to."

"Good idea," Mattie said. "The sun's a killer here. But the weather says it'll be cool. Only a hundred and six today. Otherwise I wouldn't go."

Lily handed Mattie the tube of suntan lotion. "Please cover everybody once every few hours. I learned the hard way in Mexico."

Mattie said, "You sure you don't want to come?"

"I can't. I'll be working."

Sarai asked, "Looking for stuff about Zarah, right, Mom?"

"Yes, Sweetheart."

Hack said, "And we'll be having a big day in Phoenix—the Desert Botanical Garden, lunch somewhere fancy, and then the Museum of Musical Instruments."

"Don't forget the Art Museum," Sarai said.

"Something special there?" Lily asked.

Sarai said, "An exhibit of genuine original Chuck Jones cartoon cells."

Lily asked, "Who's Chuck Jones?"

"The Bugs Bunny guy," Sarai said. "He drew Bugs and Yosemite Sam for the old Warner Brothers cartoons. You know, the

154

cartoons that were actually funny."

"Right," Hack said. "We watched those funny cartoons Saturday mornings when we were kids. And now they're in the Museum. We thought we were laughing at lowbrow humor, but it turns out they're highbrow art."

"And he was a Marine," Mattie said.

The other three looked at her. Hack asked, "Chuck Jones was a Marine?"

"No, Bugs was. I watched those cartoons with my grandpa when I was a kid. He was a Marine during World War Two. He told me they made Bugs an honorary Marine. After we won the war, the Marines discharged Bugs with the rank of Master Sergeant—which is pretty high, I think."

Hack said, "That is high. After two years in combat, my grandfather only made Sergeant First Class."

Lily said, "Sam says Bugs is a Jew. Bugs lives in a Jewish neighborhood and he speaks with a Jewish Style New York accent and whenever Yosemite Sam tries to kill him Bugs talks his way out of it."

Mattie said, "Grandpa said Marines fight their way out of things."

"Jewish marines can talk and fight," Sarai declared with her usual formidable air of certainty.

"Like your grandfather Sam," Lily said to Sarai.

Sarai said, "Grandpa was a Marine?"

Lily kissed her forehead. "Yes, Sweetheart. Like you said, he can talk and fight both."

Hack said, "And now Master Sergeant Bunny is high art hanging high in a highbrow museum."

Lily and Sarai hugged. Sarai went with Hack and Mattie out the door and left Lily left alone with her laptop. It was already ten o'clock and she faced plenty of work.

She made a pot of coffee and poured herself a cup and as a courtesy to the Vauxhall Arms placed the cup on a plastic coaster on

155

top of the brown faux wood desk. She pulled her swivel chair up to the desk and powered on the computer. She plugged Sam's flash drive into the laptop's USB port and stepped through the process of using the decryption key to access the flash drive files.

One screenful after another, she began to read.

The next thing she knew it was two in the afternoon and her back ached with anger at her.

Like most standard chairs, the hotel chair didn't really fit Lily. The feet at the ends of her short legs didn't touch the floor, which meant they hung beneath the chair and swung around loose to no place in particular. No support there. And long ago she'd discovered the hard way that sitting with one leg curled beneath the other put her legs to sleep.

Worse, the chair was low compared to the desk, and even after she'd cranked the chair up as high as it would go, the angle forced her to look up at the screen. Three hours of craning had crimped her neck.

Finally, and for this she blamed only herself, she'd been so absorbed in her work she'd forgotten to get up and walk around or even stretch in place every once in a while.

Lily stood and bent forward at the waist and stretched and sat on the carpet and did fifteen minutes of yoga exercises. While trying to restore her circulation and retrieve her freedom of movement, she thought over what she'd found so far.

As she'd been flicking the mouse to move from folder to folder and document to document, poking through the entire drive just to get a sense of everything the drive might hold, she'd happened on what might be Amir's photo. At least she supposed it was his photo. There was no caption. But after all, it was supposed to be a file about Amir.

Seeing the man's face in black and white had delivered an unexpected emotional jolt. Lily had never met Amir. She knew a little: that he'd come originally from Iraq by way of France and that a year or two ago he'd moved next door to Hack in Ojibwa City,

Minnesota. Terrorists had murdered Amir for reasons no one knew—or at least no one said—and framed Hack for the crime.

Lily knew all that, but Lily had never thought about Amir's face or even considered the obvious fact that of course he would have one. His was just a name she associated with the general catastrophe that had hit her family this past January.

To Lily he'd been even more faceless than the usual news media murder victims because he'd come from the Arab Mideast, where bodies piled up not just by the hundreds as in Chicago or America's other most violent cities, but by the thousands and hundreds of thousands.

Of course, she'd known in a cerebral sort of way that all those hundreds of thousands of corpses she read about and seen video of had accumulated one individual human soul at a time into the mounds in the news. As Amir's faded monochrome image reminded her, they died one human being and one soul at a time, each with private hopes and loves and hates.

She wondered if all the news coverage of all the mass slaughter and mayhem had jaded and desensitized its consumers. She made a private resolve: it would not do that to her. No matter what.

Even in this drab file image from some dreary anonymous bureaucracy Amir's face—if that's who it was—but then it was someone, wasn't it?—somehow impressed her. Silly, Lily supposed, but just by looking at the photo she could tell she liked him. Sarai had known him and Sarai had loved him; she called him "Uncle Amir." And a double recommendation: he'd also been Hack's friend.

Even the man's trifle of a mustache looked somehow endearing, even if a bit silly.

Along with the lone photo, the flash drive held a hodgepodge of hundreds of folders and thousands of files. There was no evident pattern to which files she found in which folders. A lot of folders intermingled reports from Arabic and French newspapers. Lily read neither Arabic nor French. And sprinkled here and there were other documents from what seemed to be foreign intelligence agencies, some in languages Lily didn't even recognize, even a few in Hebrew, which she recognized but couldn't read.

The drive also included some Portuguese-language reports from Brazil and some material in Spanish about something called "La Zona de la Triple Frontera," which turned out to translate into English as "The Tri-Border Area," a zone adjoining Paraguay, Argentina and Brazil. It seemed that several free-trade Latin American areas with large Middle Eastern populations allowed Islamist terrorist groups and organized crime mafias and corrupt officials to thrive in a mutually beneficial symbiotic relationship and to coordinate their terrorism and drug smuggling and human trafficking. The human trafficking included exploiting and selling sex slaves.

One published report in English from the U.S. Library of Congress explained:

Islamic terrorist organizations use the TBA to raise revenues through illicit activities that include drug- and arms trafficking, counterfeiting, money laundering, forging travel documents, and even pirating software and music. The Iranian sponsored terrorist group Hezbollah used the TBA as a base for carrying out two major terrorist attacks in Buenos Aires in the early 1990s—one against the Israeli Embassy on March 17, 1992; and the other against a Jewish community center on July 18, 1994.

Of course. The AMIA attack the ZNN reporter what's-her-name had missed in her expert extensive research.

Lily had yet to see anything to indicate Amir personally was ever in the Tri-Border Area. But someone had thought the subject sufficiently relevant to include the article among this cache of documents.

What connection could there be? Maybe there was a relationship between Amir and Hezbollah, but wouldn't it be a hostile one?

Before getting back to her computer, Lily took a big cushion from the couch and put it on the floor in front of her chair. Now she had a place to prop her feet while she worked.

A few hours later, about five in the afternoon, she found an English-language document describing a man named Amir ibn Yusuf and his activities in Iraq. The document was only three pages long. She couldn't tell who wrote it; wide black lines obscured the letterhead and other words that might have identified sources.

According to the document, after the Iraqi Army collapsed in the face of the notorious Sunni terrorist army ISIS, the Shia militias had become the primary effective Iraqi opposition to ISIS. But the Shia militias also committed systematic widespread war crimes themselves. They were hardly better than ISIS, if better at all. The Shiite militias destroyed homes and neighborhoods and carried out mass executions as well as mass and individual kidnappings of Sunni civilians including women and children.

The man the document called Amir had been an Iraqi activist who organized opposition to the Shiite militias Iran financed and armed within Iraq. He was Sunni, but able to work out some arrangement with Shia militias loyal to Iraq rather than to Iran and therefore fighting the pro-Iran militias for their own reasons.

It seemed Amir's opposition to Iran's militias together with his apparent ability to build ad hoc bridges between Sunni and Shia had made him useful to the Americans.

But of course, those same qualities had put his life in uninterrupted danger. The little document ended with this statement:

"The subject may become valuable again as conditions change. Consideration must be given to possible temporary asylum or other arrangements to preserve his capacity to serve as a useful actor in the future."

That was it.

Since Lily was looking for information about a child, the fact that pro-Iranian militias kidnapped children resonated.

Lily checked the computer's clock. Almost six. Time for another break. It had taken her eight hours to find one photo of someone who might be Sarai's Uncle Amir and one document about someone named Amir but not necessarily the same Amir.

Her cell rang. She checked her caller ID. "Hack. What's up?"

"How's it going with Amir?"

"Barely even started. You can take Sarai to dinner and I'll keep right on working."

He said, "I have an unusual request to make."

"Which is?"

"Sarai wants to hear Mattie sing."

"Mattie sings?"

"You didn't know that?"

"Like for money?"

"Of course for money. How do you think I got to know her?"

Lily said, "I guess that makes sense. No one mentioned it to me."

"As a friend of mine once pointed out to me, sometimes you got to ask."

"I agree with your friend. So she's singing tonight?"

"Yes. We have a gig. And it's in a bar."

"Ah," she said. "Hence the deferential supplicating tone in your voice."

He hurried on. "But it's a really nice bar. Very friendly. Family friendly. It's very nice place and we'll eat there and then she can hear Mattie sing and watch me play piano with the band and we'll all watch out for her."

"What kind of bar is this?"

"A country western bar."

"Like with chicken wire?"

"No. No chicken wire. No fights. Nothing like that. As I said, family friendly."

Lily thought for a second. "You promise you won't let her go too hard on the booze?"

There was a moment of silence, like Hack wasn't sure she was kidding.

"No booze. Only water. Bread and water. And porridge."

Lily said, "I trust you, Hack. And Mattie too, now that I think about it. Remember, I saw what she did to your terrorist 'Ear Boy' pal."

"Yes. And let that be a lesson to him."

Lily said, "Let that be a lesson to any man who messes with her."

"Or messes with Sarai, I think."

"I think too. So go ahead."

He said, "Great! Thanks!" and hung up right away, like he was afraid she'd change her mind, which she realized she probably would have with two more seconds to think about it.

"Have a good time," she said to the dead phone in her hand. Lily sighed. Maybe some time she'd like to hear Mattie sing too.

Lily ordered a small pizza through room service and made another pot of coffee and went back to work.

30 Pedro's Water

Late in the afternoon, Zarah knelt in her now-customary stealing position on the edge of her thicket. Pedro lay facing away from her in his sleeping bag in his corner under the shelf by the stove. He was snoring. A big black water bottle enticed her from its place on the ground by the white rock in the middle of the clearing.

Zarah launched herself forward and grabbed the bottle and turned on the spot and sprinted back into her thicket.

The bottle was long as her chest and a half as thick. She wrapped both arms around the heavy black thing and wormed her way among the bushes through the thicket to the other side and crossed the clearing to her own home thicket and went in. She sat in the safety of its center with her booty and screwed off the top of the bottle and peered in. A beautiful clear liquid glinted inside; the bottle was full of water.

Zarah hoisted the bottle high as she could with both arms and poured some of the water down onto her head. It splashed in her hair and dribbled down her face into her eyes and down her neck. She smiled.

When was the last time she'd smiled like that?

With her father? Before he'd disappeared and left her mother and her behind, promising they'd all be together again soon?

The moment of wild careless delight flared and died. Water was to drink. She lifted the lip of the bottle to her own lips and took three long swallows. She waited ten minutes and drank three more swallows. She sealed up the bottle and lay it next to her and curled up to sleep.

Which she didn't. She meant to and she wanted to and she almost did, but tiny creatures with tiny claws pinched her insides. Ants crawled on her arms and she jumped up to brush them off, but she saw none. She lay down again, but she couldn't settle. She twisted on the ground and rolled over and back and over and back again. Her eyes popped open and stared through the branches into the sky. Her hands shivered. Her knees shook. She found herself drumming her heels on the hard ground.

What was this? Fear? After all, she'd grabbed a big bottle sitting alone in the middle of his clearing instead of just a few packages out of a box full of them. This time Pedro would notice.

And then what? He'd come looking.

Not fair. Not fair at all. What right did this big stinky man Pedro have to camp in luxury in his fancy clearing while she starved like a rat in the parched desert bush? He had everything anyone could ever need or want, delicious meals and snacks and the fruity nectar to drink and music whenever he wanted. He even had people to talk to every night. Zarah talked with no one. He slept in a sleeping bag and she made do with her abaya on the hard ground. And he didn't have to be afraid of wolves or wild pigs because he had guns.

That's right, guns. And what if he came after her with one of those guns? Not that he'd need one. Pedro was much more than twice her size and any time he wanted he could snap her little girl's arms and neck with his bare hands like she snapped dry twigs for a fire.

So unfair. He was just as bad as Ali and Aida and all the others before them farther south and before that in Africa across the ocean and before that in her home country.

Cowering in fear from threats and blows and now running and hiding like a wild animal in the dark. But no more. It was time she did something.

Zarah stood and picked up the black water bottle and clutched it once again to her chest and carried it through her thicket and across the clearing to the other thicket and through to its edge and stopped. Pedro had his back to her at his stove, just like the first time he'd seen him, humming and frying something delicious.

Zarah stepped into the clearing and threw the bottle down on the ground. Instead of the dramatic crash she'd planned it thumped and bent against the ground and rolled. She shouted, "Pedro!"

He turned where he stood and looked at her, his face

expressionless, registering nothing, not even surprise.

She said in Spanish, "This is yours."

He said nothing. He didn't even blink.

"I stole it from you. I've been stealing your food. I was hungry. I am sorry."

He just stared.

Zarah turned around and stalked down the eastern side of the hill toward the houses and people. A sour taste pinched her tongue. Was it something from the water? The water. Of course. Pedro had something in his water. Something to keep him awake through the night. And it had made her do the crazy stupid thing she had just done.

Zarah wanted to run, but she didn't. She just kept stumbling dizzy down the hill over the rough ground, terrified that at any moment she'd fall and never get up again. Nausea surged up her body to her mouth and bent her double and she expelled the remnant of water she'd not yet absorbed into her system.

As Pedro watched her go, a mild sorrow brushed him. Sad little mouse. That's how he thought of her. He'd known for several days someone or something had been pilfering his food. The quantities were so small he'd assumed it was some kind of a little rat or other desert rodent. He'd never imagined a human little girl.

But he had a job to do. The Jefe was not running a charity. Part of Pedro's job was to protect this base camp. The girl couldn't be allowed to tell anyone about it. Pedro had his own small son and daughter back home. The Jefe and the Jefe's own bosses would punish Pedro's own children if Pedro did not do his job. The sun was setting behind him, but there was still plenty of light, and she was still only about fifty meters down the hill. An easy shot. He picked up his AR15.

31 Amir ibn Yusuf

Instead of the random hit-or-miss approach Lily had started with, Lily now decided on an organized procedure. She wanted to make sure she checked every document on the flash drive, even if she couldn't read it. This time she started from the upper left-hand corner of the display that listed all the folders. Then she moved through all the folders left to right in the first row and then on to the second row left to right and so on. She skipped almost all the items not in English, except for those in Spanish, which she stumbled through the best she could with the help of a translation website.

She was working on her sixteenth folder when she found a report about a man named Amir. His full name was Amir al-Tikriti. Except for the name, the entire document was redacted to the point there was no useful information.

The American media had called Sarai's Uncle Amir by the last name Mohammed: Amir Mohammed. That was also the name Hack had called his friend. If this al-Tikriti was the same man, he must have taken the new surname for his new life in America.

His choice made sense. She knew little about Arab naming customs, but she guessed that in the Muslim world the surname "Mohammed" would be generic and common enough to anonymize him and make him harder to track down.

She searched on the Internet and quickly hit another explanation. The last name "al-Tikriti" was a geography-based name, like the name "London" or "Kent" for someone from England. It suggested a family from the city Tikrit in Iraq. In post-Saddam Iraq the name "Tikrit" had become a despised one because the brutal dictator Saddam Hussein and many of his most vicious henchmen had spawned in Tikrit. Another reason to take a new name.

Lily searched the Internet using the search term "Amir al-Tikriti" and found an English language interview from four years earlier on a website she'd never heard of. The writer was some kind of free-lance journalist. He seemed knowledgeable about Mideast history. His questions revealed he could even read Arabic-language newspapers. He asked very detailed questions about names of people and details of Iraqi politics that meant nothing to Lily. But it was obvious this Amir al-Tikriti had nothing good to say about Iran or its militias in Iraq.

One exchange caught her attention:

Q: Do you consider yourself personally in danger in Iraq?

A: Of course.

Q: Have you considered leaving?

A: I'd prefer not to. My fight is here.

Q: But you are in danger.

A: As is everyone.

Q: But because of the enemies you're making, aren't you in particular danger?

A: Not only in Iraq. Anywhere. There are people who if you oppose them in any way, they don't forget. Their world view won't let them. They think in worldwide terms because they have a worldwide aim. They believe with absolute faith Allah has made it their destiny and the world's destiny that they will establish their world-wide Muslim caliphate and they will be in charge.

Q: Eliminating the non-Muslim world?

A: Exactly.

Q: Islamists, you mean. As opposed to Muslims in general.

A: "Islamists" is an English word that can be useful in distinguishing these people from Muslims in general. And yes, I am in danger here, but I will be in danger anywhere. What concerns me more is that my family is in danger here also.

So this Amir had a family. He didn't say "my wife," he said, "my family," which suggested he must have had at least one child. But the interview provided no name for either wife or child.

Most of the other documents in this sixteenth folder were English-language magazine, newspaper and website articles. She found the names Amir al-Najim and Amir al-Rawi and an Amir al-Mashadani, but they seemed to be Saddam's men or aligned with the pro-Iranian militia. She didn't rule them out completely but looked hard for another al-Tikriti.

She didn't find one in the next hour. But she did hit on another Amir who looked promising in a copy of a small document that looked like some kind of French identity card.

Lily remembered that Hack had told her Amir Mohammed said he'd spent time in France. By pretending the French was just badly spelled Spanish Lily could read the card well enough to see that it was an identity card for an Amir named "Amir ibn Yusuf," which Lily learned from a quick Internet search meant simply "Amir son of Yusuf". This Amir was married to a woman named "Hiba bint Mustafa," which meant "Hiba daughter of Mustafa." Maybe he'd used that name to cover his identity—though not successfully, since he'd apparently fled France to come to rural Minnesota. Assuming this was the same man.

The shooting pains in Lily's neck reminded her to check the computer's clock in the lower right corner of the desktop screen. Almost midnight. She stood up and stretched and did another yoga session and drank the last half cup of cold bitter coffee and sat down again.

Two hours later she hit the jackpot in the twenty-first folder—another longer document in French. It looked like a letter, but the letterhead was blotted out in the usual thick black. Nevertheless, two words jumped off the page: *"Fille"* and *"Zarah."* She didn't need much French to know that *fille* means daughter. Then at the bottom of the second page: *"Zarah bint Amir"*—Zarah daughter of Amir.

The French was too dense to read by pretending it was Spanish. She needed someone to translate. Maybe Sam knew someone.

32 Zarah's Dream

Pedro saw the little wild girl stop with her back to him only about fifty meters down the hill. She was leaning over with her hands on her knees. Her shoulders convulsed. She was retching water onto the ground.

The girl's stop gave Pedro his own chance to pause and consider. He swung the AR over his shoulder by its sling and took the phone from its side holster. He punched in a call to his immediate *Jefe*.

The man's voice answered "And?"

"And this is Pedro."

"And?"

Pedro told his Jefe about the little girl and what she'd done and said. "I think she drank some of my water. She's tiny and it took only a tiny dose of amphetamines to make her crazy."

"Could be."

"Should I shoot her?"

"Is it part of your job to shoot little wild Mexican girls?"

"She's not Mexican."

"North American, then. No matter."

"She's not North American either."

"Then what?"

"I don't know, but Castilian is not her first language and I have heard North Americans speak it many times and she is not one of them either. No one told me what to do if this happened."

"No one thought of this happening."

"That's why I called."

A pause. "Let her go. But I'll pass the word. There is somebody who has let it be known he wants to know about a wild Spanish speaking thief in the desert who is neither Mexican nor North American." The jefe hung up.

Pedro re-holstered his phone and walked back to his little stove. He took off his rifle and leaned it against the big boulder. The

onions and peppers had burned black. He dumped them out on the
ground and started over. The next time he went home to Mexico
he'd have a funny story to tell about the little wild desert girl who
stole his food and got stoned on his water and burst into his camp
and apologized and then ran down the hill.

By this time, Zarah had straightened up and begun staggering
further down the hill. She walked for about 30 minutes. The night
was dark and the air already had cooled. Expelling some of the
water from her system had helped a little, but she still felt weak and
sick. She found a soft spot on the ground beside a towering alif
cactus and lay down. In an instant she was unconscious.

Then she was sitting up. She was leaning against the giant
cactus. But she knew that couldn't be right because the giant cactus
had rings of thorns all up and down it and you couldn't lean against
it without horrible pain. But she felt no pain at all.

In fact, she felt happy inside for the first time in what seemed
forever. She turned and saw it was because Father was sitting beside
her leaning against the same cactus. They were both staring up at the
millions of stars. Moonlight streamed down on his round face and
his thinning dark hair so that his big forehead shown. Even though
she hadn't seen him for years, she knew for sure it was him because
of the little mustache.

He had a big smile, which was unusual. Usually he only flashed
a quick little smile when she caught him off guard when she did or
said something he thought smart or funny. The smile seemed to flare
for an instant and then disappear. It was like he never actually
decided to smile. The smile just came out of him on its own without
his having anything to say about it one way or the other. Father's
quick smile that came and went was one of the things she missed
most about him. No one else she'd met did it just that way.

He asked, "So what now?"

"What do you mean?"

"Are you just going to lie there and die?"

"I don't know. Did you die?"

"I cannot answer that," he said.

Which she thought meant yes. It made her sad. "So where are you?"

He said nothing.

"Where?"

"Here," he said. "Right with you. Right now. Always."

She woke. She wasn't leaning against the cactus any more. She was lying on the ground facing up towards the dark sky just as she remembered. The warm night air smelled moist and sweet. The moon glowed its yellow-white warmth and the stars shone sharp and bright in the clear black sky.

Her head seemed clear too and her insides felt okay—empty, but okay. The return of her hunger agony to replace the nausea actually made her feel better.

She hoisted herself up on her feet and started walking downhill to the east again. But she felt the weakest she'd ever felt in her life. She wondered if this was how little Omar had felt right before he fell over dead. She wobbled on her legs and stumbled and almost tripped from a short shallow hole hardly deeper than the breadth of her fingers.

She brushed against a plant and a few thorns sank deep into her upper right arm. The fiery sting jolted her a little more awake for about ten minutes, but then she returned again to her walking stupor until she finally stumbled one last time and fell onto the hard ground. She rolled over and stared up the black star-sewn sky for a long time. She realized she finally was going to do what she'd failed to do back in the Compound after little Omar died—she was going to die like him. But at least she'd left Ali and his Compound far behind. She'd beaten them that much.

This time it wasn't Father but Mother who came. A dark woman's face blotted out the sky. Although she looked much older now, Mother still wore the same concerned and loving expression Zarah sometimes allowed herself to remember and treasure.

Mother reached down and touched Zarah's forehead with her

finger tips and caressed her brow and asked in Spanish, "Little girl, what are you doing here?", which was strange because in Zarah's whole life back home Mother had never spoken to Zarah in any language other than Arabic.

Zarah said nothing. She sighed and lay still and happy one last time under her mother's gentle touch.

Mother said, "I come looking for desert fruit and I find you."

Zarah smiled.

"Little girl, will you let me help you?"

"Si," Zarah said.

"Bueno," Mother said.

"Are you my Mother?"

"I'm sorry, but no." But the woman's voice was soft and low like Mother's, and she sounded so kind Zarah almost didn't mind. The woman who wasn't Mother knelt down and lifted Zarah's head onto the soft warmth of the fabric on her lap and put a cup of water to Zarah's lips.

Zarah sipped.

The woman asked, "Can you get to your feet?"

"Si." And with the woman holding her arm Zarah was able to stand.

Zarah asked, "Who are you?"

"Alma," the woman said,

"And you're not my mother?"

"No. But I am someone's mother," the woman said and led Zarah the rest of the way down the hill.

33 Sarai's Big Phoenix Day

Sarai loved the morning Arizona heat. She could see it bothered Dad and Mattie from the sweat streaming down their faces and the hints they kept dropping about checking out the ice cream at the Botanical Garden Café.

Not even the promise of ice cream could lure Sarai off the Garden paths. So the two grownups had to shrug and slump and amble along after her as she gawked at the flora and read out loud each and every little sign and big sign explaining life in the Sonoran Desert.

It turned out all kinds of animals and plants made their homes in the desert. There were quail and little rodents and even little green lizards. She thrilled to spot so many lizards darting here and there across and near the paths. It made the desert vivid and un-Minnesotan. Her home state was boring by comparison.

And the cactuses. Sarai had seen cactuses only in movies, mostly old westerns Hack and Mattie liked to watch at night—some of them even in black and white. She didn't mind the black and white. She'd even tried sketching with charcoal in black and white herself. It was just another color scheme.

She recognized the signature cactus from all Dad's and Mattie's westerns. The signs said it was a "saguaro." She saw lots of saguaro in the Garden and dozens more up in the nearby hills that surrounded the place.

Some saguaro were young ones that came only knee high like little green spiny pencils. Other huge ones rose to twice Sarai's height and bore big green round branches. The tallest of all sprouted its branches in tubes thicker than Sarai's torso. Vertical rows of sharp thorns ran up and down the trunks and tubes. A sign on the ground in front of the biggest saguaro said it was over one hundred twenty years old. Older even than Grandpa.

But even more than the saguaro Sarai loved one kind of small cactus. She found a bunch of them spread low to the ground. A little sign stuck in the ground nearby announced they were "prickly pear."

Each prickly pear sprouted clusters of thick flat green leaves. The leaves were flat shaped and about the length and width of pancakes, but much thicker. Long thin white thorns sprouted from small lipped holes in the sides of the leaves.

Some of these thick green leaves had beautiful yellow flowers blossoming out of their edges. A few bore fruit, each about the size of her little girl's fist, a slightly purplish red, plump and luscious looking. Sari guessed someone gave them the name prickly pear because each fruit had a hollow concave top mounted with a crown from which sprouted long prickly thorns like skinny spears. Small bumps poked out of its reddish skin and each bump grew its own short stubby thorn.

Sarai had known cactuses had thorns, but not about the flowers and fruit. The movies never showed that. Maybe they filmed the westerns only in winter. She said to Dad and Mattie, "The sign says the prickly pear fruit is really delicious. I wonder how it tastes."

Dad shrugged. "Not easy to find out. I'm not sure how you'd get all those little thorns off."

"I had a delicious prickly pear margarita the other night," Mattie said. "So they must have a way."

Dad said, "I bet they have a machine."

Sarai unslung her back pack and laid it on the path. She took out her sketch pad and packet of different colored pens and laid them on the ground and sat cross legged and started to draw the biggest of the prickly pear plants.

"Looks like we're here for a spell," Dad said. Mattie shrugged and they sat on a bench in the shade on the other side of the path and watched Sarai draw the prickly pear and chatted about things Sarai couldn't hear. But it sounded like they were having fun, laughing and poking each other. Sometimes the two of them were worse than the kindergartners in her school.

After she sketched and colored the prickly pear plant, Dad and Mattie and she finally did go into the café for ice cream—chocolate macadamia nut for Sarai—and then after a bit of bargaining between

Dad and Mattie, they drove across town to the Musical Instrument Museum.

In the hallway about thirty feet down the hall from the front desk stood a Steinway grand piano with a little placard inviting everyone to take turns playing it.

While Dad and Mattie and Sarai waited in line to buy tickets, Sarai heard someone stumbling through a Beethoven tune she'd heard some other kids play in school at the amateur shows. It was called "Fur Elise." Sarai glanced over and saw a girl about Sarai's age sitting head down in front of the Steinway, plunking at the keys.

The three of them went into the Museum and wandered the air-conditioned halls looking at instruments from everywhere in the world. About ninety percent were drums or other things to hit. Dad banged on every single one he was allowed to. It was pretty boring, although once in a while he made fun intricate rhythms.

Sarai quickly grew tired of the Museum and wanted to sit and sketch the colorful exhibit from Mauritania but she didn't get the chance to sit long enough because Dad kept wanting to hit the next thing in the next display.

He oohed and ahhed over one huge exhibit that displayed what must have been about a million electric guitars all different colors and patterns. Each and every one had been played at some time on some recording by some ancient rock guitarist Sarai had never heard of. As Dad chattered, Mattie kept smiling and nodding like she was thrilled as Dad, but once when Dad wasn't looking at her, she snuck Sarai a wink.

Dad and Mattie weren't married, but Sarai thought they already acted like any other husband and wife she'd seen in her home neighborhood, although a little handsier.

After about an eon of this, Sarai said, "I'd like to visit the restroom now, please."

Mattie said, "Good idea. I'll take you" and gave Sarai a head shake to follow as she walked away. A few feet down the hall Sarai reached up and took Mattie's hand. Sarai saw Mattie glance back at

Dad with big eyes like she was thrilled and scared at the same time or something and they followed the signs to the women's rest room hand in hand.

It turned out the restrooms were right by the main desk, so they had to pass a teenage boy at the Steinway tinkling "Fur Elise" only a little better than the earlier girl.

When Mattie and Sarai came out the tiniest girl yet was banging out "Fur Elise" the worst yet. Mattie and Sarai passed her and when they got a little way down the hall they looked at each other and burst into laughter. They laughed their way down to Dad. He saw them and raised his eyebrows and said nothing about the laughing. Instead he asked, "You two had enough of this place?"

Mattie and Sarai both said "Yes, please!" at almost the same time.

The three of them had to pass the main desk one final time and there was a little Chinese-American-looking boy plinking "Fur Elise" no better than any of the ones that came before.

A young blond man was sitting in a white shirt and black neck tie behind the front desk. Dad walked over and spoke to him. "Say."

The young man said, "May I help you?"

"We've got a bet you can settle."

"I'll help if I can."

"It's a pool. How many 'Fur Elises' do you hear on an average day? My friend says seventeen. I put my money on fewer."

The young man crossed and uncrossed his eyes. "You lose."

Dad laughed. He walked over stood by the piano until this most recent kid was done messing up "Fur Elise" and took his place on the bench and thundered out a couple of minutes of a Beethoven-sounding piece that was loud and fast and boisterous and thrilling. The little boy stayed and watched. Dad looked at and said to him, "Practice practice practice," and the boy nodded like he meant to do it for real.

Then Dad stood up and grinned at Mattie and Sarai. "Anyone for dinner?"

"What about Bugs?" Sarai asked.

He said, "Tomorrow, Sweetie. Mattie and I have to get to work on time."

Sarai said, "Tomorrow with all of us together, right, Dad?"

Mattie said, "Absolutely."

Dad drove them across town again and the Phoenix traffic was terrible and Dad was muttering under his breath some words so nasty Mattie poked him big middle knuckle first on his right shoulder and he said "Ouch!" and pretended he couldn't use his right arm for a while.

They didn't arrive at the Hedgehog Barrel until after six P.M.. A nice plump blond waitress named Jennifer served Dad and Mattie big burgers with fries and beer and cooed over Sarai like Sarai was a princess. Sarai ate a tuna sandwich, which made Dad and Mattie laugh hard about something but they wouldn't tell her what. Sarai got to go backstage and meet Dudley and the other guys in the band. They all treated her like a princess too.

Then Sarai got to hear Dad's band—well, the poster outside called it Dudley's band, but Sarai was sure it was really Dad's band or maybe Mattie's—because Mattie was the singer and weren't all the most famous musicians the singers?

Mattie was wonderful. Sometimes she was bold and brassy and a few times she even got nasty. What was the coolest was how in her songs she acted the parts of different people instead of the shy sweet woman she always seemed to be around Sarai. On the fast songs she moved to the rhythm like she was dancing in place. On the loud ones, she burned with all kinds of passions like the women in TV soap operas. On a few, she stood stock still and held the microphone in her hand like it was a fragile and delicate little hummingbird in her hand and she was afraid if she breathed too hard on it she'd crush it.

Dad often dismissed the tunes Sarai and her friends listened to as "factory made." He meant companies manufactured them with machines. Sarai had never heard a live band like this where people made live music right in front of you. It looked impossible.

Sarai watched and listened from the farthest corner of the big room where Jennifer and other waitresses and even the manager took turns sitting with her and bringing her whatever she wanted until Dad noticed and came over and proclaimed to everyone in the vicinity that his daughter had gobbled enough peanut butter cookies and guzzled enough high fructose corn syrup for one night.

About midnight Sarai curled up and fell asleep on a little wooden bench along the back wall. Later she woke up just for a minute or two in the backseat of the car and saw the backs of Dad's and Mattie's heads in their front seat headrests. The gentle rocking of the car and mild rumble of wheels on the road under her told her she was safe. She fell asleep again and didn't wake up again until the next morning in their hotel room in her bed next to Mom's.

Mom's bed was empty, so Sarai went to look for her. Mom was still in the swivel chair dozing with her head down on the desk in front of her and her feet on the pile of blankets under the desk. Sarai said, "Hi Mom" and kissed her cheek. Mom opened one eye and peeped at Sarai and lifted her head and smiled. Mom stood up and the two walked over to the bed. Mom fell into her bed and Sarai hopped in with her and they nestled and both went back to sleep.

34 Jabali Reports

Jabali called on the Mujahid's secure satellite phone.

"Yes?"

Jabali said, "There's been a possible sighting of the girl."

"Again?"

"The Jefe told me to tell you."

"So tell me."

"The Jefe keeps scouts high up in the hills. They camp up there and look down on everything around and guide the illegals who smuggle the drugs up from Mexico and the guns and money back down."

The Mujahid said, "I know all that."

"The other night one of the Jefe's scouts caught a wild little girl pilfering food and water from his camp east of where the Compound is."

"Where the Compound was, you mean."

"Yes. Where the Compound was."

"You think she's Amir's girl?"

"Maybe. She spoke Spanish but not like a Mexican or an American."

"I see. What happened to her?"

"The last time the guide saw her she was running down the hill to his east."

The Mujahid said, "So you will search for her there, correct?"

"I already have. With many men."

"Any sign of her?

"None. The scout said she was sick from starvation and the drugs in the water she stole and pretty much dead."

"Pretty much dead is not dead."

Jabali said, "By now she's completely dead for sure. The coyotes and the other wild animals would grab her in an instant."

"You found her body?"

"The animals will have eaten her body. In the desert there would

179

be no remains."

"Not even bones?"

There was a pause. Jabali said, "Maybe."

The Mujahid said, "Keep looking."

35 Dinner with Laghdaf

Lily sat across from Laghdaf in the rich brown leather of a booth in the Vauxhall Arms Bistro. Lily warmed her arms against the powerful air conditioning with a cashmere sweater over her Lilla P woven gauze short sleeve dress. Laghdaf had come from court still in his three-piece charcoal courtroom suit and lavender shirt. With great care he removed and folded his necktie and placed it in his pocket. He left his shirt collar buttoned all the way up.

"Thanks so much for taking time for me," Lily told him. "I know how busy you are with the trial."

Laghdaf said, "Sam asked. But I'm afraid I've got only an hour or two right now," he said. His liquid vowels seemed to melt even the hardest consonants of his speech into a deep mellifluous song. "It will be another all-nighter. I'll have more time after the trial."

"I might be close to something," Lily said. "And Hack says you read French."

"True."

"You could help me."

He smiled. "Please allow me to take a few moments for dinner. Then I'll read whatever you want me to read, and if I can, I'll tell you what it means."

"Of course," Lily said. They both ordered the Chilean Sea Bass. For wine, Lily drank a glass of the 2006 *Domaine Jean Collet et Fils Chablis Grand Cru Val*mur. Laghdaf had a cola, but it was no ordinary cola; the menu declared that the Hotel served only a custom concoction from a local micro-Cola firm. Lily knew about micro-breweries, but she'd never heard of micro cola makers. She supposed out loud it had been only a matter of time and Laghdaf laughed with her about it.

They traded bare-bones life histories. Laghdaf had immigrated from Mauritania and studied law in the U.S. Lily had no brothers or sisters and just the one daughter Sarai. She showed him Sarai's picture. He showed her a tattered faded print of himself as a toddler surrounded by eight brothers and sisters.

They both skipped deserts. Sarai insisted on signing for dinner. They stood.

Laghdaf said, "Where is this reading material of yours?"

She said, "It's in my room."

"Then let's proceed," he said. Without speaking they went rode up the elevator and walked down the hall and entered her room. He took the same chair Hack had grabbed the night before. She powered up her laptop and marched through the rigmarole to access the flash drive. She navigated to the French document that mentioned Hiva and Zarah.

He said, "Please let me see all of it." She turned the computer to face him. He leaned forward and used the keyboard to scroll up and down through the document.

He said, "Where did you get this?'

"From Sam. Via Hack."

"For what purpose?"

"They didn't tell you?"

"Tell me again, please. All of it. As if I know nothing."

So Lily explained: Sarai's belief she had a sort-of cousin named Zarah who was the daughter of her Hack's friend and Sarai's sort-of uncle Amir who'd been murdered; Sarai's obsession with finding this probably imaginary Zarah; Lily's decision to help her daughter despite her own doubts; Sam's inviting her to Phoenix; Hack's handing her the flash drive; and finally, what she'd learned so far.

Laghdaf, "You've taken on something that is almost certainly impossible."

Lily said nothing.

He said, "For your daughter? You will show her one more time you will do anything for her, even if it is impossible? Or for yourself because of some dissatisfaction in your life? Or to prove something to someone? Maybe yourself?"

Lily smiled. "No psychological analysis, please."

Laghdaf nodded. "You Jews are a strange people, are you not?"

"I don't know what to say to that. Or how it's relevant. Isn't every people strange?"

"Yes. It is truly a strange world full of strange people. Do you know where this flash drive came from?"

She said, "Hack said somebody collected all these documents together for my Dad to help defend Hack's friend against a murder charge. They dropped the charges, but Dad kept the documents."

"That somebody was me."

"Hack didn't mention that."

"He may not know. But this database concerns more than one American legal case and one Iraqi little girl. I have spent years collecting this material and I have written and spoken to many people to get this information—many people in many organizations, governmental and nongovernmental. Some in the sunlight and some hiding in darkness. Some legal and some illegal. Some of them I begged from. Some I tricked. Some I robbed. It's all about a subject dear to me: human trafficking in general. And human slavery in particular."

Lily examined the man's solemn face a moment and guessed the answer, but asked the question anyway: "Why is this subject so dear to you?"

"I was trafficked. I was bought and sold. I was a slave." He smiled. "And I am proud to say that. In my own way I am like a Jew, since Jews are the only nation I know who defines your origins as slavery. Like me. Proudly."

Lily couldn't think up a perfect response, so she made none. Instead she asked, "Would you like some coffee?"

Laghdaf nodded. "Please. Black."

Lily made a pot of fresh coffee and poured a cup for each them. Then sitting with Lily at her desk in her lovely room in the swank Vauxhall Arms Hotel, Laghdaf told her his story:

"I was born in Northwest Africa, in Mauritania, which has a long history of slavery. These days they set up special anti-slavery courts supposed to eliminate slavery. But these courts do almost nothing. Mauritanian law officially bans hereditary and other forms of slavery, but courts rarely enforce these new laws.

"I was born into one of the traditional slave castes. My "Black Moor" community—for that is what some call us—is subject to hereditary practices rooted in ancestral master-slave relationships. As a small child my masters forced me to work without pay as a cattle herder. I escaped that servitude to become one of thousands of lost hungry children wandering the streets of Mauritania's capital Nouakchott. A Koranic school teacher called a *marabout* latched onto me there. But the *marabout* didn't teach me any Koran. He just enslaved me and forced me to go out and beg on his behalf."

It was hard to square that image with the suave slender man sitting across from her. She said, "A slave and a beggar?"

"Yes. I was one little soldier in an army of ragged children roving the city to beg for this cruel and nasty man. And for many others like him. And he was nasty. They all were."

"And he could actually sell you?"

"Yes. In fact, he did. Because he owned me."

Lily studied the man for signs of dishonesty and saw none. "This is common there?"

"Very much so. Just a few years ago, I helped prove that an employment agency recruited more than 200 Mauritanian women to Saudi Arabia for domestic servitude and then forced them into prostitution once they got there; the courts did nothing. And when a Mauritanian in Saudi Arabia attempted to file a complaint against her employer, even her own Mauritanian embassy refused to help her."

"You know about these cases personally?"

"I pursued them. You see, by the time these cases came up I had escaped again. I was working for an anti-slavery organization."

"Here in the U.S.?"

"No. There, before I made my way to America. To become a lawyer. And one day I will go back and take with me my American education and experience and apply them there."

"How did you escape?"

"I cannot tell that entire story tonight. I promise I will tell you some other time—if you still want me to. But the flash drive Hack gave you contains a life time of material I've put together on terrorism and human trafficking and drug networks."

"All in the same set of documents?"

"All the same network. Maybe the right term is meta-network—a network of networks. The drugs and human trafficking help pay for the terrorism. The terrorists defend the drug smugglers and human traffickers. And on top of it all, the human trafficking feeds the leaders' greed as well as their hatreds and longings for revenge."

Lily remembered her argument with Julia. "Revenge against the West?"

"So they say. And against the children of the West and even against the children of their personal enemies or if those are unavailable on the children of their own people."

"For what?"

"I sometimes wonder if it is revenge against the way they themselves grew up. They can't blame their own religion or cultures or governments, so they blame everyone else. They find the excuse they need to make war against all others."

"That makes no sense."

He said. "It might make perfect sense to someone raised in an honor-shame culture."

"I don't know what that is," Lily said.

"Of course not. Anyway, that is just my private theory. But all these networks coalesce into this meta-network extending from the Mideast through Africa and then across the Atlantic to South America and then again up the spine of that continent through Central America and Mexico directly into the United States."

"Where we are."

"Yes. Right here. Phoenix, Arizona. After all, this room in which we sit is only 120 miles from the Mexican border."

"I'm sorry if I'm wasting your time," Lily said. "But since you put all this together, maybe you can tell me whether the Zarah in this

French document is our Zarah."

"My time is not wasted at all," Laghdaf said. "Because that is easy. The answer is yes."

"That's it?"

"That's it."

"And you're sure?"

"Yes. I am sure. This document is talking about your Amir and your Zarah."

"How can you know that?"

Laghdaf just smiled. "There's an American expression I like. You can take it to the bank."

"Because of another document?"

"Yes. In Arabic."

"Does it say where Zarah is?"

He shook his head. "You have done something wonderful, Lily. I am truly amazed. In all this mass of material I spent years putting together, you have managed to find the only references to Zarah I know about, at least in the languages you know."

"And you read the Arabic?"

He gave a sly smile. "The marabout was not as effective as he hoped in preventing me from learning to read. I snuck looks and listens and held coins back from him to buy lessons from a real marabout's students. And later I was lucky enough to find a genuine teacher. A good man."

"Can you show me?"

Laghdaf said, "Please let me drive."

Lily said, "I'm sorry?"

"It's an expression. You don't know it? Let me drive the computer," he said.

Lily swiveled the laptop so it faced him again. Laghdaf clicked some keys and navigated from folder to folder. He swiveled the screen so they could both see an Arabic language newspaper article.

He said, "This is a copy of a clipping from Iraq a few years ago. The story tells how a young girl was kidnapped away from her mother on the streets. The father was long gone from the country and the mother was alone and defenseless against the militia men."

"In broad daylight?"

"Yes. The article explains. In the chaos of a war zone, the event would not even have been newsworthy but for the father's identity and the belief that he was the reason the militia targeted the other two. The article names the father as Amir bin Yusuf. The kidnapped woman was his wife Hiva. The kidnapped daughter was his daughter Zarah."

Lily looked from the screen full of alien-looking writing to Laghdaf's somber face and then back to the writing. She stood, but then a mild dizziness dropped her back in her chair.

Sarai was right. Against all logic and against all the odds, Sarai was right. There really was a Zarah. Amir's daughter. This Zarah might be suffering terribly, but if she was still out there, they could find her.

Lily scolded herself. This is serious. Act the part of a grown up. You've taken on a job; pretend you're a professional.

She took a deep breath and asked in the calmest and most even voice she could muster, "What would have happened to Zarah?"

"Who's to say? Assuming she's still alive, the human traffickers took her ."

"The meta-network?"

"Yes. The meta-network spread over four continents. That sells drugs and weapons and also"—Laghdaf gave a sad shrug.

Lily finished for him. "Women and girls."

"Yes. And boys too."

"And Zarah's mother? Hiva?"

Laghdaf's shrug was a shrug not of indifference but of helplessness. "I wish I knew. The militia had her in their power. They could have done whatever they wanted with her or enslaved her and taken her anywhere."

"Or killed her?"

Laghdaf nodded.

"Is there anything more about Zarah or Hiva in any of these documents?"

Laghdaf shook his head. "There is nothing more on this drive to tell us where Zarah or her mother might be. Unless—"

"Unless what?"

"Between you and me we know several of the languages of the documents. I know English well enough and French and Arabic and languages local to my home country. You know English even better than I, and some Spanish too, right?"

"Some," she said.

"But enough to recognize Zarah's name if you saw it?"

"Oh yes. That much for sure."

"And you haven't?"

"Not yet."

"You won't. But there is one language neither of us reads at all—not even the alphabet. But Sam reads it."

"I did see a few documents in Hebrew."

"Yes."

"So we can ask Sam to look at the documents in Hebrew."

Laghdaf shook his head. "He already has. And found nothing. But there is someone else who maybe can help you. My friend. Maybe a surprising friend, the way they brought me up in Mauritania. This is a strange man who I know from experience hates slavery as much as I hate it. Someone who has helped Sam and me from time to time."

"Who?"

"Isn't it obvious? Another strange Jew."

36 Bad Apple In The Hedgehog Barrel

Hack and Mattie took Sarai for her promised Saturday afternoon visit to the Art Museum and found the Warner Brothers exhibit. Sarai sat on a bench in front of the Chuck Jones Bugs Bunny cells and began to copy one into her sketch book. But then she caught a glimpse of the Bob Clampett's nearby Tweety Bird cells. She forgot about Bugs and shouted "Tweety!" and spent the next ninety minutes stationed in front of the bird's exhibit, studying and copying the megastar canary in all his bright yellow poses.

Lily stayed in her hotel room working with the flash drive files. Around five, Hack and Mattie dropped Sarai off at Sam's office for dinner with her grandfather. Lily was going to consult with Laghdaf about some big deal item Lily had found. When Hack asked, Lily pressed her lips together and wouldn't say what. After dinner, Sam was going to bring Sarai back to Lily's hotel room for the night and he and Laghdaf would go back to trial preparation.

After they dropped Sarai off at the hotel, Hack and Mattie drove over to the Hedgehog Barrel and ate and then played the gig. Hack's goal at his first Saturday night gig was to relax and enjoy it. By now, Hack had pretty good grasp of the band book.

It seemed to Hack Mattie sang with more ferocity than usual. She got tenser and even grumpy as the evening wore on. She spoke to the band only in terse tune names and focused most of her energy on the crowd, which was the biggest they'd performed for. Customers crammed the place, and the nastier Mattie got, the harder they clapped and cheered.

About half an hour after midnight, Dudley walked over to Hack sitting behind his keyboard. "Almost time to close up, brother. Want to do that song of yours again?"

Hack said, "Sure. Why not?"

Mattie rolled her eyes and once again stalked over to the wall and leaned against it.

Marty stepped over to Hack and whispered, "Dude, I beginning to think Mattie doesn't like your song."

Hack said, "Really?"

From his stool behind the drums, Bob said, "Take a look."

Hack glanced over at Mattie and tried to catch her eye. She refused to meet his glance and glared off into space.

Dudley said, "You sure you want to do this?"

Hack said, "I spent the first and worst part of my adult life letting women tell me what I couldn't say or do, censoring and editing myself. I'm done with that and I'm not going back. One thing about Mattie is she's never been a scold. If she's going to start that now, it's her problem."

"Brave words," Marty said.

Bob said, "I admire not only the way you play your instrument, but your pluck."

Hack looked at the man's bass and said, "Go pluck on your own instrument."

Bob grinned and Dudley hit the opening guitar lick and once again Hack sang his sad comic tale of a man's poker losses, fisticuff failures, and risky woman choices. And none of it even counted as gamblin'—he knew from the start he was gonna lose anyway, so he'd just have to pay his dues and play the blues.

That story sung again, Mattie came back and kicked the band into what had already become their standard closing song "Celebrity."

When Hack saw Marty and Bob slip through the club's back door to the parking lot, Hack followed. A bare incandescent bulb lit the few yards nearest the door and left the rest of the parking lot in darkness.

Hack said, "I've been wondering where you two slip off to on breaks. You sneak outside for a cigarette. I quit a while back, but I still enjoy the high from the occasional second-hand smoke. Mind if I stand nearby and share a taste of your self-destructiveness?"

"Sure thing, partner," Marty said. "We live to share." Then, to Bob, "Time to light up."

"Sure," Bob said. From his pocket he removed a small tube. One end rounded off to a short black tip. A transparent plastic section colored rose by the liquid inside it separated the tip from the opposite long black end. Bob stuck the short black tip into his mouth and took a quick inhale.

"What's that?" Hack said.

"Primer puff," Bob said.

"No, I mean what is that thing?"

"E-Cigarette," Bob said. "We're giving vaping a try." He handed the thing to Marty, who stuck its tip into his mouth and took a slow steady draw for about three seconds. He kept his lips sealed and waited a few more seconds and exhaled a mist that took on a pinkish shade in the white light cast by the bare bulb. He said, "I'm breathing mostly water vapor."

Bob said, "No tars. Not as harmful to your health."

"What good does that do me?" Hack said. He sniffed. "Is that raspberry?"

Bob said, "Good ears and a good nose."

"I hate raspberry," Hack said. "You're taking all the fun out of secondhand smoke."

"Hey piano man!" a husky male voice came out of the dark parking lot.

The three musicians turned.

A skinny guy stepped in his twenties stepped into the light. His blond hair straggled down onto his neck. A slightly chunky woman about his age followed him, tugging on his arm. The guy shook his arm loose and said again, "Hey!"

The woman said, "Ralph."

"Hi, Ralph," Hack said.

Ralph answered, "I said 'Hey'!"

"As you prefer, Ralph," Hack said. "Hey!"

"My girlfriend likes you," Ralph said.

"Thank you, Ma'am," Hack said and nodded to the woman. If he'd had a hat he would have tipped it.

She said again, "Ralph."

Ralph focused two watery eyes as well as he could on Hack and then glanced from Hack to Marty and Bob. "In fact, she likes all three of you. She says you're all hot."

The woman said, "Ralph, I meant the band is hot. Not the men."

"Don't tell me what you meant," Ralph said without looking at her. "I heard you." To the three musicians: "She thinks all three of you are hot. Nice and hot."

"That's nice to hear," Hack said.

Ralph said, "And I don't."

Hack said, "You don't think we're nice?"

Ralph said, "I don't think you're hot." Ralph shook his head. "No. And I don't like any of the three of you."

Marty said, "It's good you noticed."

Ralph said, "Noticed what?"

"That there are three of us," Bob said.

"That's why I always carry this," Ralph said and with his right hand reached into his pocket and tugged on something that looked like the rounded pearl handle of a revolver.

"Ralph!" the woman snapped.

Ralph had the pistol handle half-way out of his pocket when a gray garbage can lid popped into the light behind Ralph and clunked him in the head. Ralph grunted and slumped to the pavement and grabbed his head with both hands and began to moan. "Hey! That hurts!"

Mattie stepped into the light and sailed the lid away like a frisbee. Iit clattered on the asphalt from the darkness. She bent down and reached into Ralph's pocket and tugged the revolver the rest of the way out gripped it around its cylinder and lifted it into the air. She said, "You won't be needing this, Ralph."

"Hey—that's my daddy's," Ralph said.

With a deft move of her right hand, Mattie jacked open the cylinder and dumped the rounds into her left hand. She extended the empty pistol handle first towards the woman, who shook her head and muttered "another crappy blind date" and turned and walked away. Mattie shrugged and extended the pistol handle towards Hack.

He said, "What am I supposed to do with that?"

Marty said, "You never know."

"Might come in handy," Bob said.

"I don't even have a permit to carry a gun," Hack said.

"This is Arizona," Bob said.

Marty said, "Don't need any special piece of cardboard."

Bob said, "Your permit's the Second Amendment."

Hack said, "You sure about that? It doesn't sound right. I'm not an Arizona resident."

Mattie offered the pistol to Marty, who shook his head and patted his hip. "Already got mine. Below-the-waistband holster."

Hack looked at Bob, who said, "I'm covered too. But if you're not, you might consider hanging on to that one. A fine Smith and Wesson like that's close to 100 percent reliable."

Marty said, "Works better loaded."

Hack took the pistol from Mattie and snapped out the cylinder again and reloaded the rounds one by one. "I'll need some way to carry it concealed, I guess."

Bob said, "Got just the thing in my trunk."

Hack said to Mattie, "By the way, that was a fine swing. You kept your arms inside, you had nice wrist action and you showed excellent follow through."

"I visualized beforehand," she said.

"Where'd you come from, anyway?"

"I was in the parking lot having a smoke when I saw what was going on."

"A real cigarette?"

She raised her eyebrows. "Of course. What else?"

Hack said to Marty and Bob. "See? A real cigarette."

Mattie said, "I'm going home." She passed between the men and opened the back door and went through it.

Ralph sat up halfway. "What about me?"

Marty and Bob ignored him and followed Mattie through the door.

Ralph moaned, "Hey, I'm bleeding here."

Hack paused an instant, then followed the others through the door. The last thing Hack heard before he closed it behind him was, "What am I gonna tell my daddy?"

37 Alma's House

Zarah woke with her head on a pillow, lying on a soft pile of blankets on the floor. Zarah had been resting several days on Alma and Miguel's floor next to the old couple's bed, which took almost all the space in their little metal single wide trailer. Alma and Miguel also owned a little wooden chest in the corner and a small table on top of which sat a television with rabbit ear antennas poking up from its back.

Zarah loved lying on Alma's and Miguel's floor. Alma fed her and caressed her all the time. Miguel was a solid-looking man who came and went for no reason and whose entire stock of facial expressions seemed to consist of only one—a warm friendly grin he bestowed on Zarah each time he came or went through the door.

This time Zarah woke up because Alma was poking her shoulder with a finger. Alma said, "Time to eat." She held a spoon to Zarah's lips.

Zarah sat up and sipped from the spoon. Soup. Delicious. Alma spooned the soup and Zarah sipped the hot broth and chewed each little juicy chunk of chicken with delight before swallowing.

When Zarah finished, she said, "Alhamdulillah," and lay back down.

As she had every time before, Alma raised her eyebrows at the odd word but made no comment. She said, "I think you should get up now."

"Do I have to?"

"Yes, you have to."

"Why?"

"You can't stay on my floor forever."

"Why not?"

"It's not good for you."

"Why not?"

"That's not life."

"One more day, please?"

Alma laid her soft hand on Zarah's forehead. "No, that's too much."

"Please?"

"Well."

"One more hour?"

"Yes. One more hour."

Zarah smiled and closed her eyes and laid her head back on her pillow. Alma was even easier than Mother had been. Maybe because she was older.

Late that afternoon Alma rousted Zarah from bed—this time no excuses—and took her outside. There in the trailer's shadow Alma had planted a garden about six by three meters. Alma held out a little spray bottle full of water. "Time to work," she said. "Should I tell you how to do it?"

"No need," Zarah said. "I know." And she did know, from her gardening chores in the Compound. Eager to show Alma she was worth something, Zarah didn't wait for another word. She took the bottle from Alma, who shrugged and crossed her arms and watched with a doubtful expression.

Careful to step only on the bare dirt between the tomato and melon plants, Zarah crouched and sprayed the lightest possible mist over the leaves to clean off the desert dust. She knew to apply the mist only to the leaves and to avoid spillage that might saturate the ground below the soil surface and drown the roots.

Alma smiled, and Zarah felt good about working. Zarah thought she knew a lot about gardening in the desert. She knew she would have to water the tomatoes every day and not miss a single day. She knew to water in the early morning before the sun came up. She knew to water the earth around the plants where the roots reached into the soil and not on the plants themselves because the little drops of water could act like magnifying glasses that focused desert sunlight on the plants and burned them. And she saw that Alma must know a lot too, because Alma had posted little stakes and tied shade cloths to the stakes to protect the plants from hard summer desert

196

winds.

Then and there Zarah decided to do everything for Alma. Alma was the kindest woman and Miguel was the kindest man Zarah had met since home. Zarah did not only garden work but any other work she could think of. If Alma washed a dish Zarah was there to dry it. If Alma made the bed, Zarah grabbed the other end of the blanket to help straighten it out. It was fun.

The first two days Zarah knew her, Alma wore slacks and a colored polo shirt and sneakers, not that different from Zarah's jeans and white tee shirt. But one morning, Alma opened the little wooden chest in the corner and pulled out a neatly folded dark dress and unfolded it and put it on. She took out a long shawl and wrapped it around her shoulders. She twirled for Zarah like a girl and held out the shawl. "Do you like my rebozo?"

Alma's rebozo was a rectangular straight woven piece of fringed cloth about two meters long, kind of a cross between a scarf and a shawl. The indigo intermingled with its black fabric made it shimmer in the light.

Zarah fingered it. The fabric felt like the silk Mother had shown her one time once long ago, but even softer.

"Watch," Alma said, and wriggled her wedding ring off her left ring finger and handed it to Zarah. Alma said, "Hold out the ring."

Zarah lifted the ring in front of her and Alma took her rebozo by one end and passed it end to end through the ring and then untwirled it and put it over her shoulders again.

Zarah laughed—it was magic. How could a cloth so wide and long pass through a tiny space like in that ring?

Alma said, "This rebozo was my grandmother's. She gave it to me."

Zarah reached with her two hands under her tee shirt and pulled her amulet up over her head. "Grandmother gave me this." She handed it to Alma.

Alma turned it over in her hands and inspected it. "It's beautiful."

"She promised it would keep me alive."

Alma replaced the string with the amulet around Zarah's neck and patted her cheek. "It must have," she said. "After all, here you are."

"Yes, I am." Then, "Why are you dressing so fine?"

"Oh, it's Sunday. Miguel and I go to church. You can come too if you like."

Zarah hesitated.

"It's all right. You don't have to if you don't want to."

It had been years since anyone said that to Zarah. "Then I want," she said. But she didn't really; she just wanted to make this kind woman happy.

"It is your choice," Alma said. "But what will you wear?"

Zarah looked down at herself and her worn jeans and torn tee shirt. "I've got nothing. I had something, but I lost it in the desert."

"What was that?"

"My abaya."

"What's that?" Alma said.

"My abaya. It's what I wore sometimes at home." Then with no warning at all sorrow overwhelmed her. The loss of this one hank of torn dirty drab cloth hit her like it was the loss of everything she'd known in her own home and all she loved there.

First ashamed and then embarrassed by her shame, Zarah sat down on the floor and turned to face the wall, surprised by the flood of her tears in the presence of this kind woman. But it seemed that after so much cruelty with no tears at all, kindness brought out the tears.

"Zarah," Alma said. Zarah felt the touch of Alma's soft hand on her shoulder. Zarah put her own hand on top of Alma's. "I'm sorry," Zarah said. "I'm not ungrateful. I just lost something important."

"No, you didn't," Alma said. "Look."

Zarah turned to look up and Alma handed her the abaya, now all washed and pressed. Torn patches had been sewn up in gray thread so fine Zarah could hardly see it.

"When I found you, this was lying on the ground next to you. Is this something you can wear to church?"

Zarah stood and slipped her abaya over her head. "It's perfect."

38 The Woman In The Song

A few hours after he and Mattie got back to their hotel room from their Hedgehog Barrel gig, Hack was finally getting some sleep, and better yet, thrilling to his most wonderful dream ever. He was playing in a band with Haydn and Mozart on violin and Segovia on guitar and Louis Armstrong on trumpet and Charles Mingus on bass. Hack was trying to fit his piano ideas into the unique musical synthesis the five geniuses had worked up when an atrocious drummer butted in—insistent and badly out of rhythm.

Hack muttered, "You're stepping on my beat."

The bad drummer was Mattie's stiff strong finger poking him over and over in the back.

Hack clenched his eyes and tried to keep his breathing regular.

Mattie said, "You're not fooling anyone."

"I'm asleep."

No dice. She said, "We didn't finish our conversation the other night."

"There was no conversation. You wouldn't talk."

"I'll talk now."

"Maybe now I don't want to."

She said, "You asked what I was thinking about."

"Maybe when I asked I wanted to know and maybe now I don't."

"Maybe then I didn't want to tell you and maybe now I do."

"But that was then and this is now."

She said, "Then was only two nights ago."

"And now I'm even more exhausted than I was then and now I need to sleep. And you stepped on my beat."

"It's your awful song."

He sighed and sat up and swiveled to point his face and eyes towards the sound of her voice. In the blackness he couldn't see her face or anything else, but Mattie was close enough to feel the feather-light touch of her breath on his face. After a hard night's

200

singing and clobbering troublemakers with garbage can lids, she gave off a heady delicious aroma savoring of light sweat and salt which mixed in with her natural delicious Mattie scent and one other newer fragrance. He ignored the stirring below and said, "Nice perfume."

"*Annick Goutal Eau D'Hadrien,*" she said. "It retails for four hundred forty-one dollars and eighteen cents per ounce. But I got it half price at the Hotel Shop. And I only bought the quarter ounce bottle."

"You mean the song I sang last night? That song 'It Ain't Gamblin' When You Know You're Gonna Lose'?"

"Yes. That's the awful song I mean."

"What's so awful about that song?"

"It stinks."

"Dudley likes it."

"He would."

"As it happens, I like it myself. And the crowd liked it too."

"How can you know that?"

"The way they responded."

"By the time you sang, there were like eight people."

"Not true."

"And they were all men."

"Men count."

"Not this time."

He said, "So what's wrong with the song?"

"I just have one question. Just answer me this one question."

It was not in Hack's experience that any woman ever had just one question. But he supposed if any woman might be the exception, it might be Mattie. He plunged. "Go ahead."

"It's about the woman."

"What woman?"

"The woman in the song."

"What about her?"

"Is she me?"

"What?"

"You heard. Is she me?"

"The woman?"

She enunciated with exaggerated slowness. "Yes. The woman. In the song. Is she me?"

"No way. No how."

"Do you think you're gonna lose with me? Is that it? Being with me does not even count as gamblin' because you know you're gonna lose anyway? Is that the point?"

"There's no point. It's just a song."

"Am I her? The woman you think will stick you with a lifetime of singing your blues and paying your dues?"

"No. No way it's you."

"But think about it. You met me in a barroom just like her."

"No I didn't."

"Maxes' Madhouse in Ojibwa City isn't a bar?"

"We didn't meet there. We met in high school, remember?"

In an accusatory tone: "But you never paid any attention to me in high school."

That much was true—in high school Hack had been terrified of Mattie. But this didn't seem the best time to mention that.

Then, in a tiny voice he could barely hear, she asked, "Do I have a lot of miles on me?"

"Are you…"—he caught himself and stopped before he blurted the perilous word 'crazy'—"mistaken? I mean, you're mistaken. Where'd you get an idea like that?"

"Aren't you listening? From the song. Don't you listen to your own song?"

For the moment Hack ran out of things to say.

Mattie didn't. "But I suppose I'm not such a terrible drag, even if I'm only an old worn out tire. After all, I'm still pretty light on the tread wear. So I got that going for me."

Hack said nothing.

"But let me remind you I started life as a steel-belted all-season radial."

"You're still all-season to me."

"That's a joke, right? This is no time for your crappy Hack jokes. And you're that guy, right?"

"The guy in the song? No way."

"Then who is he?"

"Nobody. He's just that character. You know, like in all the old country songs. He's generic. Generic Country Guy. Maybe a sad and regretful outlaw who's made more than his share of bad choices. He drives a pickup with a shotgun on a rack in the cab behind him and only his dog is loyal and he ran a whiskey still while he was in prison for petty larceny and he drinks too much of his own product and he always takes up with the wrong woman."

"Women he meets in barrooms, right?" Her voice rose in triumph.

Maybe if he focused on song details. "Think about it. Have you ever heard of me getting in an actual fist fight with anyone, much less a muscle-bound bozo?"

"I guess not—if we don't count that terrorist Amalki guy."

"That wasn't on the wrong side of town. It was in the woods."

"I suppose."

"And it wasn't a fist fight, it was a knife fight."

"That much is true."

"See? And you've never seen me play poker, have you?"

She paused. "But since we started seeing each other, you've had no money. When you were married to Lily you both had great jobs and lots of money. How do I know what you did then? For all I know, you were the biggest high roller at The Treasure Island Resort and Casino. Maybe you pulled up in that cute little red Audi Fox of yours and all the Casino people rubbed their hands together with glee and rolled out the carpet and comped you in for all the steak and booze you could handle."

He said, "Listen carefully. Before we were together, I didn't play poker. Now that we're together, I don't play poker. As we stroll through life hand in hand towards the future, I'll never play poker. Or blackjack or roulette or slot machines. I didn't think about it while I was writing the song, but maybe part of the point of the song—if it has a point, which it doesn't—would be that gambling is hopeless."

"But you're gambling with me."

"The single unique worthwhile exception. And it's two way. You're gambling with me too."

"Did you mean what you just said?"

He'd lost track. "What did I just say?"

"About strolling through life hand in hand towards the future?"

"Of course."

A volcano of light blinded him. She must have flicked on her bed-stand lamp. She said, "Look me in the eye."

"I can't look you in the eye. I can't see your eye. Or anything else."

He felt her warm hand cupping his chin. She instructed in a gentle voice, "Close your eyes a moment and then when you can, bit by bit, open them again."

He cracked his eyelids apart and waited a moment for his eyes to adjust and then forced them open a little more. Finally, he found himself staring directly into her own dark pupils only a few inches away. Wetness shimmered there.

She said, "You know how many times I've been hurt?"

"You never say. But you give the impression it's a lot."

She kept her eyes focused square on his. "It is a lot. There's been a big convoy of assholes rolling through my life."

"I'm not an asshole."

She whispered. "I know that."

He reached out and caressed her chin with his own hand and said, "You'd better."

They kissed. It was a gentle sad sweet kiss. She turned out the light and curled up with her back to him and pulled the covers over her.

Hack turned back to his corner of the bed and lay down and pulled the covers up and closed his eyes. He needed sleep. Successive waves of exhaustion rolled over him, like—

Like?

Like a convoy of semis rolling—he conjured up and rejected one image after another—

--over a squashed dead possum in the middle of the road?

--through a wind-blown piece of discarded brown cardboard?

--through a road block manned by malevolent state troopers with their drawn guns aimed right at him?

Shut up, Mind.

Hack decided he didn't know what his exhaustion was like and he didn't care. It was just exhaustion. He emptied his lungs with a breath as deep and thorough as he could muster and then inhaled a new one.

He tried to empty his mind too but with less success. It turned out he wasn't keeping up with Mattie after all. And he wasn't just a single emotion behind—nowhere near that close. Two at least. Maybe three. Which gave him the idea for a song. He made a mental note and the relief that came with his idea allowed him finally to sleep.

39 Jabali Reports Again

The Mujahid looked up at his man Jabali. They were in the basement of his safe house. Just as before, the Mujahid sat regal in his easy chair as if it were his throne and Jabali stood stiff and uncomfortable in front of him as the inferior he was.

Jabali said, "Something happened yesterday."

"You couldn't phone me?"

"Not in this case. A sighting of the girl."

The Mujahid said, "Like the fifteen other sightings you've reported?"

"No. This is different. In a church."

"You go to church?"

"Me? No. Of course not."

"Why not?"

The two stared at each other. The Mujahid narrowed his eyes. "If you are a Christian, you should be a good Christian and go to church."

Jabali blanched. "Yes. Of course. From now on. Anyway, I was having a drink last night and I heard some men talking. About a little girl in a local church in a valley nearby."

"Why was a little girl in a church on a Sunday worth talking about?"

"The men said she didn't do or say anything right and she hung back from the other people like she didn't know what to do next and she said some weird words no one recognized. And her accent was strange."

The Mujahid shrugged.

Jabali said, "And they heard her say something that sounded like Allah."

The Mujahid considered. "Was her hair covered?"

"In that church almost all the women and girls cover their hair. But she wore a kind of gray robe different from what the others were wearing. When I saw her in the Compound, Zarah used to wear a

Zarah's Fire   Max Cossack

gray robe like the men described."

"Did the men know how this girl wound up in church?"

"She came with some old Mexican couple."

"Did they know where this Mexican couple lives?"

"The men didn't know. But the church is mostly for people in that valley. So the old couple almost certainly lives somewhere in it. Also one of the men thinks the old lady does some cleaning work part time for an outdoor garden store called 'The Thorny Path'. Once a week or something like that. Sometimes she brings the girl with her."

The Mujahid said, "Focus on the garden store."

"I was planning on that."

"Find the couple. Find the girl. If you bring the girl to me safe and unharmed you get a nice fat bonus."

Jabali grinned at the word "bonus" and turned and moved up the stairs and left.

The Mujahid watched him go. For the first time since Amir's girl had burned down his Compound and blown up all his weapons and drugs, something might go right.

40 Fairness

Hack sat alone in the back of the Phoenix courtroom. As always, on the other side of the barrier separating gladiators from spectators, Amos Owens, Laghdaf and Sam sat together on the left. Macklin and the SWASU representative sat at their defendants' table on the right.

Someone proclaimed, "All rise!" and all did. Judge Zernial emerged through a back door into the courtroom and took her seat behind the high bench. She adjusted her robes and looked out over the courtroom. She put on her glasses. Then she spoke, only once in a while glancing down at her notes:

"In this trial the parties have raised many issues. Some have great political, social and cultural significance. The facts and arguments have been interesting, thought-provoking and occasionally even entertaining. But these political, social or cultural issues that may have temporarily captured our attention have little bearing on the ultimate outcome. Accordingly, the Court will not address them here or in the Court's written opinion.

"The nub of this case is the issue of due process. After all, it was for SWASU's alleged denial of due process that Mr. Owens initiated his claims.

"What does due process mean? Simply put, fairness. Few of us are learned in all the twists and turns of the law, but we think we know fairness when we see it and when we don't.

"Are there specific requirements for a fair process? SWASU is a state university and as part of the government, what is termed a 'state actor'. Many years ago, Judge Friendly helped us out by listing the basic elements of due process, including protections any state actor ought to provide someone against whom it is considering adverse action. His list includes:

An unbiased tribunal;
Notice of the proposed action and grounds asserted for it;

An opportunity to present reasons why it should not occur;
The right to present witnesses;
The right to know opposing evidence;
The right to a decision based exclusively on the
evidence presented;
The right to counsel;
Making a clear and complete record that can be reviewed
after the fact;
Availability of a statement of the reasons for the action;
Public attendance at any hearing; and
Availability of judicial or other fair review.

Judge Zernial adjusted her glasses and looked around the courtroom. "Of course, this is a general list. Defendants have argued that they are not required to provide every single protection on this list in every single situation. But in Defendants' expulsion of Amos Owens, Defendants provided virtually none of these protections.

"Put another way, Amos Owens had no chance. And that is not fair. More to our purpose here, it breaks the law."

"The Court's written opinion is available to all. We'll be reviewing separately the damages to be recovered by Mr. Owens as well as attorneys' fees and costs. The parties should be familiar with the requirements and deadlines for filing on these matters." `

She stood. Again someone proclaimed, "All rise!" and everyone rose. She walked through the back door of the courtroom.

Hack slipped out the back of the courtroom to go tell Mattie that Amos Owens had won.

41 Laghdaf's Strange Friend

"Laghdaf told me your problem," Ari said in a thick Israeli accent. To Lily's American ears it sounded like he pronounced the "r" in "problem" as if he were rolling a "w."

Ari was a broad man only about six inches taller than Lily, but looking to weigh about one hundred eighty pounds, most of it apparently muscle. He was built a lot like Hack. Unlike Hack, he shaved his head bald. From the shadow of fringe around his ears, Lily could tell he was presenting his baldness as a fashion choice rather than the concession to necessity it obviously was. On top of his head he wore a little blue and white yarmulke. She wondered what kept it on.

It was only ten in the morning, but the Arizona sun already flamed down. Lily was miserable. The two sat side by side on a bench outdoors in a small downtown park and watched the sprinklers oscillate as they watered the grass. Into Lily's mind popped an image of herself jumping off the bench and running under the spray. But that might ruin her sleeveless beige Lynn Shift and, more important for the moment, any credibility she might have with Ari.

Ari gave no sign of discomfort. Lily supposed it was because Israelis were used to the desert and horrible summer heat. For all Lily knew, Ari found the Phoenix summer a trifle nippy for his taste.

Ari said, "Laghdaf and I have worked together on a few things, and I owe him some favors. As I do your father."

She asked, "So you'll help us?"

He shrugged. "Hard to say how."

"We're trying to find a missing woman and child."

"So Laghdaf told me," Ari said. "The family of this man Amir ibn Yusuf. But why would you imagine I can help?"

"I know you guys have spy satellites and all kinds of intelligence assets in the Mideast. You have to. You're always warning the Europeans about upcoming terrorist attacks on their soil or spilling

210

Iran's nuclear plans to the world."

"Yes. And we Zionists also control the weather. But that's just a hobby we pursue for amusement in our spare time."

She soldiered through the sarcasm. "I saw in the news that you can telephone civilians who live next door to bad guys and warn them to get out of the line of fire before you wipe out the terrorists with air strikes or rockets."

"Those are important measures incorporated into specific operations and worth the effort."

"And one woman or child isn't important or worth the effort?"

He shrugged again. "I would never say that."

"If you can help me and don't, you are saying that."

He looked at her and nodded as if his worst suspicions had been confirmed. "You argue like my mother."

"I am a mother."

He said, "I believe that"

"But unlike your mother, I'm not scolding you."

"Yes you are."

"Is it working?"

He shrugged and turned to look at the sprinklers on the lawn again.

She said, "If I give you the name of a person, can you tell me where the person is?"

He gave another shrug, this one almost imperceptible.

She thought, Ari's mother tongue is not Hebrew, but a vocabulary of shrugs. And there are nuances; each shrug says something slightly different from the shrug before or after. Probably some Mideast thing.

But then Ari spoke. "What you're asking for is a very serious thing."

"I know that."

"So what's the name?"

"Two names, actually."

He nodded in apparent sadness. "So now you've doubled it to

two names. Soon you'll raise it up to a dozen or more. Have you considered moving to Israel? You'll fit right in."

"I promise I'll stop at two. I'd be thrilled and very grateful for any information about either one of just two people: the woman might be Hiva bint Mustafa. The daughter might be Zarah bint Amir."

Lily thought she detected a tightening around Ari's eyes. Had he recognized one of the names?

He said, "Do you know how many men named Amir live in the Mideast?"

"Amir al-Tikrit. Or Amir ibn Yusuf. But I think the same man used both names. I'm not sure. But he's dead now."

He said, "I see." Lily didn't know what he saw. But she read that as somehow meaning something. At least it wasn't a shrug.

He asked, "Have you actually got a specific someone in mind? A possible wife or daughter you've met or seen in life or at least in a photo?"

"No," she said. "I'd like to, but I don't even know where to begin to look. And the odds I ever will meet or even see one of these two people are infinitesimal."

"Yes," he said. "Infinitesimal indeed. But you are determined."

"I am."

Ari reached into his briefcase. He removed a small cardboard box and handed it to her.

She took it. "What's this?"

He paused as if rehearsing in his mind every word he was about to say, then spoke with obvious deliberation and care. "If you should ever happen to satisfy these infinitesimal odds you mentioned and come upon some little girl about nine or ten years old you suspect might be your Zarah, please ask her to suck for an instant on the stick in this kit and mail it in the pre-addressed mailer. It will reach the right people."

Ari stood. He shrugged one last time, but this time he also gave her a sad smile that instilled in his hitherto unexpressive square face a hint of human feeling. "Don't lose hope," he said. "The beginnings of my little country included thousands of people who succeeded in surviving and eventually flourishing despite starting out with only the most infinitesimal odds in their favor. I personally know hundreds of stories. And since you're a Jew, so do you."

She said, "Yes, I do."

"Including from your own family, of course," he said.

"Yes."

He nodded. He turned and walked away. Lily didn't move. She watched him dwindle on the city sidewalk, briefcase in hand, growing progressively smaller until he disappeared into the pedestrian crowd.

An odd hope stirred within her. She tried to decipher his entire array of words and shrugs. Had he given clues? What would be the point of a DNA test unless there was someone with whom to compare the results? And he had come to their conversation prepared. He had checked out something based on whatever Laghdaf had told him before meeting her.

On the one hand, the way he spoke suggested he knew something. On the other hand, Lily knew nothing about who Ari was or what he did or knew, only that he had teamed in some capacity with her father and with Laghdaf. On the third hand, a good relationship with either Sam or Laghdaf or both stamped Ari with the best possible credential.

Lily stood and crossed the lawn to the edge of the area covered by the spray from the sprinklers. Just out of reach of the direct spray she stepped into the cool mist and let the mini-droplets cool her face. Then she surprised herself by taking several full steps forward until her heels sank into the dirt under the wet grass. Two more steps forward and the full force of the spray showered her dress and drenched her head and doused her face.

To her astonishment, Lily delighted in her immersion. After long moments she backed away until she felt firm dry grass under her feet again. She bent down and removed each of her soaked Christian

Louboutin heels in turn. She carried the shoes and walked in her stockings down the sidewalk towards her hotel. She ignored the strange looks she knew she was getting. She didn't care.

After about a hundred yards, sidewalk heat began to singe her feet. She stopped and slipped her soggy heels over her feet again. Her waterlogged fifteen-hundred-dollar shoes wobbled under her and she had to limp back to the hotel.

Once in the icy cold of the Vauxhall Arms lobby she stopped and took her heels off again and carried them up to her room. She changed into the warm white hotel bathrobe and dropped the Lynn Shift dress and Christian Louboutin shoes into the little trash basket under the little sink.

Then she reconsidered. She retrieved the dress and shoes. She hung the dress in the closet and laid the two shoes on two glossy magazines. After they dried, they might make nice additions to next morning's tip for hotel staff. Someone else might make good use of them. Someone else might love them.

42 *Trodding The Thorny Path*

Later that Monday Mom said to Sarai, "I need a break. All I've seen of Arizona is this hotel and one park. The concierge told me about a fun place and I rented a car."

"Really?"

"I told him what you like and he promised you'd love it."

"Sounds okay, Mom," Sarai said.

"You sure?"

"No need to ask twice, Mom. You're the mom, remember?"

The trip out took almost an hour. Mom drove and Sarai sat quiet in the back strapped into the child safety seat that came with the rental car.

Mom said little. She just turned on the radio and hummed along with ancient pop songs. Sarai didn't mind. The landscape fascinated her. Sarai had not anticipated the strangeness of Arizona. Little grass grew except for occasional big green parks and golf courses. All the other land was khaki-colored or cinnamon or beige or coffee or some other shade of brown. In some neighborhoods thick iron bars made gray vertical stripes in all the windows. Sarai hoped St. Paul didn't get to be like that.

Tan dust covered the sides of the roads and what passed for front yards. Very few houses had lawns. Shrubs and cactuses and lots of rock divided the house fronts from the streets. The houses were mostly low and flat and wide instead of tall like the older two and three-story homes in her St. Paul neighborhood.

Instead of peaked Minnesota roofs, flat ones topped the houses. Sarai asked why and Mom guessed they didn't need peaked roofs because no snow piled up on them. The people didn't have to worry about their ceilings caving in on them after a March blizzard.

Once out past the city, the country landscape was even stranger. There were no forests or real rivers or streams, just occasional canals paved in gray concrete holding thin blue ribbons of water or sometimes wide empty waterless dirt channels Mom told her were

215

called "washes." There were farm fields, but they sprouted crops
Mom said were cotton or alfalfa instead of corn or soybeans like
Minnesota farmers grew.

Sarai asked, "Mom, is this already the desert?"

"Yes, Sweetie."

"It's greener than I expected."

"I know what you mean. Me too."

"Mom, may I ask you something?"

"Of course."

"I've been scared to ask. But have you found anything about
Zarah?"

Mom turned off the radio. "Maybe," she said.

Sarai leaned forward against her seat restraints. "Really?"

"And I've been cautious about telling you. I didn't want to raise
your hopes. But you were right all along. The man you called Uncle
Amir did have a daughter named Zarah. Zarah bint Amir. Zarah, the
daughter of Amir."

"Where is she?"

"No one knows. While Amir was hiding in France bad men in
Iraq kidnapped her away from her mother."

"Kidnapped to where?"

"I don't know."

"Does anyone?"

"Her kidnappers, I suppose. But you were right. I want you to
know that much. And that's all I can really tell you because that's all
I know. But I haven't stopped looking. I promise. I never will."

Sarai said nothing because she could think of nothing. She sat
looking out the car window. She'd been right all along. So what?
Instead of feeling good she felt sad. Maybe a kidnapped Zarah was
worse than no Zarah at all. She'd imagined a Zarah she could meet
and be best friends with. Sarai didn't know everything that happened
to a kidnapped girl and she didn't want to.

Sarai began to wonder if it was her fault. Maybe she'd imagined
this other sad little girl into existence in the first place. A girl with

no father and torn away from her mother by bad men. A lost girl.

The rental car had a GPS and Mom listened to it and executed each instruction until they turned right down a gravel road. They hit a few ruts and jolts and Mom slowed the car. On the right Sarai saw a big wooden sign hanging from a wire hung between two tall brown wooden poles. Burned black into the dark brown wood were the words "The Thorny Path." Sarai said, "There it is."

"I see it," Mom said and turned off the road into the gravel driveway and into a big open unpaved area covered in sand and gravel. She pulled to the left and parked and turned off the engine. "Made it."

Sarai unstrapped herself from her seat and opened the back door and got out and looked around. The grounds stretched back at least a hundred yards from the road to a wire mesh fence in the back. Stubby green trees and bushes stretched along the sides. Orderly rows of young saguaro and prickly pear and barrel and hedgehog cactuses spread under the branches of the trees in the middle of the grounds. Some wire mesh cages were visible under the foliage.

Mom clicked the key fob to lock the car and walked around behind the car to Sarai. She said, "I'm sorry, Sarai. I didn't want to make you sad, but you have a right to know what I know."

"Don't be sorry, Mom."

Mom said, "But we are here. And the concierge promised there'd be live birds. Very special ones."

Sarai said, "Really?"

"Since we're here, let's have fun." Mom took Sarai's hand and they started walking across the grounds towards the trees.

They'd gone about twenty yards when Sarai heard a shout. Mom and Sarai turned.

A man walked towards them from the left side of the enclosure. When he got to within about fifteen feet he stopped.

He was a fat Mexican-looking man who looked a bit like that cartoon character who was always trying to kill Bugs—not the bald one, but the one with a big mustache that drooped down both sides of his lips like two old fashioned curved swords. At his right side he wore a big black pistol in a holster.

He and his gun frightened Sarai. She grabbed Mom's hand. Mom squeezed back hard.

Mom asked the man, "May I help you?".

The man looked Sarai over in a way that made her feel strange.

Mom said, "Sir. May I help you?"

The man said in an American accent, "This is your daughter?"

Mom said, "Who wants to know?"

"I suppose I must seem rude to you, but could you please ask your daughter to remove her sun glasses? I have been hunting all over this valley for a lost little girl—my niece—I am helping my brother out—and I saw you and your girl from a distance from behind and I thought this girl might be her. The resemblance is strong. The other girl—my niece—is also dark skinned and dark haired."

Mom said "I don't know about that. I've already told you this is my daughter."

Sarai wanted this all to end quickly, so she took off her sunglasses and held them in her hand and, trying to show no fear, stared into the man's eyes. She didn't like what she didn't see.

The man said, "And the cap?"

Sarai took off her Diamondbacks cap and shook out her hair and glared at the man.

The man said, "I see I was mistaken. I apologize."

Mom said, "Then this conversation is over."

He said, "What is your name, little girl?"

Sarai said nothing.

Mom said, "You have no reason to know her name."

The man said, "You are right." But he didn't leave.

The man glanced past them and Sarai turned to see what he was looking at. An older man in the green vest of a salesman came walking their way from the trees.

Mom said, "Well, we've answered your questions and we'll all be on our way now."

The man said, "Of course." He turned and walked back the way he had come towards the fence at the side of the enclosure.

Still clutching Sarai's hand, Mom tugged her in the direction of the car. She said, "Time to go."

"But I haven't seen any birds."

"Another time. I promise."

"When?"

"Soon." She stopped. "I promise. We'll come back here and you can see all the live birds you want. Okay?"

"Okay."

They got back in the car and Mom started the car right away and turned and watched Sarai buckle herself into her child safety seat. The whole time, Mom drummed her finger on the top of her seat. Then Mom roared the engine and took off out through the gate and made a hard left back towards Phoenix. As she drove she looked over her shoulder two different times until she seemed satisfied and slowed to her normal driving speed.

Sarai asked, "Who was that man, do you think?

"No idea," Mom said.

"He shouted something at us, didn't he?"

"Yes."

"I didn't hear exactly what he shouted."

"I did."

"It sort of sounded like he called me 'Zarah'."

"That seems unlikely."

Sarai asked, "Did he?"

"Never mind what he said."

Just like a parent, leaving out the most interesting part.

43 Hondo

"What kind of ex-husband are you, anyway?" Mattie asked Hack.

"Getting ahead of yourself, aren't you?"

"What do you mean?"

"You planning for me to join the multitudinous ranks of your ex-husbands?"

"Multitudinous? Just like you to hide behind a big word. Anyway, you do want to marry me, don't you?"

They were sitting up leaning on big pillows in their hotel room bed watching John Wayne strut and shoot his way through the nineteen fifties western movie "Hondo."

Hack said, "What makes you so sure?"

"Are you kidding? But why? I mean, why do you want me for a wife?"

"I admire your way with a garbage can lid."

She said, "You should. But you'll have to be a better ex-husband to Lily if you're going to qualify as one of mine. She told me about that dude that scared the crap out of her and Sarai out in the desert. You should have been there with her to watch out for them both."

"I didn't even know they were going out there."

"Seems to me it's part of an ex-husband's job to protect his ex-wife from assholes."

"Do any of your exes do that for you?"

She said, "They feel sorry for the assholes." She paused. "Probably professional courtesy,"

He said, "Understandable."

She snuggled up against him. "Anyway, next time we'll all go together and keep an eye out for the guy."

Hack asked, "Why should there be a next time?"

"Sarai didn't get to see any of those special live birds like Lily promised. And maybe I'd like to meet the dude myself."

Hack said, "You bringing your garbage can lid?"

220

A pause.

Hack asked, "Is your birthday over?"

Mattie said, "Yes. I think I finally caught up."

"With what?"

"With all the birthdays I missed."

Another pause.

Hack asked, "How many ex-husbands do you have, anyway?"

"Watch the movie," Mattie said. "Here comes my favorite part. This stud Apache warrior rides his mustang bareback into this lonely white widow woman's farmyard. He wants to marry her. To impress her he does an acrobatic mount and dismount."

Hack said, "Do you think that would work for me?"

44 Zarah's Happiness

Zarah was happy settled in with Alma and Miguel. Nice days seemed to blend one into the other.

Miguel was almost always away working. It turned out he worked several jobs. On the days Alma walked to her own job nearby, Zarah went with her once in a while, but she usually stayed behind and took care of the chores. She did the gardening. She made Alma's and Miguel's bed and then her own little bed on the floor. She dusted and swept. If there were dishes, she washed them outside in the pail.

Sometimes she sat on the edge of the bed and watched television. If she moved the rabbit ear antennas around she could pick up different local channels. Zarah liked the Bugs Bunny cartoons best. She especially liked it when Bugs tricked and beat up the little angry man who looked so much like Jabali.

The shows helped her learn good a lot of new words in English. It seemed funny to hear Bugs talking in English instead of his native Arabic. Zarah guessed the television people must have had someone say the English words and replaced the Arabic words in the cartoons somehow. She was curious how they'd done that.

One day Alma brought home some pens and a little child's coloring book full of animal drawings. Zarah thanked her and sat cross legged on her mattress and colored in everything very quickly. Alma watched awhile and said, "You're very good at that."

"I used to be," Zarah said.

"You always stay exactly within the lines. And you choose the right colors for things."

"It's easy."

Zarah didn't want to be greedy. But this one time she couldn't help it. "I used to draw my own pictures, too."

"I'm not surprised," Alma said.

The next day Alma brought back a big pad and more pens in many more colors.

222

From then on Zarah drew her own pictures before she colored them in. Sometimes she drew Bugs. Sometimes she drew cactuses and their flowers and fruit. She drew the way the land back home looked from Grandmother's camp where they'd sat together, or hardest of all, tried to draw the market stalls with mounds of food or the kitchen where she'd helped out back home.

But she never made pictures of real people—only cartoon people. She never drew Grandmother or Mother or Father.

45 Mattie's Bill Comes Due

Hack was sitting on a chair in the waiting room of Sam's borrowed office still trying to finish his Travis McGee novel *Darker Than Amber* when Professor Groucho came out of the Sam's inner office door and took a few steps past Hack.

Hack said, "Hey, Professor. You're not wearing your glasses."

The professor turned and said, "Sorry?"

Hack stood and stuck out his hand. "You don't remember me? We met in my rental Ford in Lot AB2 on campus."

"Oh, sure." The man shook Hack's hand. "Ron Handy."

"Nice to learn your name, Professor Handy."

"Former Professor Handy, if the High Priestess Sterns-Marquardt gets her way."

"Sorry to hear it."

"It may turn out okay. I think I've got a good case."

Hack said, "No surprise there."

"No. They never learn, do they?"

Hack said, "Why should they? They're playing with the taxpayer's money."

Handy sighed. "It would be nice if Sterns-Marquardt herself suffered some personal consequences."

"She's also playing with the wrong people, so don't rule it out. Her playmates don't suffer fools."

The man brightened visibly. "Happy thought. Nice seeing you again."

"Good luck," Hack said.

"Thanks. You too." The man turned and left.

Hack knocked on Sam's door.

"In," Sam said from inside and Hack opened the door and stepped in and sat in the visitor's chair in front of Sam's desk.

Sam leaned back in his swivel chair and folded his hands in his lap. "My favorite ex-son-in-law. What can I do for you today?"

"There is something I want to talk about. But before I get to that, anything more I need to do in the case?"

"Your work is done. We're about to file on damages. We'll do well. And you should be gratified to hear I've passed your Groucho papers on to some trustworthy law enforcement people."

Hack said, "I am gratified. Do you think the University will punish Professor Stein-Marquardt?"

"She'll be fine. She's got her 'intersectionality' to fall back on. It's this decade's mandatory academic theory. None dare dissent."

Sam intertwined his fingers behind his head and leaned back further. He seemed relaxed and even expansive—a winner taking a few moments to savor his victory. A good chance to dig into Sam's thoughts.

Hack said, "What the hell is Intersectionality anyway?"

"A theory that ranks human beings by race, class, sex, religion and any other category these superannuated Chairman Mao fanboys can conjure up. The more different categories in which you claim to be oppressed, the holier you are."

"How does Amos Owens fit into that."

"Muslims are the favored victims *du jour*. So when Owens asked a question about how Islam treats gays, the Professor and her colleagues deemed this gay black scholarship kid a privileged oppressor."

Hack said, "His first time in that situation, I'll bet."

Sam said, "Zealots always want to torture the inexhaustible variety and complexity of human experience into some straitjacket scheme."

"I've noticed. You have a theory on why they do that?"

Sam looked up at the ceiling. "Sometimes they're frauds. Sometimes they're sincere. Sometimes they mistake their own petty personal frustrations and inadequacies for manifestations of some galactic-scale injustice. Sometimes it's a personality disorder. That's why you can't dent people like Sterns-Marquardt with facts."

"Or, in my experience, with logic," Hack said.

"Logic is good. I studied formal logic in school. I also studied

225

feminism, communism, socialism, fascism, conservatism, all the 'isms' we had back then. And I decided there's only one useful ism."

Hack asked, "Which is?".

"The only good ism is a syllogism."

Hack said, "I thought you were going to say Judaism."

"Used to describe the religion, Judaism is a word invented by a nineteenth century German professor. He was naming something he didn't understand. Before he coined it, in four thousand years, no Jew ever used that word."

"I didn't know that."

"The isms loose in my younger days killed tens of millions of people. Now the same semi-mediocre intellectuals have conjured up new ones like postmodernism and intersectionality."

Hack said, "Nice new words."

"Postmodernism and intersectionality are the the syphilis and gonorrhea of the modern university."

Hack asked, "So what'll we use for penicillin?"

Sam said, "I've asked myself whether we could abolish all university departments with the word 'studies' in their titles."

"Would that work?"

"No. Another thing that's inexhaustible is human stupidity. Lucky for me."

"How's that?"

Sam smiled his shark-like smile. "Keeps me in business."

A pause, then Hack handed Sam a sheaf of papers.

Sam looked down at them. "What's this?"

Hack said, "The real reason I dropped by. Our hotel bill so far. Mattie went haywire in the Hotel Shop on your credit card."

"Hm…Cecilie Bahnsen Dress, Tom Mix hat, Tony Lama boots, Annick Goutal Eau D'Hadrien perfume—and a few nice pieces of jewelry." Sam looked up at Hack. "So?"

"You can take the money out of what you owe me. You didn't bargain for this spree of hers."

"I didn't bargain for Mattie helping save Sarai's life this past January either."

"That comes free. They're my family too."

"Nevertheless." Sam tore the sheets in half and dumped them in the waste basket to the right of his desk. "Tell Mattie 'happy birthday' from me."

Hack started to say, "Thanks, I will. And—"

Sam jumped up and headed for the door.

Hack said, "Sam, hold it a minute, please!"

Sam turned. "Is there something else?"

"You didn't hear me say the word 'And'?"

"Not really," Sam said. "And?"

"And I was wondering. You remember all those lies ZNN told about me this past January?"

"Who can forget?"

"Can I sue ZNN for slander?"

Sam blinked once. He came back around his desk and sat in his chair. He punched the cell phone lying on the desk top. "Laghdaf, if you have a few minutes, could you come in here, please? I've got Hack with me and he's asking for our help on something."

Laghdaf's liquid baritone flowed through the phone. "Sure thing, Sam. Give me twenty minutes, okay?"

Sam said, "Of course," and jabbed the phone to click off the call. He smiled and leaned back in his chair again. "This is going to be fun."

46 The Hope of the Mujahid

The Mujahid sat alone in his safe house. He knew he should get out of Arizona as soon as possible, but it might be just a few more days.

Because of the idiot woman professor at SWASU who'd blabbed in the courtroom, the Jew lawyer for the sodomite Khaffir athlete had gotten his hands on all kinds of critical information exposing the Mujahid's Anti Islamophobia League, his pet political project and a mainstay of his plans for America. Sooner or later someone was going to sue AIL itself. If the Khaffir authorities dug in deeper, they would even prosecute.

The Mujahid had thought about killing the professor, but she hardly seemed worth it. Anyway, it was the other female who had started his truly big troubles—Amir's girl. He admitted to himself he'd made a bad mistake in trying to sell her. His greed had gotten the better of him. He should have had her killed like he'd had her father Amir killed, or better yet, cut her throat himself and savored the experience.

Hadn't the Prophet said, "Two hungry wolves sent into a flock of sheep are no more destructive to a man than his own greed."

The girl was some kind of bad seed—Amir's revenge on him. How could a nine or ten-year-old girl bring such catastrophe? Zarah's fire had destroyed not only the Compound he had stowed her away in, but all his carefully accumulated treasures. It had also brought the Khaffir authorities in. Each new day brought new reports of disruptions in his business and raids and shutdowns of other compounds and his bases all over America.

The only thing keeping the Mujahid in Arizona was his hope that in the next few days Jabali would do his duty and find Zarah and bring her to him so he could slice her throat as he should have done in the first place. That would be a fitting end to Amir's line.

47 *Once Again Trodding The Thorny Path*

Sarai could tell Mom was sad again. Sarai had to tap on her shoulder a bunch of times to wake her. Mom got out of bed and dressed in slow motion in her shorts and long-sleeved tee shirt. The only thing she said was "Let's go, Sweetheart," in a kind of monotone. On the elevator ride downstairs, she didn't speak at all. Sarai grabbed her hand and Mom just smiled a faint smile and bent and kissed her on top of her head.

When they ran into Dad and Mattie downstairs at the breakfast buffet, Mattie suggested they should all four eat together and Mom just nodded. They each got their meal and they sat together around a little square table. Dad and Mattie and Sarai handled all the chatter. Mom ignored her eggs and nibbled a plain butter croissant and sipped her black coffee and stared off somewhere. She was almost as bad as she'd been at home in St. Paul.

Sarai saw Dad and Mattie exchange glances. After Dad asked Mom about her plans for the day and Mom didn't really say anything in particular, Mattie said, "Lily, we're taking Sarai out to the Thorny Path again."

Mom said, "I'd like to come too."

Mattie said, "After what happened before, you're not scared?"

Lily said, "Terrified. So what?"

Sarai put in, "It'll be a special day. All four of us together."

The trip out took almost an hour. Dad drove and Mattie navigated with a road atlas in her lap. She said it would help her learn the way better than using a GPS. Nobody else said anything about the child safety seat so Sarai didn't bring it up either. She just buckled herself into the seat belt in the back like a regular person. Mom sat to the left of Sarai. Mom still didn't say much.

Sarai didn't mind. She liked the scenery. About half way there, she said, "It sure is green for a desert."

Dad said, "There's different kinds of deserts. The desert around here has more water than most of the others. All kinds of animal

229

life."

Sarai said, "I know. I even saw a wild coyote."

"Really? When?" Dad asked.

"Just now. We passed him by the side of the road. He was loping along in the opposite direction like he was headed somewhere really important."

Out of nowhere, as if to make the point she was part of the group, Mom said, "I saw him too."

Dad said, "You think he was going after Road Runner?"

"Or maybe Bugs," Sarai said.

Mom said, "Don't worry, Sweetheart. Bugs can talk his way out of any trouble."

"I'm not worried," Sarai said, and snuggled up as close to Mom as her seatbelt allowed.

Mattie looked up from her road atlas at Dad and said, "Left here, then straight half a mile. Then turn right at the next intersection."

Dad followed Mattie's directions and turned right down the same gravel road Mom had used. He slowed the car for the same ruts and jolts as before. On the right Sarai saw the same wooden sign hanging between the same two tall brown wooden poles. Sarai shouted, "There it is."

"Got it," Dad said and turned off the road into the gravel driveway and into the big unpaved space. He pulled to the left and parked and turned off the engine. Dad clicked a button to unlock all the doors and Sarai pushed hers open and got out. The adults got out too.

Mom said, "Hack, why are you wearing that long sleeve shirt?" The other three wore just tee shirts, but Dad had an unbuttoned long-sleeved blue shirt that hung over his tee shirt all the way down so it covered his side and rear end.

Dad said, "I'm getting too used to the heat. I could swear I feel a chill." But big globules of sweat had already begun to gleam on his forehead.

Mom came around the rear of the car and fixed a big sun hat

over Sarai's head. She handed Sarai a tube of suntan lotion. "Everybody grease up."

Everyone passed the tube around and did as commanded. Sarai said, "I hope I get to see the birds this time."

Dad said, "Go for it." He waved his hand towards the rest of the grounds.

Sarai turned and ran onto the grounds. Mom shouted, "Slow down, Sarai."

Sarai passed stubby green trees and bushes and the orderly rows of little saguaro and prickly pear and barrel and hedgehog cactuses. She glanced back and saw Mom and Dad and Mattie half-jogging close behind.

Screened-in cage-like enclosures dotted the grounds here and there in the shade of trees. Each cage was about fifteen feet square and ten feet high. Sarai counted at least a dozen. And in nearly every cage fluttered and squawked one or two huge gaudy multicolored parrots.

Perched on a branch in the first cage on the right was an apple red parrot with a white throat. The next cage held one feathered in a shade of shiny violet so dark she thought it was black until she looked closer.

Inside the next enclosure were two even more beautiful ones—a nearly identical duet splashed with all the colors she'd seen in the prism her science teacher Ms. Akamian had shown her. Ms. Akamian had handed her the little clear glass triangle and told Sarai to look at a light bulb through it. Sarai had seen a rainbow with more gradations of color than she had ever imagined possible.

The two parrots were living rainbows. From head to tail the hues of their plumage followed the same order of the spectrum as Sarai had seen through the prism. Their heads glowed red and then the colors ranged down their torsos through green and then yellow and then blue to their mostly deep purple tails. To complete the spectrum, they wore pale beaks and masks of white eyeshadow.

The sign in front said, "Flamingo Land Parrots."

For the first few minutes, Sarai was so absorbed in the swaggering and squawking Flamingo Land Parrots she didn't notice the Mexican girl about her own age moving behind her and standing at the next cage over.

When Sarai did become aware of the girl, Sarai didn't turn her head. She didn't want to stare, so she peeked out of the corner of her eye. The girl was Sarai's age or older and a bit taller. She had beautiful hair the same dark shade as Sarai's but even longer. She was very thin, in fact, thin almost like girls in foreign countries Sarai had seen on TV who didn't get enough to eat.

If the Mexican girl noticed Sarai, she gave no sign. She watched the parrots a moment and then moved off to another cage and other parrots.

Sarai considered trying out her classroom Spanish on the girl. But it might be rude. Just because the girl came from a Mexican family didn't mean she didn't speak English. But it would be fun to speak Spanish with a real Mexican person, like Señora Hernandez had promised she'd get do to some time.

Sarai took off her backpack and got out her sketchbook and pens and got ready to sit down and draw the stunning Flamingo Land Parrots when she heard someone nearby speak.

The voice said, "Hello."

Sarai glanced over in the direction the voice came from.

No one there. Just another cage with another parrot.

She sat cross-legged on the ground and picked up her sketchbook. Again the voice said "Hello."

Sarai glanced over again. Again the parrot said "Hello." Of course! Parrots talk. But in the movies they always had squawky voices and said things like "Polly want a cracker." This parrot sounded just like a human being and it said something a person would say.

Sarai collected her supplies and stood and went over to the new cage. The parrot said "Hello" from its little perch and Sarai said "Hello" back. The parrot said "Hello" another time and so did Sarai.

A little sign posted in the dirt in front of the bird's cage read, "Ruby Macaw." The parrot was mostly red with a white beak and deep blue-green plumage tinged with yellow and turquoise. Very thin red candy stripes crisscrossed the nickel–sized white patches around and below its eyes.

Sarai sat cross-legged again and set up to draw. She traced a black outline of the bird to start her sketch when a shadow crossed her page and blocked the light. She looked up.

"Lo siento," the girl said and backed away.

"No problema," Sarai said.

The girl turned as if to leave and Sarai took a breath and made a stab in Spanish. "Qué hermosos loros! [what beautiful parrots]"

The other girl stopped and turned and gave her a shy smile. "Si, ellos son."

Sarai liked the girl's smile and gave her one back. "¿Tienen muchos en su país?" [Do they have many in your country?] Her teachers had cautioned Sarai it could be rude—some kind of "micro-aggression"—to ask questions about someone's home country, but she hadn't understood why. When she asked Dad, he laughed it off. He said, "People love to talk about their home countries. Maybe because they love to talk about themselves."

The girl said, "No, pero los he visto en muchos otros lugares." [No, But I have seen them in many other places.]

It was working! Just like in class. A real conversation in Spanish with a real Spanish-speaking person. A traveler, it seemed. And Sarai understood everything she said, just like Señora Hernandez had promised.

"I see you're drawing," the girl said in English. "I like to draw too."

English— the girl must have recognized Sarai's accent—that was disappointing. Sarai might as well answer in English too: "I draw a lot. Would you like to see?"

"Yes," the girl said. "Please."

"You can sit down, you know," Sarai patted the ground to her right. The girl sat cross-legged next to her. Sarai opened the sketchbook and began to turn the pages one after the other. "Here's my Dad."

"Yes." The girl wore a very intent expression, as if she was seeing something new and interesting to her.

"And my Mom."

"She's bonita—pretty."

"Yes. They're both right around here looking at other stuff. With my dad's girlfriend Mattie."

As soon as she said this last part, Sarai realized that talking about her dad's girlfriend might sound odd to some people, but nothing in the girl's expression changed.

Sarai riffled some more pages. At each page Sarai paused and the girl examined each picture. Sarai wondered if the girl were interested in the quality of Sarai's work or in the things she had drawn.

"Wait," the girl said. It was a sketch of Amir Sarai had started but never completed. The girl looked at it a moment. A hint of sadness showed in her thin face. She said, "That's a nice picture. Is that another picture of your dad?"

"No. My uncle."

"I see," the girl said. "Are you going to draw the parrots?"

"Yes."

"You know, I like to draw too."

"Maybe we can do it together," Sarai said.

"Yes," the girl said. "Thank you."

"It'll be fun." Sarai began to flip through more sketches.

After a few more, the girl stopped her again. "I know him."

"You know Bugs Bunny?"

"Yes. He's from my home."

"He's Jewish, you know. Like me."

"Really? You are a Jew?" The girl glanced with obvious curiosity at Sarai. "I never met a Jew before."

Sarai was used to hearing that. She always thought it odd. Of course, she knew lots of Jews herself.

Sitting close and face to face with the girl, Sarai was getting a very good look at her. The girl's cheeks were so lean and gaunt Sarai saw the flexing of tendons and muscles beneath her skin whenever she spoke. Unlike the kids in Sarai's school and neighborhood or for that matter so many other Mexican kids Sarai had observed since she'd come to Arizona, there was nothing round about this girl. No softness. No baby fat. She was all hard edges like intersecting planes. Her face would be fun to draw.

But then the girl smiled and she was beautiful in a strange new way Sarai had never seen. Despite the girl's wild look, it was a shy and sweet smile, and Sarai fell into an instant best-friend crush.

Sarai heard a woman's voice from behind, calling, "Zarah."

Both girls turned and looked up. It was an old Mexican-looking woman, even shorter than Sarai's Mom. And much rounder. The woman smiled and said the name again. "Zarah. ¿Quién es tu nueva amiga?"

Sarai turned to the girl and forgot all about speaking Spanish. She blurted in English, "Did she call you Zarah?"

"Yes," the girl said.

"Your name is Zarah?"

"Yes. What's yours?"

"Sarai."

"That's a nice name. It's almost my name, isn't it? Does it mean princess?"

"Not just princess, but 'my princess'. My mother told me that. But how did you know?"

"Not hard. My name means the same thing."

Sarai said, "But Señora Hernandez—my Spanish teacher— taught us princess in Spanish is '*princesa*'."

"That's true. I learned Spanish. But that's not my first language." Zarah's face was serious again, but hinted at an amused expression like she had a secret she'd share with Sarai but only if Sarai figured it out on her own first. Zarah said, "I bet you can't guess my original language."

A wild surmise struck. Sarai's heart rocked against her ribs and threatened to knock them apart. But it couldn't be. "I maybe could guess better than you think."

"Go ahead. Try." Zarah cocked her head to the side, like she was giving Sarai a small test Sarai would have to pass to become her friend—but if she did pass, her loyalty would recognize no limit.

Sarai felt a stab of fear. What if she was wrong? She played it safe. "French?"

"No."

Zarah had seen parrots. Maybe she came from Brazil. "Portuguese?"

"Not even close."

That was stupid. Zarah said she'd seen parrots but not in her home country. Brazil had lots of parrots. "Okay. I think I do know. But I'm afraid to say."

"Why? What is there to be afraid of?"

"It's hard to explain."

Zarah sighed. "Everything is hard to explain."

True enough.

Sarai looked at Zarah and took a deep breath. "Arabic?"

Zarah stared. "That's right. That's very good. How did you know? Did you recognize my accent?"

Sarai shook her head.

The elderly Mexican woman said, "Zarah, ¿de qué estás hablando con tu amiga?"

Zarah answered, "Perdoname, Alma." Then to Sarai, "Alma doesn't speak English. She wants to know what we're talking about."

Sarai said, "I understood her." Then, "She's not your grandmother?"

"No."

"Or your mother?"

"No."

"Is your mother here with you?"

"I don't know where my mother is."

"I'm sorry."

"I am sorry too. Thank you."

"And your father?"

"I don't know that either. I think maybe in France."

Hadn't Uncle Amir said he'd been in France? Sarai jumped to her feet. "Can you wait here?"

"Why?"

"Please? It'll take just a minute."

"Whatever you want."

Sarai turned to run, then stopped. "Promise you won't move?"

"I said so."

"Not an inch!" Sarai said and sprinted away, looking for Dad and Mom and Mattie. She ran and found all three of them by the very next cage only a few yards away together talking with a salesman in a green vest—some grownup chatter about "vases" and "yard plants" and "seasonal." She shouted, "Dad! Dad!" and ran to him. He turned. "What, Sweetheart?"

"Dad!" She hugged him around the waist. She pulled back but couldn't breathe to speak.

Mom and Dad and Mattie were all staring down at her. Mom tugged her gently away from Dad and leaned over and took Sarai's shoulders in gentle hands and said, "What's wrong, Honey? Are you hurt?"

"No." Sarai's throat was so tight she could barely get the word out.

"Okay," Mom said in a quiet soothing voice. "So you have to tell us or we can't help."

Sarai shook her head over and over. She worked at catching her breath, like she'd had to do sometimes when she'd been little and couldn't stop crying. "Just one minute." She slowed her breathing as much as she could.

The adults waited the minute. Then Mom asked, "Sarai, did

237

something happen?"

"Yes."

"Something bad?"

"No."

Dad said, "You've got to help us out, Sweetheart."

"Come with me," Sarai said. What if Zarah disappeared before they got back? "That's all. Everybody just come. Right now!" She broke free of her Mom and ran back towards the ruby macaw cage without looking to see if any of the adults followed her.

After the new girl Sarai had dashed off, Zarah just sat as she had promised. She looked up at Alma and they shrugged and smiled at each other.

Something had happened, though. Something puzzling. Something important. And the something seemed to excite Sarai, which meant it might be dangerous to Zarah. She wondered whether she should be frightened, but she'd lost all fear, so she just got angry instead. She'd just started a good life with Alma now. Was something going to wreck that too?

In her scramble away Sarai had left her sketch book behind in the dirt. Zarah picked it up and began to flip through its pages. Sarai had talent. The lines were smooth and the size and shape of things looked real. And the drawings were very close to real pictures of real people, the way people actually looked. Zarah stopped when she saw the sketch of a little girl Sarai had skipped past. It looked familiar. She held it up to Alma and asked in Spanish. "Who does this look like?"

Alma leaned over and looked. She took her glasses out of her pocket and put them on and leaned close to the drawing again. She shrugged and answered, "Well, it could be you, I suppose. Or some other little girl with long dark hair who looks like you."

"A lot of girls look like me," Zarah said.

"Yes, many. Millions, I suppose. Not always the same nose, though. And not so many around here."

Zarah flipped more pages until she got to the picture of Sarai's uncle again. The round face could have been the face of any nice man, except for the little moustache. That was very familiar. And the chess pieces, if that's what they were.

Sarai dashed up and stopped dead in front of them. "Good! You didn't leave."

"I said so," Zarah said. "It is okay I looked at your pictures?"

"Sure. As much as you want."

Three grownups walked up and stood. Zarah made some guesses. One woman was the woman from a drawing. Sarai had said she was Sarai's mother, which was easy to believe, since she was a slightly taller adult double for Sarai. The man must be Sarai's father. He was stocky with a bearded face, with the friendly open expression a lot of Americans seemed to wear for no particular reason anyone not American could imagine. The third was another American woman, also pretty but taller and strong looking almost like a teenage boy—the woman Sarai called her father's girlfriend?

Zarah waited for someone to say something. But all of them just stood looking at one another. Sarai's mother smiled. Sarai looked around at everybody else like she knew something no one else knew. But Zarah wasn't going to guess what that was. She'd learned never to guess. She'd wait and see and then deal with whatever happened next.

What happened next was Jabali.

48 Jabali

Jabali appeared as if out of nowhere like a nightmare in the day. He still wore his big greasy moustache. His black holster was empty because he was waving his big black pistol with the squarish grip at everyone and shouting, "Sorpresa, Zarah!" as if he thought he was clever and funny and charming instead of just another pig-like animal.

Alma agreed. She hissed, "Cerdo!"

Jabali gave her a casual light whack on the forehead with the metal barrel of his pistol. She fell. Zarah ran to her and knelt by her. Alma said, "Estoy okay, Zarah," and propped herself with her palms on the ground behind her and sat up and stared at Jabali. But she didn't try to stand.

To Zarah's shock, Sarai ran and stood in front of Zarah between her and Jabali with her fists on her hips. Sarai glared at Jabali and said, "I know you." Sarai was acting towards Zarah like Zarah had acted with little Omar. And it seemed to Zarah even less likely to succeed.

Jabali looked at Sarai. "Two for the price of one," Jabali said. "Even better." He looked around. "Everyone here speaks English, true? He glanced over at Alma. "I mean everyone that counts."

The mother spoke. "What do you want?"

"I want this girl. Zarah. An important man has been sent me to get her."

The mother said, "For what?"

Jabali said, "You know what."

The mother said, "There are three adults here. What if we say no?"

Jabali looked at her. "I recall that this girl so foolishly standing between me and what I want is your daughter. The other one is no one's daughter. So I offer a deal. If you let me take the one, no problem. If you try to stop me, I will take both. See? Simple. A good deal for us both."

Jabali eyed the other man. He stood still and said nothing. His girlfriend stepped in front of him as if to protect him. The mother walked over and stood in front of Sarai so that there were now four in a column—the mother, Sarai behind her, Zarah behind Sarai, and finally Alma still sitting half propped up on the ground.

Jabali said, "This is stupid. You are all stupid. Maybe I will just shoot you all anyway. He stepped toward the mother, who backed up, which made Sarai back up. But Zarah could not move from Alma. Now there were five—Alma, then Zarah, then Sarai and her mother and Jabali facing all four of them, his face purpling with terrifying rage.

Zarah despaired. There was really no fairness or justice in this world. Maybe she should have just died after Omar died like she tried to. All of it was wasted—the escape and the trek over the desert hills and the scavenging for food and water until Alma saved her. And now maybe Alma would be murdered too as this terrible world's punishment for her kindness. Maybe Zarah should just give up. She'd die right now rather than go anywhere with Jabali. Let him shoot her—but only her, not any of these good people she'd hunted for and finally found.

She focused her remaining rage on Sarai's father. She'd seen so many men like him all over the world. He just stood by. He said nothing. He did nothing. He just hid behind his pretty girlfriend like a coward and let Jabali wave his gun at the girls and women—even if Jabali killed all the girls and women, it was clear from this spineless man's expressionless face he was just avoiding trouble in the hope he could escape with his own worthless life.

Zarah recalled her vision of her own father in the desert—he'd promised he was always with her. Where was he now?

Sarai's father said one word so quiet Zarah barely heard it: "Mattie." She stepped left and he stepped right and shot Jabali three times in rapid succession.

The shots came so fast they sounded almost like one continuous explosion. Three times Zarah saw the gray metal cylinder turn and

saw the hammer rise and fall. With each of the three blasts a new
hole gaped in Jabali's chest. Jabali fell backwards onto his back and
shivered several times and lay still.

The blasts echoed through the desert. Nobody said anything.
Sarai's father walked over and looked down at Jabali lying on the
ground. He pointed his revolver at Jabali's head in a trembling hand
and cocked the hammer with his thumb.

The girlfriend murmured "No" and he looked over at her. His
eyes glowed like the distant fires Zarah had seen from the
Compound that first night out in the desert. Then the glows died. He
thumbed the hammer back down on the pistol and pulled his shirt
back and stuck the pistol in the holster at his side under his belt. He
swung his long shirt tail back to cover his pistol. He said, "I better
go check on the salesman and make sure he's okay." He stalked off
on stiff legs.

Sarai was trembling. She turned and looked back at Zarah with
her own eyes wide. She said, "That's my dad."

"I like your dad," Zarah said. And in her own mind Zarah gave
quiet thanks to her own father and a quiet apology. She never should
have doubted him.

Sarai introduced her mother Lily and her dad's girlfriend Mattie
to Zarah and to Alma. Everyone gathered around Alma to help her.
Jabali's blow turned out to have been a glancing one that left only a
mild swelling and trace of blood on Alma's forehead. Alma stood
and walked around in little circles and shook off the other women's
attempts to support her. "Estoy okay, estoy okay," she kept saying
until everyone accepted that she really was okay.

Then she took her phone out of her purse and pressed a button.
Zarah asked, "Alma. who are you calling?"

"Miguel," Alma said.

"Who's Miguel?" The girlfriend asked.

Alma glanced towards Jabali. She said, "El cuerpo."

Sarai's mother said, "Should we call the police?"

Alma shook her head. "No policia. Miguel better. And sus

amigos. His friends. Then no problema. Big desert."

Sarai's mother and the girlfriend looked at each other. Mattie nodded a brisk nod and the mother shrugged a shrug Zarah had seen many times before, as if the person was going to go along with something she wasn't sure about because after so many disappointments she just didn't care that much anymore. The mother turned to the girls and said, "Okay Sarai, now please tell us. Who is your new friend you care so much about?"

"Zarah," Sarai said.

"Really," Lily said. "Somehow, that makes sense."

"Yes," Zarah said. "My name is Zarah."

"Tell her where you're from," Sarai said.

Zarah said, "Why?"

"Please!" Sarai's eyes were bugging almost out her head.

Zarah said, "I was born in Iraq."

49 *With A Little Help From Her Friends*

Zarah held Sarai's hand as the two girls followed Lily down the long hospital corridor.

Zarah had been terrified the entire flight to Tel Aviv. Israel was the country of the Jews, and she had never heard a single good word about Jews her entire life, not in Iraq, nor in Africa, nor in South America nor in Mexico, nor had she ever met a Jew until she met Sarai.

But Sarai and her mother Lily were Jews. And Sarai was Zarah's friend, although Sarai kept insisting they were cousins. Sarai explained it three times but Zarah never understood. It was hard to picture herself as cousin with a Jew, although she had loved and trusted Sarai from the first instant she saw her and then even more so after Sarai and her family had jumped between her and Jabali. That was hard to understand too. But one of the ways she had survived through everything was knowing whom to trust and whom not to trust and she hadn't been wrong yet. Otherwise how could she have made it this far?

After Sarai's dad shot Jabali, Miguel and some other men came in a pickup truck and took the body away. Then Lily and Alma talked a while and Alma came and hugged Zarah and told her to go with Sarai and Lily. She'd be safer with them, far from whoever had sent Jabali.

The very next day Sarai's dad came and drove Lily and Sarai and Zarah and the girlfriend Mattie all the way to Sarai's house in Minnesota. It took four days. A huge bearded friend of Sarai's dad with the funny name Gus came out the house and said everything was safe. Sarai's dad and his girlfriend drove off to return to Phoenix. Gus stayed in the house with Lily, Sarai and Zarah. When Zarah got to know Gus he seemed like a very nice man. And he was funny.

Lily put Zarah in her own brand-new soft bed next to Sarai's in Sarai's bedroom upstairs. Zarah stayed with Sarai for many days in the most beautiful house Zarah had ever seen in the greenest paradise she'd ever lived in. Everywhere they went, everyone in the town smiled at Zarah all the time and treated Sarai and her like two princesses.

One time, Lily asked Zarah to suck on a stick. Once Zarah woke in the middle of the night and saw Lily standing by her bed in the darkness. Lily was holding a bunch of four bananas she had pulled from under Zarah's bed where Zarah had hidden them. Lily said. "We'll find a safe place for you to live and then you'll never have to do that again," and bent down and kissed her cheek and stood there in the darkness besides the bed until Zarah fell back to sleep.

Another time, Zarah overheard Lily say to Sarai "Not even a hint. Nothing to get her hopes up." Zarah didn't know what Lily meant by that, but she didn't need to. She could wait and see; she had gotten very good at waiting.

At the end of the second week Lily—who more and more reminded her of Alma—came and made her a promise. And the promise was too wonderful to refuse. So, no matter how scared Zarah was, she would take her chances and fly with Lily and Sarai to this country whose very name terrified her.

The three of them had come off the plane and through the airport and the Customs where people checked their luggage, including the suitcase Lily had given her. Although Zarah had traveled the world, this was the first time she carried a suitcase. Zarah saw the tall letters in the weird alphabet on all the buildings and then they got into a car and she sat stiff in the back seat with Sarai's hand clenched in hers. Nobody said much.

As they drove, sometimes she saw Arab letters and that made her feel safer. It turned out all the street signs included Arab letters along with the weird Jewish letters and that helped too. She still remembered how to read the Arabic letters.

Once Lily drove them through a neighborhood where all the store fronts and buildings had Arabic signs and Zarah recognized many people as Arabs. So there must be a lot of Arabs in Israel,

245

which was something she hadn't known. So she wasn't as alone here as she'd been in so many other places.

From the driver's seat Lily clicked on the car radio and found an Arab music station and turned around and smiled in a reassuring way. The music seemed old-fashioned to Zarah, not like the fun new music Sarai and Zarah played for each other on Sarai's phone. Zarah didn't mind. Lily was just being nice.

For several hours Lily drove past green fields and small villages and into a small city with mostly Jewish signs on stores and businesses and then to the edge of the city where there was a huge wide whitish-yellow building with a giant parking lot. Lily parked and the three got out and walked across the lot to the building Lily said was a hospital.

They entered through the big doors and went down a long hallway to what looked like a special section of the hospital and there were young Jewish men and women soldiers with big rifles but they paid her little attention, except one older fattish man who grinned and winked. Lily showed the soldiers some papers and spoke to the older one in English and the soldiers let Lily and Sarai and Zarah pass them into the halls.

Most doors they passed were closed. But Sarai halted in front of one half-open door through which they saw someone in a bed completely bandaged, the person's arms and legs hanging from straps, tubes poking into him. The person was missing one arm and both legs.

Now it was Sarai's turn to clutch Zarah's hand. Her eyes grew wide. "It's okay," Zarah said.

Zarah understood that growing up safe in America Sarai had never seen the death and suffering Zarah had seen. Zarah knew the stench of decomposing flesh and untreated wounds and the moans of the injured and the sight of streets littered with piles of corpses. She knew the flies and the other creeping and flying creatures that fed on death. This was normal to her.

No, this hospital didn't frighten Zarah at all—quite the opposite.

For Zarah, the smells that were strange were the unfamiliar smells of medicine. The injured were not writhing and moaning on the ground but sat in chairs or lay on white beds while efficient and often smiling nurses and doctors tended to them. And everything was clean—no maggots and no vultures and dogs who tugged the limbs of the dead and fought over their meat.

And she heard her home language all around her—different but familiar. One nurse smiled and said, "Good morning" to her in a strangely accented Arabic and Zarah replied, "Good morning."

It made no sense. She knew she was in Israel, the home of the Jews—the city Tsfat, Lily had explained. Very near Syria. Which itself was next to Iraq, Zarah's home.

She asked Lily, "If this is Israel, why is everyone speaking Arabic?"

Lily said, "To make the patients comfortable. Hearing Hebrew could frighten the children in particular. They are raised to fear Jews."

"Are the doctors Arabs?"

"Some. And some are Jews or Christians or Druze."

"Druze?"

"Another different people who live on both sides of the border with Syria."

Zarah didn't know who Druze were. "And these Druze speak Arabic too?"

"Yes."

"And the injured people?"

"The patients? They are mostly Arabs and Druze."

"Jews too?"

Lily smiled. "I don't think there are many Jews in Syria any more. There used to be, but the dictators chased them out."

"So these wounded people are all from Syria?"

"Almost all. Wounded in the war there. But it's possible some come from other places farther away. The doctors and nurses have a rule never to ask anyone where they come from or what side they fought for in the wars. But it seems there are a few from other countries who somehow wound up in Syria. I told you."

This was where Lily's promise came in. Zarah refused to name the promise even in her own mind, for fear the mere act of thinking it as a conscious thought in her mind would make it fade and disappear as it had faded and disappeared every time she had prayed for it and wished it before, over and over again, sweltering in the backs of trucks, stuffed into packing cases, carted over long distances and awakening in the dark to the hard cruel hands and nasty curses of hard cruel men and women who made her dodge and duck to stay alive, or then in the Compound and afterwards through her nights hiking across what she had since learned was an American desert.

For all the most recent years of her life she had learned to suppress the thought and keep it unformed—just a yearning with no name or definition, not even an unspoken sound in her mind. Now, because of Lily's promise and the smiling faces of the kind men and women surrounding her in this place she was tempted to think it and name it, if not out loud at least in her mind.

But she didn't. Not yet.

They stopped in front of a closed door. The door opened out and a woman dressed in white like a doctor came out. She and Lily stepped away a few meters and spoke for a moment. The doctor turned and said to Zarah in Arabic. "It's been a long time, hasn't it, Zarah?"

"Yes."

The doctor smiled. "Let's not waste a single second more."

Zarah glanced at Sarai. Sarai wore a solemn and serious look. Sarai let go of Zarah's hand and said, "Go ahead."

Zarah walked to the half-open door and stepped through.

And it was really true. Lily's promise. And when Zarah saw the smiling dark-haired woman in the bed Zarah allowed the word to form in her heart and soul and mind and she ran forward and she let the word flow into her mouth and after so many years she once again spoke it out loud. "Mother!"

Zarah climbed onto the bed and jumped into her mother's arms.

THE END

Preview of the Next in the Series

Simple Grifts

1 Gus Dropo

The first time Gus laid eyes on Professor Soren Pafko, Gus's inner sociopath detector went haywire.

It wasn't the scale and relative luxury of Pafko's office, which took up the entire top floor of a minor mansion some nineteenth century lumber baron had bequeathed the College.

But how many college professors rate a private bathroom? And Gus could see both a tub and a walk-in shower through the door.

Nor was it the placards leaning against the wall. In his time, Gus himself had picked up his own petty cash picketing for dollars, although it seemed unlikely that poverty had driven Pafko to stoop so low, considering the thirty-thousand-dollar Krencker-brand bicycle over in the corner.

Nor was it the big poster of Chairman Mao with its sinister black Chinese letters, nor the giant one of Che Guevara, though Gus recalled that his buddy Hack Wilder—who unlike Gus read history books—had once mentioned that, despite his movie idol looks, Che was just your standard-issue psycho killer.

Gus had seen dozens of Che posters around the Ojibwa campus. Everybody who displayed one couldn't be psycho.

It wasn't even the huge red banner hanging on the wall behind Pafko's desk, emblazoned with a black fist crossing over a black sickle, below them this legend in bold black cursive: "Democratic Communists of America."

No, it was the man himself.

Professor Pafko was an animated smiling man who beamed at Gus with a show of warmth. He leaned his hands on the enormous walnut desk in front of him. He rested his chin on his tented fingers

250

and peered over at Gus with merry bright blue eyes that sparkled with the over-abundant good will of a dime-store Santa.

Pafko's ensemble—and it was an ensemble—leaned towards earth tones: tan twill slacks and brown tweed jacket but a red checked flannel shirt proletarianizing his look.

The man looked trim. Gus supposed the bicycle loomed large in the man's almost superfluous fitness, along with abundant hours in the gym and, Gus guessed, a miser's diet. Pafko compensated for the balding spot in front with a feeble not-quite-pony tail which trickled down the back of his neck and failed to reach his shoulder

On his side of the desk, Gus teetered on an eco-friendly wicker visitor chair, undersized and rickety beneath him. Gus kept shifting his weight to reduce the jabs from the rattan poking his thighs. He wondered how long before the frail thing collapsed and dumped him butt first onto the plush Afghan rug.

Pafko nodded from behind his digital tepee. "Yes. LG Dropo. Fine young man."

"You flunked him."

Pafko nodded. "Not me personally, you understand. It was my Teaching Assistant Mason Offenbach who made the initial determination."

"So, I should be talking to this Offenbach dude instead of you?"

"Actually, I'd prefer not. This is Mason's first semester teaching here, and he has no experience coping with the local parental variety. I can answer any questions."

"And you have the final say anyway?"

"It's a collective decision."

"But you didn't overrule him," Gus said.

"I rely primarily on Mason's insights."

Gus paused to forge a mental path through the maze of circular reasoning. Then, "Since you are the ultimate decisionmaker and the adult in the room, I'm here to see you. Normally I stay out of LG's business. He's smarter than me anyway. But he's after early admission to the University. The 'F' could kill his chances."

"The 'F' will kill his chances." Pafko leaned back in his swivel chair and spread his hands out before him in a friendly gesture signifying openness and cooperation. "And I want to help LG as much as I can."

Gus said, "So my natural first question is why does he have to take this 'Diversity and Inclusion' course in the first place?"

"The University requires it for early admission." Pafko spread his hands out in a repeat of the previous gesture, this time signifying the unfortunate supplemental reality that, despite his powerful desire to help, there was nothing he could do. "And this was just an introductory course. If he does make it into the University, he'll have to study the subject in depth to graduate."

"I looked at your stuff. What's social inequality or intersectionality or race marginality got to do with engineering?"

"We are all grappling with the extent to which problematic and hierarchical western male-oriented ways of thinking generate traditional engineering."

"There's some other kind of engineering?"

Pafko tilted his head in an expression apparently intended to suggest he was giving Gus's question deep thought. "There must be. After all, there is more than one way of knowing. What we once accepted uncritically as objective scientific knowledge turns out to be gendered, raced and colonizing. We need to decolonize in order to build a community for inclusive and holistic engineering education."

"We do?"

"Indeed. And Mason reports that your son has been quite vocal in rejecting that most fundamental principle. LG has absolutely refused to concede his own colonialist privileged upbringing and to see things from other perspectives."

"LG does that?"

"Yes. In fact, in a class discussion, he said something other students experienced as colonialist, sexist, racist, cisnormative, phallocentric, transphobic and white supremacist."

"All at once?"

"He claimed that people who accused math and physics of being white supremacist"—Pafko consulted a yellow sheet of paper off his desk—"in your son's words, 'they're too lazy or maybe just plain too stupid to do the hard work'." Pafko laid the paper back down. "He labelled people's concerns 'sour grapes'. He said they wouldn't or couldn't 'hack it', to use his offensive expression."

"My."

Pafko said, "As you expect, people were offended."

"I bet."

"Yes. Students felt their own perspectives disrespected. He was erasing them. We can't have that." As he spoke the final sentence, Pafko was nodding his head. He clearly expected that it would be just as obvious to Gus as it was to him what we could have and what we could not have.

"I see." But Gus didn't really see what Pafko was yammering on about. What he did see was that LG was getting screwed for expressing an opinion, an opinion that sounded obvious. He supposed now wasn't the time to say that last part.

"I'm glad you see." Pafko leaned forward and placed his elbows on his desk and tented his fingers again and beamed at his precocious adult remedial.

"So, what's the solution?"

"An apology would be a good start."

"I agree."

"Great!" Pafko leaned back again but kept his fingers tented.

Gus wondered if the man's fingertips were glued together, like the guy in that comedy movie—what was its name? "And when will you and this Offenbach guy be apologizing to LG?"

A frown clouded Pafko's sunny expression. "I'll take that as an ill-conceived attempt at humor. No, what we need is a demonstration that LG understands his position of privilege."

"LG grew up in a hundred-fifty-year-old house on the edge of the jackpine wilderness. When I first got it from my own father, there was no indoor plumbing. I just put in central heat two years ago. We get by on my salary as a part-time maintenance man at the College here."

Which was only partly true, since Gus augmented his intermittent meagre paychecks with often spectacular earnings from private enterprises. But Pafko had no more need to know about those than did the IRS.

"I suppose it's no surprise that white fragility enters the picture here," Pafko said in a warm supportive tone.

"Fragility?" No one had ever called Gus fragile before. Coming from this twerp, he wasn't sure what to make of it.

The professor continued. "Yes. Most white people face challenges having their assumptions challenged, if you'll excuse the play on words. LG will benefit from recognizing his privilege as a white male. Hopefully that recognition will become the first step in a process by which other students can become comfortable with him. He can begin to grow out of the limitations of his upbringing."

"His upbringing by me, you mean?" Gus leaned forward and stiffened his thighs to hold himself up above his flimsy chair and tented his own fingers in front of his face. Now Pafko's office contained two men gazing at each other over digital tepees.

Pafko gave no sign he found anything odd in their postures. "Don't concern yourself too much, Mr. Dropo. I've dealt with this situation many times these past few years and I've got a good handle on how to handle it, if you'll excuse another play on words."

Gus said nothing.

Pafko continued, "In fact, I designed the Diversity and Inclusion course myself."

No surprise there. "What happens now?"

"Your goal and my goal are the same. We both want LG admitted to the University, where he can take advantage of the University's rich vital exchange of ideas and experiences from individuals of diverse backgrounds."

That last bit sounded memorized. Of course—Gus had seen it embossed in one of the University's multi-colored foil-stamped University brochures. Gus said, "So what next?"

"LG apologizes and retakes the course."

"What if he doesn't?"

Pafko leaned back, serene as any potentate on his swivel throne. He smiled. He beamed. His blue eyes sparkled and twinkled. "No apology, no University. No university, no degree. No degree, no engineer."